17/5/18

D0714955

'...ight-plotted, too-close-for-comfort thriller that races to the finish ... pacey and disquieting'
Stylist

'A really enjoyable read'
Martina Cole

'[A] suspenseful Hitchcockian tale ... [one of the] top ten crime books to take on holiday'
Daily Telegraph

'Jo Nesbo, Stephen King, Patricia Cornwell, Ali Knight'
Independent Books of the Year, 2011

'Knight's promising debut ... crackles from first page to last ... She could be very good indeed'
Daily Mail

'Knight's knack with plot ensures that everything rattles along nicely in Nicci French territory'
Independent on Sunday

'Tightly-plotted, high-pitched psychological thriller' ★★★★
Daily Mirror

'A fast-paced whodunit'
Woman and Home

'A psychological drama that grips from first to last'
Choice

'This thriller will have you on the edge of your seat desperate
... I was left
...nd'

523 051 75 7

Also by Ali Knight

Wink Murder
The First Cut
Until Death

About the author

Ali Knight has worked as a journalist and sub-editor at the BBC, *Guardian* and *Observer* and helped to launch some of the *Daily Mail* and *Evening Standard*'s most successful websites. Ali's first novel, *Wink Murder*, was chosen as one of the *Independent*'s Books of the Year 2011. She lives with her family in London.

Visit Ali's website to find out more about her and her psychological thrillers at www.aliknight.co.uk and follow her on Twitter @aliknightauthor.

ALI KNIGHT

The Silent Ones

HODDER

First published in Great Britain in 2015 by Hodder & Stoughton
An Hachette UK company

First published in paperback in 2016

1

A CIP catalogue record for this title is available from the British Library

Paperback ISBN 978 1 444 77717 8

Typeset in Plantin Light by Palimpsest Book Production Ltd, Falkirk, Stirlingshire

Printed and bound by CPI Group (UK) Ltd, Croydon, CR0 4YY

Hodder & Stoughton policy is to use papers that are natural, renewable and recyclable
products and made from wood grown in sustainable forests. The logging and manufac-
turing processes are expected to conform to the environmental regulations of the
country of origin.

Hodder & Stoughton Ltd
Carmelite House
50 Victoria Embankment
London EC4Y 0DZ

www.hodder.co.uk

For Stephen, Joseph, Luke and Isabel

Two hundred and fifty thousand children are reported missing in Europe every year.

Source: the European Commission

I

There were two guards in front of Olivia and her lawyer
behind her, the sound of their hard civilian shoes clattering
on the wipe-clean floor tiles. She swung her hands easily by
her sides; there were no handcuffs, though she was sure this
mother would expect them. They'd probably put them on
her outside the door, just for show, to keep the mother calm,
to stop her thinking she was having it easy in a high-security
hospital rather than a prison. Mothers dispensed their moral
outrage so cheaply.

Their little convoy paused outside a door as a guard
fumbled for the right key. It amazed Olivia how clumsy people
were. She suspected it was a reflection of their brains. She
was the calmest here – none of them wanted this meeting to
happen; one thing she'd learned over the years was that the
prison system loved the status quo. Deviating from it upset
everyone.

They entered the windowless room and she was made to
sit on a chair fixed to the floor. Her lawyer took a seat next
to her. A long blacked-out window on the wall to her right
would have the hangers-on peering through; there was
probably a crowd. Maybe she'd give them a show.

'Upset her and your privileges will be withdrawn,' said one
of the guards who had walked down the corridor with her.

Olivia didn't bother to nod. 'We're ready,' he said to no one in particular.

The door opposite her opened and a large black lawyer came in, followed by a small woman with a set mouth and dark hair. Her eyes met Olivia's and the woman faltered in the doorway. Olivia noted with detachment that she had stopped breathing. Olivia smiled, spread her unchained hands wide, palms up. 'Come on in, I won't bite.'

The men in the room stiffened; the woman's mouth gaped and then closed. Olivia turned to the window, already enjoying herself. The woman's lawyer indicated that she should take a seat and sat down after her.

The mother was shrunken and shrivelled and old before her time, thin in the cheeks with tight lines migrating from upper lip to below her nose. She had her hands on the table. She shifted in her chair and looked straight at Olivia. 'I'm Carly Evans's mother. I wanted to ask you one last time to tell me where Carly is. So she can come back to us.'

She said it with pride. She was defiant. That got you nowhere, Olivia knew.

'You talk about her as if she's still alive.'

The black lawyer's eyes bulged, the guard's mouth dropped open a fraction, but the mother didn't move.

'I believe she is.'

Olivia grinned. 'And what do I get for revealing this precious titbit?'

The lawyer found his voice. 'You would get extra privileges, more time to attend courses, longer periods outside.' He looked like he would rather be anywhere but here.

'I have always felt myself a spiritual person,' Mrs Evans said, and Olivia lost interest immediately and drifted off for a few seconds. Her own lawyer had grown old since she'd last seen him a few years ago; he'd lost his hair and presumably his wife too – she noted that the wedding band was gone.

'Are you listening?' the mother said, as if the bereaved should be offered special treatment. 'I've got cancer, and I'm dying. I'm here today because I believe that despite what you've done, in your heart, you have feelings and you feel remorse.'

'Why do you say that?'

'Because you're a woman.'

Olivia's grin was replaced by a flush of anger. She was being underestimated and that made her mad. She had been fighting against lazy stereotypes of female intuition and womanly feeling all her life, and this mother was revelling in them. The assumption that made her maddest was that to do what she had done she had to have been influenced by a man. In love or infatuated; that she was incapable of killing them by herself. That she needed the cruelty and strength of a man to kill a child.

She sat back slowly in her chair. 'That I'm a woman seems to be important to you. I'll tell you what's important. I haven't seen a bus for ten years. A river. I haven't heard the sound of wind in the trees, feet kicking a stone, the crackle of a fire. And I never will again. I stare at these walls for fourteen hours a day. Yet I am freer than you will ever be. I lie in the gutter, but I am looking at the stars.'

Mrs Evans frowned. 'I have it in my heart to forgive. Please, tell me where my daughter is.'

Olivia grinned. This was priceless! They might as well be in Scandinavia for all the liberal tosh that was being thrown around. She had often wondered whether it wouldn't have been better to have been born in Texas. They would have shoved the lethal stuff in her veins a decade ago. It would have spared her the mewling. 'Mrs Evans, you're going to have to try a lot, lot harder than that.'

She saw the tears brim in the mother's eyes. 'Please, God, I beg you.' Olivia felt the pleasure of power flush through her body. It felt as pure and sharp as freedom. 'Make it end, for me and the other families. We have weapons we can use to—'

Olivia laughed. 'Do you know the most powerful weapon in the world, Mrs Evans? This.' She stuck out her tongue and wiggled it. 'A woman's weapon, isn't it? I bet your husband's thought that over the years, your lawyer too. A tongue-lashing from a woman is a terrible thing. They say words can't hurt you, but we know that's not true. They hurt more than the sharpest tools, they can cast you into a pit of despair, or deliver you to ecstasy.'

'Just tell me and put me out of this misery!' The mother's voice had risen to a wail.

'That's enough.' The woman's lawyer stood up sharply, his chair scraping back noisily on the floor. 'This is achieving nothing. It's time to go.'

Mrs Evans didn't move, staring at Olivia helplessly. She needed the strong arm of her lawyer to get her out of the seat and out of the door.

Olivia liked having power. There was power in holding a secret, and she was going to keep it.

2

Darren stood in the living room doorway, trying to block out his mother's voice from behind him in the hallway. 'Take him for a walk, otherwise he'll bark all night and the neighbours have suffered enough. Darren!'

'In a minute, Mum.' Dad was watching golf in what must have been America, the course so green it was blinding, the sky Georgia blue. He'd seen a paint colour on a chart called that once, and had used it in a painting a few months ago. He didn't understand golf and couldn't see the attraction. He could never see the ball when they teed off, the camera swinging wildly to capture nothing except that Georgia blue. He began counting the beer cans on the table in front of Dad. Too many for this time of day.

'Darren, the dog.'

There was a ripple of applause onscreen from a lot of square, middle-aged men in baseball caps and oversized shorts.

'Darren!'

Her voice was loud enough to force him to begin moving.

'OK, OK.' He turned lazily to see Chester staring up at him, tail wagging.

His mum had got the bit between her teeth. 'I don't know what's got into you lately, honestly. You've finished that course that cost you a fortune and now you're frozen. Like now, you're not even really watching the golf, you're hovering in the doorway, neither in nor out. Take that dog out and get a life, or at least a job. Paint the house!' She was waving her hand at the patch of carpet beneath him, where all he could see was Chester and his lolling tongue and a pen lid that had bounced away behind the radiator pipe.

'OK, OK!' Darren gave in and grabbed the lead she was holding out. There was irony here, if you cared to look for it. Chester was Carly's dog; she'd begged Mum and Dad for a puppy and they had joyfully complied. Now, this lazy heap of dog was just another painful reminder that Carly was gone. Darren had just completed a fine art degree at the London Institute, spent three years immersed in trying to not show things as they really seemed – to not represent them literally. And all his mum could do was nag him about painting the house, as if a three-year course and a degree show made him a painter and decorator.

Not for the first time he had the feeling that his parents didn't appreciate how he had struggled – that the shocks of the past caused him pain too. And everything was named wrongly – his home wasn't his home, because his home had been Brighton and he had been uprooted from there in the aftermath of his sister's death; his dog wasn't really his dog, even though he was the only one who looked after him; Carly was his sister but she had been gone for years – dead but with no body and no grave, a murdered teenager who had become a saint. Life was as confusing as those invisible golf balls, everyone supposedly watching and applauding and seeing nothing.

He opened the front door and slammed it behind him, the front of the house Mum was so keen for him to paint shaking with the impact. The roads to his right were Victorian terraces. To his left they gave way to roomier streets with houses built in the 1930s, cars jostling for space in what at one time would have been front gardens. His own house was in a little row of seventies houses with clapboard fronts, an anomaly more suited to a Kent coastal village. South London was full of dreamers imagining other places, he felt. Now the peeling paint on the clapboard was like another reprimand. He jumped over the crazy paving of the front yard, edges striking skywards like a row of teeth growing awry.

He turned left, up the hill, the boxy skyscrapers of central London just about visible through the pollution haze in the distance. Shit, he had forgotten his keys. Mum would nag him about it when he returned. The day was muggy and close and he had on a T-shirt that was too thick and made him sweat. Chester was waddling, making strange wheezing noises as he grubbed about on the pavement, weaving round the skinny saplings that lined the road.

Despite his protestations, Darren loved this dog. He used to walk him miles over the Downs behind Brighton when they lived on the south coast, desperate to get out of the house and away from his mum's grief and the spectre of his missing sister. They'd moved to south London a year after Carly's disappearance, passing the exodus of people moving from London to the coast for a better life and fresher air. He always felt he was going in the opposite direction to other people.

He crossed the street at the top of the rise but Chester didn't follow, sitting instead by the edge of the road, paws dangling over the gutter. 'Come on,' Darren called to him.

Chester didn't move. Darren crossed the street and bent down, ruffled his ears. 'Come on, old-timer.' Chester gave a low whine of pain and got to his feet, turned in a circle, his breath coming in jagged gasps. 'Chester?' Darren put his hand out towards him as a violent shudder passed along Chester's back. Darren fancied the dog looked up at him with despair in his eyes. Another whine escaped, louder and more desperate. Chester's legs collapsed under him and he stared up at Darren, as if disappointed. Darren managed to say 'No!' before the dog's painful panting stopped and he was still.

Darren crouched down over Chester, shocked. The dog was ten years old. Too young to die, surely? He bent down and picked the dog up in his arms and walked back down the hill to the house. Chester was surprisingly heavy. Darren rang the doorbell with his chin and his mum pulled it open, ready to let loose a stream of invective about the forgotten keys, but instead she stood stupefied as Darren came in, the body of the dog large and awkward in the small hallway.

'He just keeled over in the street at the top of the hill.'

Mum had her hand over her mouth as Dad came out of the living room. She put a shaking hand on Chester's head. Darren could see her lip beginning to go, the quiver that always began one of her crying jags.

'He died right in front of me.'

He could see his mum's face crumpling like a paper bag and he knew he had to say something to try to make it better. 'He didn't suffer, Mum.' The lies we tell, Darren thought, to make it better. Death was not easy, or quick. 'He died right away.'

As soon as he'd said it he wished he could take it back. He heard her jagged in-breath and the wail that came after it. 'Mum, I didn't mean—'

'Darren—' Dad was trying to butt in.

'I've got the body of her dog but I haven't got her!'

Darren felt his knees give way and he had to slump against the wall.

'I can stand by the grave of her dog, hold him in my arms now he's gone, but not my own daughter! She never had me there.'

'Melanie . . .' Andy's long arms were round his wife's shoulders now, her wailing coming louder, as if the hallway wasn't large enough to contain it.

Anger chased after her grief as Chester had chased his tail in earlier years. 'All I get is a dog! This dog'll get a better send-off than Carly . . .'

Darren and his dad looked at each other and tried to swing into action. They had done this before, on the many occasions that had set his mum off. This time Andy dragged her into the kitchen and took some pills off a kitchen shelf, urging her to take one. Darren was still holding Chester's body, a weight in his arms so heavy he was in danger of developing back spasms.

Melanie was quieter now, her head buried in Andy's chest. Darren looked around for somewhere to put Chester, and decided on his basket. He suddenly didn't want to let him go; he felt a terrible fondness towards him, remembered the passage of the years. Tears pricked his eyes as it dawned on him that he had known this dog as long as he had known his own sister.

'He had you at the end, Darren, Carly just had the Witch,' Mum sobbed.

'Melanie please, let's think about Chester,' Andy said.

That's what his mum called Olivia Duvall: the Witch. Her real name was never mentioned. What the Witch did to Carly, what the Witch was watching on telly, how the Witch could sleep – that was how his mum always referred to her.

His mum wiped her face with the heel of her hand and came and knelt next to Darren by the dog basket.

'Can you shut his eyes?' she asked. Darren reached across Chester's nose and got his eyes shut. 'Do you think it was a heart attack?'

'I don't know,' he said. 'He was walking along like normal and then he sat down by the kerb. He was struggling to breathe. He was moaning and then he slumped over.' So much detail. He could describe every little step in the sequence; there was no guessing, no filling in the blanks with horrid speculations. Hanging over all of them was the contrast to the great yawning chasm of information about what had happened to Carly.

'God I'll miss you, Chester,' Darren said. They had a quiet moment, the three of them, there on the floor with Chester's body. Darren put his arm round his mother's shoulders. Her eyes were red but she wasn't seeing the dog, he knew she wasn't. Her eyes showed the fervour of ten years of intense prayers that had never been answered and never would be now. She wanted her daughter back. 'Mum, we'll do anything you want. You can decide. How do you want to bury him?'

Melanie suddenly found some strength and stood up tall. 'I'll tell you what I want.' She glared at him and Andy as if they were at fault somehow. 'I want to stand here in this garden, with my daughter by my side, and I want her to look down on the body of her dog, because she is living and he is dead. I want us to stand here as a family.'

Andy and Darren glanced at each other and then away. Darren felt the impotence settle on him like a wet coat, the torment of the unanswered questions, the feeling that he could have done more, that he should have tried harder to find his sister.

Living back home since his course had finished had made him realise how stuck his mum was – how stuck all of them were. Mum and Dad were stunted by their grief. He needed to grab life by the throat, but he was burdened by a sister whose own life had been cut brutally short. He felt trapped by the weight of his mum's false dreams, of her deluded hope, and of his dad's drink habit – he kept finding bottles of spirits secreted in the recycling bin and crushed beer cans hidden under newspapers.

Andy took Melanie to go and lie down. Darren got the shovel from the shed and dug a hole in the corner of the garden by the dead bush no one had bothered to remove last year. His dad came out and stood around pushing at the soil with his boots. Darren watched him. 'You OK?'

Andy looked back at the house. 'It's a good thing you're here, Darren, things have been tough recently.'

'Don't be hard on yourself, the breast cancer diagnosis is a big thing to take on board.'

He nodded, distracted, looking back at the house to make sure Melanie wasn't in a position to hear them. 'I'm worried, Darren, really worried.'

Alarm spiked up Darren's back. 'Is the diagnosis worse than I've been told?'

Dad shook his head and struggled for words. 'No, it's not that. I'm sorry, Darren, but I'm finding it impossible lately. She hasn't got over Carly. Her grief hasn't gone away, it's worse if anything. I can't live with it, Darren.' Darren stopped digging. 'She needs to accept that Carly is dead. That she's never coming back.' Once Dad had started he couldn't stop. 'My life is a daily battle to keep her mood up, but what's that doing to me, Darren? She won't go and see a professional to work through it. Instead there's a procession of clairvoyants and Tarot readers and priests and shamans coming to the house and fleecing her of our money, preying on her weakness and vulnerability.'

Dad kicked the mound of mud in frustration. 'She never asks what I want. I'll tell you now, Darren, what I want. I want Carly's bones, so I can end this thing. I want your mum to stare at those bones, so she can accept, grieve and move on. Carly is gone. And she's never coming back. Because, Darren, if she doesn't accept it, it's me who's going to be gone.

'And this fiasco with the prison visit, nothing was ever

going to come of that. You knew it, so did everyone else. She spent months with lawyers writing endless letters, buoying herself up for meeting the Witch, and she was simply humiliated. I'm forty-eight years old, Darren, there are decades of life still to live, and I want to live them well, even though my beloved daughter is gone. And I owe it to you. You are young, you have your whole life in front of you.'

Darren crouched down by Chester's grave, by the pile of London clay he'd dug, the hard brown streaks marbled with black topsoil, and said a silent prayer. For years he had prayed that Carly would be found, that she would walk, like a miracle on water, shimmering and bright, back into their lives. Now he prayed for something different. He prayed that he could find Carly's remains. Banish his dad's bottles and his mum's false hope.

Darren studied his mud-encrusted hands, the black curve of dirt under his fingernails. Since he had come back home from college he had been aware of the increasing distance between his parents and his low-level panic was now beginning to feel forceful. It was a double abandonment. Mum had endured a complicated birth with Carly that had forced her to subsequently have a hysterectomy. His parents had always told him that this trauma had been a gift – they had adopted him, loved him and brought him up as their own. They were the only family he had, but now it felt as though it was all falling apart and that there was nothing he could do to stop it.

3

They buried Chester in the garden at sunset, wrapped in his blanket. They cried together as a family, acknowledging that there was another funeral they had never had, for a girl they had lost and who they wanted back so much.

After the improvised service, Mum and Dad said they were going to Melanie's sister's and Darren encouraged them to go – he was desperate to smoke a joint and float away from his cares for a while.

Once they'd left he took the stairs two at a time and lay on his bed and let the marijuana pull him away from his worries. Wandering out of his bedroom again and past his parents', he noticed the cardboard box half pulled out from under the bed. It was the box about his sister's abduction. Inside were press cuttings, magazine articles, police reports, victim support letters, sympathy cards from the public. The box should have been put away in the attic, Darren thought, but Mum had kept it here, right under her head. She had slept surrounded by it all for the last ten years.

Dad was right, it was infecting her, radiating its bad karma, probably causing the cells to mutate in her breast with the grief. It was no accident that those cells lay over her heart, Darren thought, feeling stoned now. He sat down cross-legged by the box and began looking through it. He found pictures of his mum looking shockingly young, his dad standing next to her, photos of all five women and girls and the one photo of Olivia Duvall, used over and over again. She was very ugly, with one side of her face enlarged and one eye half closed. She had short, dark hair. She fitted perfectly the image of the 'freak of nature' killer that the press and the public wanted her to be.

He found the police reports into the case. He started to read them again, but began to feel ill and put the paper down.

Olivia was tried for all five murders together. The trial was controversial; none of the bodies had been found, but there were scraps of physical evidence at her house: a tiny torn section of a pair of Isla's pants in the cellar, a hairband belonging to another girl, trapped behind a radiator, two strands of dark hair clinging to the elastic, the blood and the bone fragments in the garden . . .

Darren swallowed and tried to concentrate. Olivia's house and garden were taken apart so thoroughly by Sussex Police there was nothing left of them by the time they'd finished. The house was later demolished.

Olivia accepted she was guilty, baldly said she'd murdered all five and never said another word. She had never revealed what she'd done to them, or where she'd put the bodies. She showed no remorse, had no understanding of what she had inflicted on the victims or their families and was judged to be legally insane. She was sentenced to life with no opportunity for parole and had been sent at first to a high-security hospital in the Midlands, but been moved three years later to Roehampton, a secure psychiatric hospital in south-west London.

He had been eleven when Carly had disappeared. She had been fourteen.

He pushed the box back under the bed.

He went back into his bedroom and lay down, computer games boxes cascading onto the pairs of trainers on the floor. He picked up his laptop and looked up Olivia's name on Google. There were 1,753 million results. They tended to fall into distinct categories: articles denouncing the freak of nature that she was – how someone trained as a social worker to save and improve the lives of the disadvantaged could terminate them so coldly; campaigners who claimed she was innocent, her confession the misjudged ramblings of a disordered mind; the smaller numbers who believed that she hadn't acted alone, that a man must have been pulling the strings behind her. The newest search results covered the attempts by the other families to get her to reveal where she had put their daughters' remains, led by Orin Bukowski, Isla's father, and his pressure group, The Missing. Under Google Images he found a succession of photos of Orin and a small group of protestors from The Missing climbing the outer wall of Roehampton Hospital to highlight Olivia's lenient treatment. They'd unfurled a banner saying 'Victims must come first', and stayed on the wall for seventeen hours. They were applauded by the press for their show of defiance.

He typed 'Roehampton Hospital' into the search engine and looked at the low, red-brick buildings that seemed conspicuously free of high-security features; lots of green lawn and saplings. It looked like a place celebrities checked into and wore fluffy bathrobes as they dried out, rather than somewhere murderers and violent psychopaths went to be punished. He clicked through some more pages, read the biogs of the staff, saw the smiling faces of the directors. He looked at the place on Google Earth, zooming in and out again. He felt angry. The Witch had ended up on Easy Street, had a view with no barbed wire. She was probably enjoying herself – watching TV and taking self-improvement classes. He saw her in his mind in a sun-filled room, a pencil in her hand, a life drawing class in progress, hiding a sly grin of victory. An image of his mum begging her for scraps of information about a beloved daughter, debasing herself even though she was ill . . . The drumbeat of rage in his skull began to reach a crescendo and he sucked on his joint with quivering hands.

He clicked on a link that said 'Job opportunities'. They were asking for a facilities manager, a financial controller, IT workers and cleaners.

He heard the front door opening and shut his computer in a hurry, as if what he was looking at was shameful.

Darren woke in the night with a start, a bad dream chasing him awake. He could hear low, urgent voices from the room next door. Mum and Dad were arguing, her voice reedy in the night. He turned to the wall and put his pillow over his head, but he still couldn't block it out.

4

The next morning his mum was black in her mood, pacing the kitchen.

'What time you call this to get up?' She was on a war footing. 'I don't know why you think you can lounge around here all day, you need a job, Darren. J. O. B. Or paint the front of the house, put your degree to good use.'

Darren put his cup of tea down. 'I got a fine art degree, Mum! It doesn't mean I'm any good at painting the house!'

'Too proud to get stuck in, that's your generation. And cut your hair. Painting the house is the only thing you can do – no one'd hire you looking like that anyway.'

Darren rubbed his blond Rasta locks protectively. 'Leave me alone!' He stomped out of the kitchen and back towards his room.

'And I don't want you smoking your gear in the house, d'you hear me!' she called after him.

He flopped down on the bed. He felt bad; she was ill and scared and he needed to be supportive, but he just wanted, for one day, to wake up and have a cuppa in peace. Living back at home was turning into a nightmare. He traced the knots and twists of his once vaguely curly hair with his fingers. He had left it for years uncombed and uncut, and it had twisted in and around on itself until it was a mass of shoulder length dreadlocks, lightened to blond by the sun and the salt water from the surfing he enjoyed. He had stopped cutting it when Carly disappeared, promising himself he would go to a barber when she came back. Ten years later, he still hadn't touched it. And now he couldn't, because he was more like his mum than he cared to admit – he was superstitious, and cutting it off would mean too many things, none of them positive.

In the creative bubble that was art school he hadn't really thought about his hair, but back home in the real world he realised it served a purpose: he was shy and he hid underneath it.

He picked up his laptop, lifted the lid and found it still open on the Roehampton website page from last night. He took a deep lungful of smoke, feeling the ends of his fingers become numb.

The job vacancies swam in his vision. No one cared what a cleaner looked like, he thought. His hair wouldn't be a disadvantage. He picked up his mobile and dialled before he had thought through what he was doing.

After he had chosen options on a menu and endured some lame classical music, a woman answered.

'I'm calling about a cleaning job I saw on the website.'

'Hold on a minute please.' She put him through and after a few rings a man answered.

'I'm phoning about a cleaning—'

He was cut off before he could finish. 'Email in a CV. You'll need previous experience.' The voice had an accent Darren couldn't place.

'Of what?'

There was a pause, a sharp intake of breath. 'What do you mean, of what? Cleaning.'

'Oh, yeah, I see.' Damn. He'd never worked as a cleaner. 'I've worked in a pub, does that count? I've cleaned the glasses, wiped the counter and stuff.'

'Toilets?'

'Yeah, you're right, sorry I forgot, I did that too.'

'Of course, everyone wants to forget that. You need to have the right to work in the country.'

'That's all OK, I'm English.'

'What you want, a medal? You need a DBS check.'

'A what?'

'Disclosure and Barring Service. It's the new CRB. They're in chaos, surprise, surprise. Their checks are taking ages. You need proof of ID. If you can't provide all that, original documents, don't bother applying.'

'Er, OK.'

'Who's your friend here?'

'Excuse me?'

'Who do you know who already works here?'

'Oh, I don't know anyone there already.' There was the first pause, Darren fancied, of suspicion. 'I'm moving in with my girlfriend and she lives nearby.' He was surprised how easily the lie tripped out.

'Can you start straight away?'

'I guess.'

The man barked out his email address, said his name was Kamal.

'Kamal what?' Darren asked.

'There's only one of me,' the man said, and put the phone down.

Darren lay back and smoked the rest of the joint. The day ahead of him existed in great acres of unformed time. He was out of sorts and there was no Chester to walk.

The phone call was ridiculous, a mania brought on by Chester's death, by his warring parents, his sick mum being humiliated by Olivia Duvall.

And then there was the insurmountable problem about who he was. A victim's brother, trying to get a job at the facility where her killer was housed! He wouldn't get within a hundred feet of the place.

He lay back on the bed, dropped the tab into a wooden cannon he'd made in A level Art and looked at the preliminary studies of a series of paintings that covered his bedroom wall. He groaned, realising the absurdity of what he had just done, but he couldn't let it go. A few minutes later, he changed the surname on his CV and pinged it to Kamal, and promptly fell fast asleep.

5

The next afternoon Darren was in the bath, a joint in one hand, trying to shove his toe up the tap. It was midweek, Mum was laid out on the sofa cushions in the living room; the pills she was taking were robbing her of energy and any desire to eat. Dad was at work. His mobile rang with a blocked-number message. He answered it.

'Is this Mr Smith?'

'Wrong number.' Darren put the phone back down on the porcelain.

A moment later it rang again. 'I'm looking for Darren Smith. It's Roehampton High-Security Hospital.'

Darren sat up sharply, sending a wave of water over the side of the tub. 'Er, yeah. That's me.' His pulse was racing. He had forgotten that Smith was the name he'd put on the application form when he was stoned.

There was a long, tense pause.

'It's Kamal. Can you come for an interview on Friday?'

'Friday?'

'It's the day after Thursday,' Kamal said, not hiding the sarcasm. Darren wanted to say no. He wanted to scream it, that it had all been a mistake. 'Come Friday at ten. Remember your documents.'

All Darren could think of to say was, 'OK.'

Kamal hung up without saying goodbye.

'Darren, stop slopping water over the side of the bath!' Mum was yelling from downstairs. 'It's dripping through the ceiling!'

He struggled out of the water, the thin bathmat failing to cope with the water draining off his long limbs. He used his foot to sweep the dishcloth of a bathmat around the soaking floor. He wrapped a towel round his middle and padded downstairs, shaking water from his hair like Chester after a dunk in the park pond.

Mum was reading a card, a friend expressing her sympathy probably, which had come with a gift box of lotions and potions. She was staring absent-mindedly out of the window, rubbing cream across her knuckles.

She turned and appraised him. 'Goodness, look at you. It's funny, I forget that you're so tall.' She sighed, a faraway smile appearing. 'So strong. I never thought I'd see a six-pack again! You're lucky your genetic heritage isn't ours. Evanses are short and Michaelses are stubby.' Darren's heart constricted as he saw what he thought was fear on her face. 'Maybe you'll avoid this fate too.' She tapped her chest and held up the card.

Darren felt goosebumps stand up proud on his arms as if a door was open somewhere. He sat down next to her on the sofa and put his arm round her shoulders. He felt a desperate tenderness for her that he couldn't express. He wanted to take away some of her pain, to soothe her, if only for a moment. 'Mum, I've got a job interview.'

Her tired eyes widened in surprise and her face creased into a smile. 'That's great. Where?'

Now Darren wished he could take it back. This was typical of him; he had acted on impulse to try to make things better and had not thought through the consequences. His mind had drained of every word except the one he couldn't say: Roehampton. He struggled to think of a job that would please her and cast around the room, hunting for inspiration. He saw a crown on the front of a pack of Tarot cards on the table. 'At King's College Hospital. In the records department.' He didn't even have the ambition to think of a creative lie, he thought.

'That's fantastic. It's a start. Think of that debt you've built up.'

'You only pay off the student debt when you start earning enough.'

'Well, they'll be waiting a long time, eh?' She stood up, ruffling his hair fondly, and left the room.

Darren picked up the card next to the gift box; it was from one of her friends. The loopy writing said, 'A little something to help you face the battle that is to come.'

Darren put the card back on the coffee table, berating himself for his dull, stupid lie. In a couple of days he would have to tell Mum that he hadn't got the job, which would make her feel worse, not better. He would seem even more of a failure to her. His eyes came to rest on the picture on the shelf by the fire, a photograph of Carly, Mum, Dad and him, on a beach in Devon, taken by a kindly dog walker. It had been shot the last summer before she was ripped from them. He had been happy then, a different person, a better person. The Witch had changed and reduced them all.

He got up fast and came out into the hall, grabbed his jacket that hung from the banister and went upstairs to his room. He rifled through his jacket looking for ID. He found a student card with a photo and his former student address on it, the name Darren Evans clearly printed across the middle. He glanced at his full-colour, top of the range printer, bought as a Christmas present by his parents for his artworks.

He opened his computer and began to work, days of in-action now replaced by a feverish concentration on forging an ID card. He played around with fonts, downloaded new ones that were subtly different. Four hours later he was placing a new ID card back in the worn plastic student card cover. He was proud of his work; it looked realistic. He knew that this card alone wouldn't be enough to get the job – he needed a passport or driving licence too, and those were beyond his artistic skills. But he had to admit it felt good, it felt like he was taking action. It would get him in the door of Roehampton for an interview. It would get him closer than he had ever been to the woman who had murdered his sister.

6

Friday dawned hot and still as Darren cycled across south London to the hospital. Roehampton was uglier and shabbier than it looked onscreen. The woman at the front desk was in civilian clothes and made him fill out a pass, gave him the top copy and told him to pin it to his chest. He sat down on a plastic chair and watched people coming and going past a security checkpoint at the other end of the lobby.

He waited for ten minutes before Kamal, a big, north-African bruiser with eyes like bitter olives, collected him and took him through a swing door down a featureless corridor to his office, which looked like every other office Darren had ever seen: a desk, a chair, a computer, too much paper and the inescapable air that hours and hours of a life had been wasted on something pointless.

'Sit down.' Kamal tapped on the keyboard and looked at the screen. 'Documents?'

Darren smiled and tried to look efficient, even though he was nervous. 'Here's something with my address on it.' He handed Kamal his student ID card.

Kamal gave the document a careful look. Darren held his breath, panic beginning to build. On the wall behind Kamal was a large sign stating that anyone providing false inform-ation would be prosecuted.

If he had been put on the spot as to why he had come to Roehampton, Darren wouldn't have been able to give a coherent answer beyond that he wanted to see where Olivia Duvall lived, smell what she smelled, see what she saw.

Kamal handed his ID card back. Darren breathed easier. 'There are fifteen hundred people who work at Roehampton, including fifty-five cleaners, who I hire. Recruitment and retention are a big problem, my friend.' He paused and stared at Darren. 'Why do you want to work here?'

Darren swallowed. 'I need a job.' How lame did he sound? 'How reliable are you?'

Darren shrugged. Not very, that's what everyone said. 'Very.'

'If you don't turn up you don't get paid, you clock in and out, so if you're late you're deducted. It's £7.50 an hour and you have to provide your own latex gloves, the uniform is provided by us but you have to wash it. Eight-hour shifts, with two breaks.' Kamal was hurrying through everything, as he'd probably done a hundred times before.

Now he was staring at his hair. 'What is that on your head?'

Darren put his hand protectively up to his dreads. 'I can cover it, if that's a problem—'

'Cut it off.'

Darren shook his head. 'I'm really sorry, but I can't do that.'

Kamal made a scoffing sound. 'You tell me, my friend, it's your religion or something?'

Darren shrugged helplessly as Kamal tapped on the computer again. 'A fine art degree.' He gave Darren a sly look. 'Can you draw an eight?' He laughed at Darren's stricken face. 'It's how you mop a floor.' He stood up, balanced one fist on top of the other and made a quick figure-of-eight motion.

'Oh yes, I see,' Darren said.

'Hand your tag in at reception on your way out. I'll contact you if a position becomes available.'

'Oh. OK. But don't you need the checks and other documents?'

'Of course. You can get started on that.'

There was a pause and Kamal looked up, as if surprised to see him still there.

Darren needed to ask one more thing. 'Tell me, just so I know what to expect. Do you ever see, I mean will I have any contact with . . .' Darren wasn't sure even what to call them. 'With the prisoners?'

'With the inmates?' Kamal narrowed his eyes. 'They won't stop you working.'

Darren sat in the chair expecting more, more grilling about his life, more opportunity to back out. But nothing happened, so he stood up and retraced his steps, making his way out of the building back to the car park and his bicycle. He almost burst out laughing as he unlocked it. What was he thinking of! He could never work here! It would become a mad story he'd tell his mates when he saw them later.

He got on his bike and coasted round the car park to the exit gate. He only saw the car screeching round the corner of the line of parked cars at the last minute. The driver jammed on the brakes as Darren clipped the car's bonnet and half fell off his bike, ending up with his bum on the tarmac.

The driver's door opened. 'God I'm so sorry, are you OK?' A girl with bouncy blonde curls and a tight white T-shirt jumped out. Before Darren could say anything she continued. 'I drive too fast, I know, I'm really sorry. Are you sure I didn't hurt you? I've knocked you off.'

'I'm fine I think.' He stretched his legs and checked his bicycle. 'The bike's OK.'

'This piece of crap car!'

He looked at her clapped-out Mazda, dented and scraped on every corner, but he really wanted to look at her. She had big blue eyes and sounded breathy, as if she had been running rather than sitting still.

'I'm Chloe. I like your hair. They let you get away with that in there?' She lifted her chin and thrust it at the building behind him.

Darren waited for the funny and clever reply that never came. 'So you work here, yeah?' he managed, eventually, getting to his knees on the concrete.

'Kitchens. Shit I'm late, sorry, sorry, I need to run.' She bent down and pulled at his hand. Her grip was tight and he got to his feet. He didn't want to let go of her hand so he shook it instead.

'I'm Darren.'

'I owe you. Ride safely.' She winked at him and ran back to the car. He watched her screech off to a parking space near the low red building, slam the door, run towards the entrance and disappear inside.

7

Darren slept easier for the next two nights than he had for a long time. He felt his boil of curiosity about Olivia had been lanced; but then it began to grow again, larger and more intrusive, and he spent increasing amounts of time on the internet reading every scrap of information he could find about Olivia.

After breakfast one morning, he knew he needed to look at something. 'Mum, I want to see Carly's stuff.'

Darren felt Dad stiffen, tea mug frozen an inch away from his face. 'Your mum and I were going to go to visit Auntie Jackie . . .'

'You don't have to be with me when I look at it.'

Darren knew that the attic in the house was Carly's space, where all that was left of her was stored, a makeshift mausoleum pressing down on their lives. No one was allowed to go in there unless Melanie was present; it was like she was guarding it, protecting the pathetic remnants of her daughter from being rifled over by family or police or, God forbid, journalists.

'Well, I can help you when we get back from Jackie's,' Melanie said, 'but I need to clear the bedroom so we can spread things out. Andy needs to move the blanket box – I can't do that on my own, it's too heavy, and I'm just too tired at the moment.'

'Mum, I don't need your help. I just want to . . . look at her things.'

'Melanie, does it matter if he has a look at it?' Andy asked.

'I don't want him to, not without me. I don't want anything damaged.'

'Mum, please!'

She rounded on him. 'Is this about the dog? Chester's death has got to me too, it unsettles a person, that sort of thing.'

'I just want to – just look at what's left.'

He saw his mum's face go stony. She picked up one of the pillboxes that had appeared shortly after the cancer diagnosis and shook it in his face. 'You know what this is?' The pills rattled and bounced around their plastic prison like Lotto balls in a Saturday night draw. 'This is my failure.'

'Melanie baby—'

'Andy, please. A mother does one thing. She looks after her child. Keeps her safe. These are the sign that I failed Carly. That I'm going to end up down there –' she jabbed a finger melodramatically at the floor '– before I find her.' Darren reached out to hold his mum's hand but she pulled away. Her illness had brought on bouts of aggression mixed with a terrible passivity. 'Oh, go up there if you want,' she said, before leaving the room.

Out of respect for her he waited until she and his dad had left the house before he climbed the ladder into the stifling loft.

The contents of the first box were pathetic really, some schoolbooks with Carly's handwriting in them now faint and at times indistinct, as if with every passing year she faded away a little more. Her skateboard poked out of another box that also contained storage boxes filled with jewelry and photos of her as a baby. There was a pile of images of her with her best friend Isla Bukowski, tongues sticking out, and back to back and hands aloft like Charlie's Angels, brandishing imaginary guns.

Propped up in the corner of the attic was her surfboard. He ran his hands across the wax that still clung to its surface, brittle and flaking with age. He put his cheek on the graffiti tag she had designed and had painted on to the end of the board. It was her initials winding round each other, the C enclosing the E in a curly topographic embrace. Maybe she would have grown to be an artist; maybe he had become one because of his sister's influence. So many what-ifs.

'Where are you?' he whispered. 'Where in God's name did you go?' He wanted an answer to that question more than he wanted anything. He hugged the board like it was her body and he cried. He had not cried over Carly for a long time, years in fact. It wasn't finished. More than anything, he needed to finish it, to get his sister a place in a graveyard before breast cancer carried his mum away. A grave was timeless, body after body in serried ranks in the grass, a stone angel gazing down. It was where she belonged. He laughed through his tears. Fighting to get into a graveyard, battling even for that.

His fingers traced over the bumps of wax and he thought again about Roehampton. He wouldn't find any answers sitting in a stuffy attic in Streatham. But there was one person who knew exactly where Carly was. Just one.

8

With no job and no dog to walk, Darren found himself staring at a weekend that looked as long as a prison sentence. He needed to distract himself and began a self-imposed exercise regime – chin-ups on the bar in his bedroom, a run round the neighbourhood, yoga when he got home. As his mum got weaker, it was as if he was trying to defy her illness by getting stronger.

On Monday he drove his mum to her hospital appointment and cleaned the house for her. He was reading an article on the internet about serial killers when his phone rang – number unavailable. He answered cautiously, wondering if it might be Kamal.

It was. He was short and to the point. 'Two people have left with no notice, I need you tomorrow. It's a simple yes or no.'

Darren didn't even hesitate. 'When do I start?'

Darren arrived at Roehampton at 9.30 as instructed and locked up his bike, scanning the car park for Chloe's car. He couldn't see it.

He spent some time with a silent woman in an office next to Kamal's, getting a pass with a photograph. He balked at seeing the name Smith, but didn't have time to dwell on it as he followed her outside to a large cupboard where uniforms of varying sizes were stacked on shelves. The uniform was scratchy nylon and comprised a loose-fitting short-sleeved top with the Roehampton logo on the front and baggy trousers with an elasticated waist, with no pockets. He was handed a pair of disgusting white plastic shoes like surgeons wore.

He lined up with a small group of fellow cleaners and Kamal came out of his office to talk to them. 'We've got a new recruit today, so I'll tell you all the rules again. In the unlikely event that you meet a patient, don't touch them. Don't accept anything they give you. They have been told not to hand things over, so if they try, don't think they're being friendly – they're not. You're not to eat anything you find in the facility. Anything. Don't chew gum. Wear your protective gloves at all times. All mobile phones must be put in the lockers. They are not to be carried at any time. Anyone found with a mobile phone will be dismissed and prosecuted. Take your watch off. It makes the time go quicker.

'What goes in on the trolleys comes back out that door on the trolleys.' He pointed to the door down the corridor. 'No cleaning agents, mops, wipes, scourers, are to be left anywhere in the facility.'

Kamal paused. 'Let's talk about the cells. Don't touch or turn the mattress. All sorts of nasties have been found in there – syringes, razor blades, used Tampax. They have a plastic cover, but things get in.' He let the sentence hang, probing a molar with a finger. 'They remove the bedding themselves, so don't be persuaded by them to touch it. Remember, they know all these rules, so don't let them play you. You don't want to be the individual who ends up on the news because of a simple thing you forgot. Now go and get changed. You've got a minute and a half.'

They filed into the changing room and Darren put his stuff in one of the lockers. Three other men were changing in the room as well and they looked at him with tired eyes and total disinterest. They all filed out and Kamal led them down a long corridor to a door, which he unlocked with a large bunch of keys clipped to his waist. Darren looked up at the security camera pointing down at an angle from the ceiling.

The group turned right down another corridor with windows on to the car park and walked past a locked door and a set of stairs. Kamal opened a service cupboard and turned on the light. Metal buckets on wheels and mops were lined up neatly against the wall. A non-brand bottle of cleaner containing a yellow liquid the colour of urine hung off the side of each bucket. 'You change the water in the bathrooms, old water must be disposed of in the toilets, not in the sinks. We clear? They say there are seventeen miles of corridor in this place,' Kamal said. 'And every bit of it needs to be cleaned.

'Now, Darek, you take Newman ward, Yassir, you're on Forsyth ward and the dayroom. Darren, you can do Porter, a nice easy way to get acquainted.'

Kamal walked away and the four men waited by the locked door. There was a loud buzzing noise and the door slid open automatically. They passed through and the door clanged shut behind them.

They were in a different world. The corridor seemed to have had the air sucked out of it and there was nothing but a smell of cleaning fluid and plastic. A big man in a dark uniform walked towards them, a large bunch of keys jangling at his waist. 'Good day, gentlemen. Let's rock and roll.'

Darren looked back at the locked door, panic beginning to conquer him. There was no going back now, he was in here for eight hours – a whole day for them to find out who he really was.

They shuffled along with their buckets, pulling them with their mops or pushing with their feet. As they passed through the next security door a middle-aged woman with dark hair and her own clothes was writing notes behind a desk. Her name badge hung low over her breasts, knocking loudly against the counter. Helen McCabe. She didn't look up, barely registering the cleaning team at all.

At the next security door the team split up. 'Where do I go?' Darren asked the man called Yassir.

'Follow me,' he said and they began to walk down the corridor, light pouring in from the windows to his right.

'Why don't the prisoners clean the place themselves? It would give them something to do, no?' he asked.

'They are not capable. Too mad, too ill.'

They reached another locked door, which opened automatically with a buzzing sound. 'Now you clean and dust, everywhere inside the locked doors. Kamal come check later so you do it well,' Yassir said.

'I have a question,' Darren said to Yassir, who looked up expectantly. 'Why is Kamal such a, how should I put this . . .'

'Ballbreaker?' Yassir answered for him, smiling.

'Tosser.' Darren grinned.

'Some people are just born angry,' Yassir replied. He turned and waved to the camera in the ceiling and the door buzzed open. 'Have a good day,' Yassir said, and the door clanged shut behind him.

Darren was alone now in a long corridor with no windows. It was very quiet. Darren had never been in a prison before. It was featureless and unpleasant; a thousand sad stories seemed to crowd around him.

He dunked the mop in the rapidly cooling yellow water, placed it in the colander-shaped hole at the side of the bucket and squeezed. He dutifully began to mop the floor in a figure-of-eight motion, as Kamal had instructed. Dull. He moved along two feet, and repeated. And repeated.

Three hours later he was so bored he felt he would die. The folly of his mad scheme to meet Olivia overwhelmed him. His back ached, and the place was hardly teeming with prisoners or people of any sort: two men in civilian clothes had walked past him about half an hour ago and ignored him; while he mopped in another corridor an unmarked door had been opened by a woman and he got a glimpse of a room with blue carpet and a chair before the door closed with a click behind her.

He had a break for lunch and ate it in the changing room, reading bullying notices about what to put in the bins and where to put recycling, no doubt pinned up by Kamal. It was like he posted reminders of himself all around the facility, just in case anyone was fortunate enough to be able to forget him for a minute.

By the afternoon he was thoroughly sick of the endless corridors that smelled of boiled cabbage and he was disorientated: windows were rare and he felt trapped, with no light and only the wall clocks to tell him the day was wearing on. A door at the end of the corridor buzzed open and a man in civilian clothes with a large name tag round his neck came out. Darren stopped mopping and stared. With him were three inmates, unmistakable in their white tops and loose-fitting white trousers. Two of the women were middle-aged; a third was younger, only a little older than Darren. He watched them, fascinated, as the group paused by a side door at the end of the corridor. The man held the door open for them and said, 'Come in, ladies.'

The door closed behind them and silence returned. Darren hurried with his mop down to the closed door and tried to listen to what was being said inside. He heard nothing at first, and then some faint laughter. He backed away. Olivia was no doubt also called a lady in here. People held doors open for her. She got to laugh. Something unpleasant began to stir deep within him.

9

The next morning Darren returned to Roehampton. He had sworn to himself at the end of his joyless and unfruitful shift yesterday that he was never going back, that Mum's illness had brought on a temporary madness of which cleaning floors at Roehampton was the manifestation. But now here he was, unable to resist taking another mopping tour of the hospital.

He changed into his uniform and lined up outside the cleaning cupboard with a new group of cleaners. Kamal wasn't there and a woman called Roksandre doled out the cleaning rota. He was given Newman and Forsyth wards. No one asked how his first day had gone; no one asked his name. Yassir was the only face he recognised and they smiled at each other. As they waited for the security door to buzz open and swallow them up, Darren knew he wouldn't be smiling much for the next eight hours.

He took out his mop and began to figure-of-eight the floor. After an hour and a half he was desperate to make the rest of the day more interesting. One thing Darren didn't lack was an imagination. He was a daydreamer, an artist. He began to trace a large surfboard shape on the lino with his mop and filled it in with water. Then he drew large crashing waves, and some rocks to avoid when catching a break into shore. Then he filled in the spaces by the closed doors with the low clouds that always hung over the shore when he, Jez, Mike and CJ took the boards to Devon to surf.

He used the mop as the oar on a paddle board for the next bit of corridor, leaning low and bending his knees as if adjusting to the movement and swell of the ocean. He looked behind him at his rapidly drying picture. Not bad. Maybe he could use this experience to create some real works of art when he got home.

There were thirty-five cameras inside the buildings at Roehampton, and a further ten on the perimeter and the exit points. Sonny's job was to monitor a third of these and make sure everything looked OK. Which it always did. He was alone at the moment, as Corey was in the small kitchen at the end of the corridor brewing the tea. They worked in pairs at Roehampton, in case someone was taken ill or needed a bathroom break.

The images from the cameras were black and white and soundless, and relayed on to TV screens that reached from desk height to the ceiling of the windowless room. After a while the rhythms on the screens, the occasional door swinging open, a group of visitors or Dr McCabe walking around, blended into a pleasing backdrop that was as hypnotising to Sonny as driving on a motorway at night. Which was why the young cleaner on camera number fifteen jerking about with the mop was something to see.

Corey came back, holding two tea mugs. Sonny used the zoom feature on the camera. 'You seen that white guy before?'

Corey sat down on his swivel chair and put his feet on the desk, something that Sonny hated. They watched Darren turn a full circle with the mop. 'He trippin',' Corey said. 'What's he drawing on the floor?'

'His resignation if Kamal catches him,' Sonny answered, shaking his head and sipping his tea.

Darren had reached the end of the corridor. There was no clock in this corridor and he had no idea if he was ahead of schedule or behind. An orderly coming the other way down the corridor opened the door with a key and he pushed his bucket through.

Darren turned to see another long corridor, this time with doors leading off on the left, with no windows. He wondered how far from the kitchens he was, how soon he might see Chloe again. His bucket had a dodgy wheel that meant it didn't push straight, like a supermarket trolley. He decided to count nineteenth-century French artists as he mopped to the end of the corridor. Maybe he could paint an imaginary Cézanne on the floor. No, that mountain Cézanne was always painting was the wrong shape for this passage. Which artist did long wide paintings?

The door at the end of this corridor had a narrow panel with security glass in it. He looked through it and saw a tall man in civilian clothes coming closer, someone behind him. Darren stood back as the man opened the door.

The woman directly behind the man was an inmate. Darren looked at her as she passed and felt a pain as if his heart had stopped. It was Olivia Duvall.

Those were the last eyes Carly ever saw.

Olivia stared at him with big brown eyes framed with long curled eyelashes, crow's feet radiating over her cheekbones. She had eyebrows that weren't overplucked, but neither were they anything Frida Kahlo would admire. Her skin was tanned, with a soft down of hair across the cheeks. She didn't break her stride as her eyes dropped to his name badge and lingered there for a moment before looking back at his face. He felt as if she had stripped him bare. Her long brown hair had no grey in it and bounced on her shoulders as she receded down the corridor, her small frame accentuated by the baggy white trousers and top that she wore.

Inside that head was his sister, crying out to be found.

The man stopped at the door at the far end of the corridor and opened it using another key from a bunch in his pocket.

Olivia was thirty feet away now, standing still, just looking at Darren as a cat might wait under a bird's nest for the chicks. A moment later they had passed through and he was alone again.

Darren had never seen Olivia in the flesh; he had not been at the trial. He had only seen the newspaper picture of her taken in the police station, after she had been hit by someone or something in the side of the head and it had developed a large swelling that distorted one of her eyes and accentuated the bags under them. She had looked how people would have wanted to see her – mad, deranged, and violent, her horrid work finally at an end. He had lived with that picture of her in his head for ten years. Only that image had been a lie. He had been lied to, and he didn't like it. One of the many thoughts that were roiling round inside him was that Olivia Duvall was . . . normal-looking. Almost pretty.

Sonny watched the young cleaner collapse against the wall. 'Bwoy look like he gonna faint.'

'Seeing that kiddie-killer will do that for you no bother,' Corey said. Sonny shook his head in disapproval. Corey had a tabloid take on the world even though he never read a newspaper. 'It's not healthy, having normal people in here mixing with these nutters,' he went on.

Sonny sighed. 'Someone's got to do it though. Might as well be the young. Maybe they can recover quicker.'

Darren had been parked with his nana during the court case; he was deemed too young to understand the details, to see the monster herself. One day Dad came home from the trial early – they found out later that he had begun shouting in court and had had to be dismissed. He came through the front door, a tension in him so great he walked like a man Darren didn't recognise. Darren and Nan followed him into the living room where he began to grab his records off the shelves, his prized collection of thirty years, and pull them from their sleeves, snap them against his knees, hurl them at the walls and smash them on the floor.

His mum and dad used to dance before Carly died; they never danced after. It was in this room that Dad and Carly would fight over music. Dad would put on a tune and would wiggle his hips and click his fingers, jiving like he was at Studio 54, while Carly would bounce, high and far, arms out and knees high-kicking, the hip hop rhythm pulsing through her whatever the track. She always existed, to Darren, in a physical way: spinning on a gymnastic high beam, rolling over cracked and uneven paving on her skateboard, crouched low on her surfboard, prancing about in this room, her long hair flying to the ceiling.

As they cued up the records and shouted out suggestions for tracks the two of them would get madder, freer, the volume control would turn and turn, their dancing becoming more and more frenetic, until it was loud enough to make Mary from next door barrel down her path and up theirs, her housecoat flapping. Dad would hold up a hand in apology and, when she was gone, give his low chuckle and turn the volume back down, boogieing down the corridor to the kitchen for a vodka and tonic.

But the sounds in the living room on that afternoon were not like the whoops of joy brought on by dancing with his daughter; they came from the pain of listening to what was being described in court. He and Nan could only watch until Dad was done destroying something he had loved doing, because without Carly it was too painful to ever repeat. When he had destroyed every single record, he collapsed on the floor on top of the pile of broken vinyl. It seemed to Darren now that he had never managed to get back on his feet.

Darren imagined his mum, the devastating news about the cancer still being absorbed, sitting opposite Olivia just a few weeks ago, in a sad room somewhere in this building, begging her for Carly, trying to prompt a sliver of pity in the Witch's heart. It hadn't worked. Yet here the killer was, strolling down a sunlit corridor, a spring in her step, receiving one-on-one attention. The injustice of it pressed down on him in a way he had never felt before. It was as if a piece of dry tinder had finally been touched by the spark it had been waiting for and exploded into life, igniting the fiercest anger he had ever known.

That night he woke with a start in his narrow bed, sweat pouring from him. He scrambled for the reading light, gasping as if drowning. Something horrible had stalked his dreams, but it vanished as soon as he flooded the room with light. The image that remained with him was Olivia's head, its high forehead, symmetrical and lined, and her big brown eyes, as she walked in slow motion past him, those eyes never leaving his face. Behind those dark pupils were the five secrets of England: Molly, Heather, Isla, Rajinder and Carly. The five women and girls, desperate to get out.

He got out of bed, his phone showing 3.30 a.m. He had worked just two shifts at Roehampton and he had already seen the Witch, could have reached out and touched her. He felt the euphoria of possibilities crackle in him. He scratched and twisted, then dropped to the floor and did twenty press-ups, the blood flowing through his forearms and biceps. He did chin-ups until he was exhausted and his muscles burned. He couldn't wait for morning. He was going back to the hospital to face the demons that were chasing away his sleep. He would go back through the gates and into her world. Carly would have wanted it. More than that, he thought, his sister demanded it.

IO

'I heard you saw Duvall yesterday.' Kamal was smiling slyly as they pulled buckets and mops out of a cupboard.

Darren was taken aback. 'How?'

'Remember, everything you do is on those.' He pointed up at the camera in the corner of the ceiling. 'Got friends in security, they saw the whole thing. They said you nearly fell over you were so surprised.'

Darren tried to smile, feeling exposed. 'Yeah, I guess it was freaky.' He shuddered. 'How many women did she kill?'

'Five. Fi-ive.' Kamal waved his hand. 'You know the rumour why she's here, got transferred from that place up north?'

Darren leaned closer as Kamal unlocked a door. 'Had a thing with a guard at the other hospital. They had to keep it hush-hush, would have caused a scandal.'

'What kind of thing?'

'Sexual thing! She is one twisted bitch, I tell you. He was doing her in her cell! Got inside the guy's head, sent him mad! He apparently still sends her love notes. Now he's out of a job and probably lost his wife too. Imagine saying that to your other half! I'm in love with another woman, and it's Duvall.' Kamal shuddered.

'She never told him where she put the bodies?'

Kamal looked confused. 'No man, they were fucking, right at it. She's an evil, mad bitch on heat.' He said it with a touch too much admiration, before turning back to the huddle of cleaners.

'Right. Darek, you do Newman, Yassir the offices upstairs. You, Darren, can do the corridors down to the dayroom.' Kamal barked out further instructions to two female cleaners and they all pushed their buckets and trolleys to the door and waited for it to buzz open. 'Wave to security once in a while. It keeps them awake. It's not like they've got much to do all day, unlike the cleaning team.' Kamal turned and moved away and the door buzzed shut behind them.

Darren pushed his bucket towards another security door and held up his ID badge. A woman at a nursing station checked it and opened the door.

He figure-eighted the floor, getting angrier by the minute. The Witch was having sex and enjoying herself while Carly lay rotting somewhere cold. And here he was, cleaning bloody corridors. He could be painting the house, doing something useful for Mum and Dad; for his living family.

Several hours later he was trying to quell his anger by imagining what the corridor would look like painted different colours, with the ceiling gunmetal grey and the walls yellow, or with Carly's graffiti tag as a motif down the wall. He was tracing the letters of her tag on the floor in a furious mop stroke when the door at the far end of the corridor was opened by a male orderly in a nurse's uniform, keys on his hip. 'Excuse me, what's your name?'

'Darren.'

'There's been a spillage, can you come through, please.'

The nurse held the door open for Darren, who pushed his bucket through the door. It closed behind him with a loud click. He was in a kind of recreation room with about ten people in it, a large space with full-length plate glass windows that gave on to an expanse of grass with a single willow tree in the middle, the low red buildings at the sides and opposite giving it the appearance of a large courtyard. Low-slung chairs with well-used leather cushions were dotted around, and four women were at a table where their card game had been interrupted by what was happening beyond them. An old woman was bent sideways over her wheelchair, staring at a puddle of vomit.

'Linda's been feeling unwell all day, haven't you, Linda?' A female nurse announced, to Linda but intended for Darren. She unhitched the wheelchair's brakes and pulled Linda backwards away from the mess.

'If you could deal with that please,' the male nurse said to Darren, indicating the vomit spread across the lino.

Darren pushed the bucket across the room, fighting the disgust churning in his stomach.

'You're a new face.'

Darren glanced up – and nearly fainted. Olivia sat in a low chair near him, staring at him. He looked around the room. One nurse was pushing Linda towards the door; another was turned away from him, talking on the phone at the main desk. Darren straightened, gripping the mop handle. He had an overwhelming urge to cry out Carly's name and shove the mop head with its old woman's sick straight down the Witch's gob, watch her writhe in pain, but he fought the desire, so strongly he felt his knees shaking.

Olivia noticed. She was staring at his legs, or maybe his crotch, he couldn't tell.

'Cat got your tongue?' Her head was cocked to the side, watching.

No one was paying them any attention, but his mind was like a bucket with a hole, draining of anything he could think of to say, and even then, what did you say to the woman who had murdered your sister?

'What's your name?' she asked. Her voice was deep, more like a man's.

Even this simple question was fraught with complications. Was he giving too much away? He struggled for a few seconds and said, 'Daz.'

She smiled as if this amused her. 'That's a washing powder, not a name.' She crossed her legs and he could see her ankles as her baggy trousers rose up. Her legs were shaved. The thought of her with a razor blade made the contents of his stomach move unpleasantly. 'You can dissolve a human knuckle in biological washing powder in less than twelve hours.'

Carly was on his shoulder, her thin arms round his neck like when he used to give her backies on his BMX, urging him on to kill her right there with the mop. 'I don't know,' was all he could manage. It sounded as if his voice was coming from far away and belonged to someone else.

Her smile broadened and he saw her teeth for the first time. She had pointed incisors. 'I'm going to call you Darren. I don't like Daz.' Her brown eyes bore into him, as if she knew every lie he had told to get close to her.

Darren swallowed the saliva that was forming too fast in his mouth. He wanted to look away, but he couldn't do it. He was closer to Carly than he had been in ten years. The secret of his sister's whereabouts was locked within the head of the woman sitting comfortably in that chair. What Carly had told her as she was held captive or begged for her life was unbearable to think about.

'You've done that bit.' She was looking at the small figure of eight he had mopped over and over in front of him. Darren looked down at the spot. Before him hovered the secret he was desperate to know, that he was convinced had made his mum sick, had made his dad an alcoholic shadow of the man he had once been. How could he get her to tell him, just a cleaner, when ten years inside and the finest psychological treatment hadn't managed it?

'You look stricken,' she said. Darren felt like he was holding on for dear life to the mop handle. He couldn't take his eyes off her face. 'Come on, Biological, you look like you want to unload a burden.'

Countless times had Darren lain as a teenager in his bed at night and wondered what he would say to the woman who had murdered his sister. If he just had that one moment . . . So many revenge fantasies had come and gone, been played out in his imagination until they were exhausted. Now years later, when he was grown and life had dulled the pain, he had the chance to actually do it.

'Come closer.' Her voice dropped to a scratchy whisper, a sly movement crossing her features.

He could have reached out and touched her. He was fighting within himself, desperate to recoil from her, but there was something he had always wanted to know and he was acutely aware that this might be the only opportunity he ever got to speak to her. He had to use the moment wisely. 'Are the girls together? It would be nice to know that they weren't alone, that they . . . that they had each other.'

Olivia had been leaning forward, Darren realised, because now she sat back. Her face had changed; the smile dropped instantly and a hard veil was drawn over her features. 'You said that like you actually cared.'

Darren took a step backwards. He had to get away from her; she scared him. He put the mop back in the bucket. The sick was gone, the floor clean. He had to go to the toilets in the corridor now to pour away the water and put in a fresh lot, and detergent.

The loud nurse was coming towards them, having taken Linda somewhere more convenient. Darren pushed the bucket away towards the door. As he waited to be let out, he looked back at Olivia, still in the chair. She was staring at him.

Once outside, he ran to the toilets and threw up.

11

Darren's sickness didn't last long. When he had recovered and changed the water in the mop bucket, he rushed back to the recreation room to try to talk to Olivia again and was buzzed in by the nurse, but she was no longer there. The last of the women were filing out of the room through a far door. Nevertheless, Darren felt, now that his stomach was empty and his fear had subsided, a sense of euphoria after his conversation with her that carried him to the end of his shift, to the disrobing in the changing room, past the security checks and out to the car park. He saw Chloe sharing a fag in the sun with some other people, shouted out her name and waved. She frowned for a moment, trying to place him, then her face broke into a grin and she waved back. 'How many people have you run over today?' he shouted at her.

She giggled. 'None, but I'll keep trying.'

She turned away and he saw her holding court in their smokers' huddle, retelling the story of his near accident, and he felt a wave of happiness crashing over him like surf. Bring it on. Such was the perfection of the world, he could have walked right up to her then and there and asked her out and he was sure she would have squealed with pleasure and accepted. But he didn't. He cycled home and bought his mum a bunch of flowers on the way.

His euphoria didn't last.

Mum loved the flowers. She put them in the living room

where their bright yellow and purple blooms brightened up the room. He noticed more cards on the shelf. News about her cancer had spread, and the motivational messages of help and sympathy had started to trickle in faster.

'Darren, Brenda came round today, do you know Camilla's working at King's too? She's doing art therapy. I told her you were in the records department. You two should hook up.'

Camilla was someone he knew vaguely from school. 'Er, it's always really hectic, Mum, I don't know.'

'Which room are you in? I'll tell Brenda.'

Jesus, that was all he needed, to be caught out in a lie by Brenda. 'Oh, one of the miles of corridor, you know. I've got her number, I'll text her.'

'Do you fancy art therapy? She could give you some advice.'

'It's not for me, Mum, thanks.' Darren gave a tight smile, the lies sliding and merging and all the while tightening round his throat.

She looked disappointed and it hurt him deeply. 'Oh well, maybe one day you'll paint the house for us.'

That evening they all watched a film together but Darren couldn't concentrate, looking instead at the flowers on the small table next to the sofa. His mum's head was inches away from the blooms. He felt that he had brought the killer into their home and she was getting comfy right here in their living room with them. Olivia, but not Carly.

When his parents went up to bed he threw the flowers away, desperate to get them out of the house, as if they were polluting it. He couldn't sleep, disgust and regret churning through him. He was lying to his sick mum to get scraps from the mouth of his sister's killer. It was beneath him, and would devastate her if she knew.

12

Darren spent most of the night turning over every tiny detail of his conversation with Olivia, trying to find meanings in her few words that he knew weren't really there. He spent hours in the dark wondering what to ask her when he next saw her. He trawled the internet, reading articles on manipulation, psychology and bullying; he researched how to frame a question and what techniques worked best. He fell asleep over his laptop with dawn beginning to streak his bedroom with pale light and woke the next morning exhausted.

'Darren, where are the flowers?'

Mum was in her dressing gown in the kitchen as he sipped his tea.

'I had to get rid of them, I was really allergic to them, I kept sneezing. I'll buy you some more later. Sorry.'

She sat down at the table and he was alarmed at how slowly she did it, like she was tender all over. 'You look shattered. Why are you up so early?' she asked.

'I'm going to work; sometimes I have to work Sundays.'

'In the records office?' She looked surprised. 'Good old NHS eh?' She stared out at Chester's grave in the garden. 'It's funny, you know, if it was me, I would, I don't know, always think I was going to find a record for Carly, like she'd been misplaced and was just waiting to be found, under another name.'

Darren grabbed her by the shoulders. 'Look at me. You're going to be OK. You will come through this. Stop being maudlin.'

She smiled a faraway smile of defeat. 'Sometimes, Darren, you can be so strong, so determined. And other times you're such a numpty.'

Kamal wasn't working this Sunday and a woman Darren had never met told him to clean the offices on the first floor, handing him the skeleton keys to the office doors, obviously not realising he'd never gone up there before. He tried to protest – being up there meant no chance of seeing Olivia – but the woman had already turned away and was attending to something else. He would have to suck it up.

Whoopee, instead of going through the buzzing doors he got to go up one floor in a lift. Wow, up here he got to push a cart with industrial-size toilet rolls on it. He was staring at an eight-hour shift of mind-numbing boredom with no benefit to it. There was blue carpet in this corridor, which deadened the sound. Not that it was necessary today, with only a reduced weekend staff at work. Darren got a mild thrill, for about a minute and a half anyway, from using a hoover instead of a mop. God, this job sucked. The corridor over-looked the car park where the bright summer sun bounced off bonnets and glared back at him, taunting him that he should be at the beach or on the bright expanse of Streatham Common, asleep. He tried to spot Chloe's car.

He saw her arrive about twenty minutes later, pull in to a bay with a screech and race for the catering wing. She was Sunday-morning late. She looked sketchy and dishevelled and had obviously enjoyed a major Saturday night. He'd like to have a Saturday night out with Chloe. His mind drifted pleasantly on that topic for a while as he worked the hoover down the corridor past glass doors and into the rooms. He would spray, dust and do the toilets once he'd finished with the hoover, he decided. Maybe this was an executive decision, like the ones Dad was always banging on about.

A security control room was at the end of the corridor and he saw two men in security guard uniforms, one old and one much younger, sitting in the room on swivel chairs.

The older man turned as he pulled the hoover past the open door. 'Oh, I thought you were Helen,' the man said when he saw him out in the corridor. 'Don't be shy, come in.'

'Wow,' Darren said, looking at the banks of TV screens. 'Quite an operation.'

The older man nodded. 'I'm Sonny, this is Corey.'

'Darren.'

'Have some cake, it's my birthday.'

'Happy birthday,' Darren said as Sonny cut him a slice of the cake that sat on a plate next to a computer keyboard.

'So, Darren,' Sonny said, smiling, 'you been here a long time.'

'Oh I haven't really, just a few days—'

He saw Sonny's face and stopped.

'I'm only ribbing you, that can seem like a long time in here. Most people don't last too long.'

'I don't know,' said a voice from the corridor, 'I've been here years.'

A woman whom Darren had seen before in the corridors downstairs came into the room with a card, which she handed to Sonny. She wore an expensive-looking white silk shirt with the sleeves rolled up and she had a short curtain of glossy black hair, which she swept off her face with a twist of her head. 'Many happy returns.'

'Dr McCabe, thank you kindly.'

Corey began to cut her a slice of cake, but she shook her head.

'Darren, this is Dr Helen McCabe,' Sonny said.

'But you can call me Helen.' She smiled at Darren.

'Darren here is new,' Corey added.

'But Darren,' Sonny sat back and shook his head, like

something was a disappointment to him. 'I no see hair like that even in Kingston, bwoy!'

Corey sniggered. 'You must have something living in there, cuz.'

Darren smiled shyly and shrugged. 'People say I hide behind it.'

'That's not difficult!' said Sonny.

'I've made a promise to myself that one day I'll cut it off.'

'Sooner would be better, cuz,' Corey said.

'Gosh, an English cleaner, how unusual. Darren, where do you live?' Helen asked.

Darren swallowed a bit of cake to give himself time to think about whether he needed to lie. 'Streatham.'

'You live with your family?' He nodded. 'Any brothers or sisters?'

Darren froze. All the heads in the room had turned his way, waiting for his answer. Should he tell the truth? He decided on a version of it. 'I had a sister, but she died. A long time ago.'

Sonny shook his head. 'I'm so sorry.'

'That's rough,' said Corey.

'If you don't mind me asking, how did she die?' Helen had her head to one side, her straight shiny curtain of hair hanging down.

'Leukaemia.'

Helen nodded, like she understood.

Sonny glanced up at the cameras as they automatically switched to different views. Looking up with him, Darren could see the dining hall and the serving counter, where a small queue of inmates stood. He stiffened: Olivia was among them. As if sensing she was being looked at, she turned and stared at the camera. Darren realised he'd taken a step backwards.

'Well, I have to get on,' Helen said. 'Have a good birthday,

Sonny. Nice to meet you, Darren.' She walked out of the room and down the corridor.

Corey pointed at the screen showing the dining hall. 'Do you think Duvall will ever tell Helen where she put those girls?' he asked Sonny.

Darren nearly choked on his cake. 'Helen's Olivia's therapist?'

'Her psychiatrist,' Sonny replied. 'And she do management stuff – that's why she here on a sunny Sunday. Very conscientious is Helen.'

'If it was me, I'd waterboard her to get her to confess,' Corey said, putting his shoes up on the desk and relaxing now that Helen had gone. Sonny pushed his feet off.

'I'd better get back to work,' Darren said, polishing off his cake. 'Nice to meet you guys.' His mind was a whirl as he walked back up the corridor. Helen McCabe. Here was a woman who spent countless hours trying to get inside Olivia's head.

He walked back to her office but she wasn't there. He walked in. She drank too much coffee; the several cups on her desk were stamped at the rim with the red lipstick she wore. He put the cups on his trolley, ready to take to the kitchen. He looked around. There were no cameras in her room or in the corridor here. The computer on her desk was password protected. He pretended to dust while looking through her in tray, one eye fixed on the door. There was nothing useful: cost-cutting memos, forms from the Department of Health. The filing cabinets lining the wall were locked and keyless, as they should be. All Olivia's secrets – all that she had ever felt able to tell, anyway – would be in there.

He became bolder. He pulled on the drawers of her desk and they opened. He rooted around for the filing cabinet key, past a box of Tampax, a spare pair of 10-denier tights and a letter from her lawyer relating to her divorce, but didn't find it. The desktop held a tube of expensive hand cream, a bottle of Evian, a card from someone called Liz telling her not to let the bastard get you down, exclamation mark! and a yellowing cactus in a pot.

He was cleaning her desk, wiping away the dust and crumbs from her lunches eaten in front of her computer, and wondering where to search next, when she appeared in the doorway.

'Sorry, do you want me to leave?' he asked.

She shook her head. 'No, I just came to collect something.'

He nodded, picked up her waste bin and emptied it into his trolley bin, waiting to see if she went to open the filing cabinets, but she took a long drink of water from the Evian bottle on her desk and then tipped a little into the cactus.

'Can I give you some advice?' She looked taken aback and ready to be suspicious. 'Your cactus. You're killing it by giving it too much water. You have to let it get really, really dry.'

She stared at the yellowing spiky thing on her desk for a moment and then she laughed. 'You're telling me I have to make it suffer to get it to flourish.'

Darren shrugged. 'I guess so.'

'I won't tell my patients that,' she grinned.

Darren grinned too, but he was thinking about what Corey had just said. Maybe making Olivia suffer *was* the answer.

13

The heat of summer was building, walls and pavements and cars radiating the warmth of the city and a sluggish wind lazily circulating the heat around. On Monday Darren was at work again, desperate to pick up as many shifts as he could before he was unmasked or forced to leave. Every morning Darren stood outside the cleaning cupboard with the other workers on tenterhooks to see whether Kamal gave him the route that would bring him into contact with Olivia. He couldn't risk asking for Newman ward because he knew Kamal would immediately become suspicious. Having to be so passive was a torture, and if someone else got allocated Newman ward he had to endure eight hours of mind-numbing boredom in the rest of the hospital. He stood like a condemned man waiting to see what Kamal would dole out.

The heat was making everyone tetchy and irritable.

'Yassir, you do the offices upstairs,' barked Kamal, 'and Darren, you do Newman ward. And today I'm checking every inch of what you clean.' He wiped a hand across his sweating brow.

Darren tried very hard to look disappointed.

He cleaned the corridors in double-quick time, keen to get to the rec room. A line of women filed past at one point and he feared he would miss her, but when the door was opened for him he could see Olivia standing by the window, feet apart, her baggy elasticated trousers see-through in the sun. The silhouette of her legs and bum was clearly visible. She turned and he could see the swell of her breasts before the effect was lost as a cloud passed over the sun outside.

Darren mopped across the main thoroughfare of the room towards the windows and towards her, passing Linda, parked nearby. She smiled vaguely at him as he mopped under her wheels. Olivia watched him the whole time, unmoving. He ran the mop across the dust on the floor-level runners that opened the plate glass door, should anyone have a key, to the courtyard garden beyond.

'Walls make people talk. I've learned things about you.'

He looked up at her. Olivia's eyes seemed to glow with flecks of yellow, reflected from the willow tree in the courtyard. He found he couldn't look away.

He blushed with embarrassment, pulled a cloth from his pocket and began to wipe the window. 'Oh yeah? Like what?'

'That you're an artist, Biological. With a degree and everything.' She said it quietly, so softly that he had to take a step nearer to hear her. 'Intelligent. So my question is, why is a bright boy like you cleaning floors in a shithole like this?'

Darren felt his stomach moving unpleasantly. If she had found out that already, then she probably knew he had a dead sister and that he was from Streatham. He began to panic. He had been unbelievably naïve and stupid, to not even consider that casual conversation in the upper offices or from Kamal could get back to her. He met her eye. He had not thought this through, this half-cocked plan to insinuate himself into the world of his sister's killer; he had never considered that she might discover who he was all by herself – and take his power away from him in one moment.

Her face had turned blank and hard, the soft grins and melodious inflections gone. Her moods were like quicksilver, benign one moment and threatening the next. He had no idea what she knew about him, how much Carly might have told her about her life and her family, how long they had spent together. *I'm trying, Carly,* he said to himself, *I'm trying so hard to get back to you.*

'I'd keep mopping if I were you, they might notice you staring otherwise.'

Darren tried to recover his composure. 'You think this job is too good for a graduate?'

'Oh yes, Biological, you're too good to be true.'

He took a step away, like she was a cobra about to attack, not liking the implications of what she was saying.

'And then there's your hair. I imagine it doesn't get like that without a lot of sun, sea and salt. You're a surfer or a swimmer aren't you?'

The gold flecks were back in her eyes now, a come-hither smile on her face.

Darren needed desperately to take control of this conversation, but he simply didn't know what to say, and stared at her like an imbecile instead.

She sensed his discomfort. 'What would you bring me in here, if you could?'

'A noose.' It was out of his mouth before he had time to consider the consequences and felt for two long seconds that he had blown all his hard work up till now.

But Olivia laughed. Darren took advantage and ventured nearer her with the mop. 'Actually, I don't want you to die. Because then those girls will never be found.'

A strange look came over her face and she gazed out of the window at the brilliant summer day she was denied. Her lip curled with disdain. 'The missing. There are so many of them.'

'Why do you say that?'

'Because it's true.'

'Cleaner! Move away from the patient please, you're here to work, not chat.' A male nurse by the desk was looking over, annoyed.

Darren moved quickly to the low bookshelf filled with tatty paperbacks, frustration overwhelming him.

'Martyn, I'm just passing the time of day with a new member of the Roehampton family.'

'Save it, Olivia, I'm not interested,' Martyn snapped back.

She looked over at Darren and something passed between them. There were so many setbacks and obstructions to his snatched moments with her. He was gathering tiny crumbs from her when he needed to gorge on a big fat cake, but he felt he was getting somewhere, he really felt it.

14

After Darren had seen Olivia twice in quick succession, she now frustratingly disappeared from view and he didn't catch so much as a glimpse of her for his next three shifts on Newman ward. At the end of eight hours of back-breaking and mind-numbing corridor-wiping on a hot day he'd put the mop and cleaning tools away, changed back into his civilian clothes and was queuing to get past the last security check before the doors to the car park.

The security checkpoint was airport-style, and beeped if something metal such as a mobile phone, laptop or watch was not put in the plastic trays that went round the side. It was manned most often by Nathan, a security guard and part-time model.

Nathan had already begun to high-five Darren when he saw him at the end of his shift. This afternoon they said hello and Darren realised Chloe was in the queue ahead of him, gathering up her things from the tray.

'How you doing, Darren, OK?' Nathan asked him.

'Yeah great. You?'

'Surviving.'

'You know you really look like that actor, Bradley Cooper.'

Nathan's smile was very white and very charming, but Chloe turned round and rolled her eyes. 'He gets that *all* the time.'

'You met Darren yet? This is Darren,' Nathan said. 'He's new.'

Chloe turned towards them both now. 'Yeah, we met.' She peered out through the doors into the car park.

Darren had to get her attention before she disappeared for the day. 'Did you do them mashed or chipped today?'

'Sorry?'

'Did you do the potatoes mashed or chipped?' he said again, feeling lame and awkward.

She smiled cautiously. 'Both. Nothing but the best for our inmates.'

Nathan was examining the tassels on her bag, listening to their conversation.

'Do they eat the mash?' Darren asked.

She looked affronted. 'Course! That's all they're going to get.'

'That depends on how well you cook it.'

Nathan was running his fingers along a tassel, Darren quite sure he was listening.

'I'd be a pretty poor caterer if I couldn't do mashed potato.'

'It's hardly *Masterchef*.'

She looked at him, annoyed. 'Cleaning the toilets here is hardly being a valet at Claridge's.'

'Is that where you'd like to work?'

'No. It's where I'd like to stay and have people like you cleaning up my crap.'

Nathan was taking an age with her bag, just so he could enjoy Darren's embarrassment. He finally pushed the bag to the end of the table and Chloe popped the turnstile over with a side wiggle of her hips, picked up her bag and walked away.

'I don't think that went well,' Nathan said, giving Darren his best sad actor face. Darren said nothing, because there was nothing to say. 'Cheer up, you could be one of those befrienders over there.' He nodded towards a short line of visitors queuing at another desk.

'Who are they?'

'They're the people who visit the inmates, keep them company, talk to them.' He saw Darren's blank face. 'The inmates're allowed to have visitors, people who make them feel better.'

Darren looked over. 'Do any of them visit Olivia?'

'She gets more than anyone else! She's famous, you know.' Nathan sighed a little. 'More famous than me, anyway. See that guy in the boots? He's hers.'

The man Nathan was talking about was tall and young, in dark green clothes and combat boots covered in a sheen of white dust. He was turned away and Darren couldn't see his face.

'I fear you haven't got a chance with Chloe mate, gorgeous though she is.'

'What's that?' Darren zoned back in to what Nathan was saying.

'That's the boyfriend. In the wanky motor.' They both stared out at the car park at a man in sunglasses behind the wheel of an open-topped Audi sport.

'Shit.'

Chloe jogged round to the far side of the car, threw her catering uniform in the back seat and got in.

'Like I say,' Nathan added. 'We're too poor and too late. He's come every day for a week.'

'He doesn't work then?'

Nathan snorted. 'He's a student, he doesn't bloody have to.'

Darren was horrified. 'He's a student driving that car?'

'That, my friend, is why you – and I – are in here, and she's out there.' They both watched as the Audi pulled away.

15

Victoria Coach Station, London

The man could make his pint last a long time as he sat at one of the pub's outdoor wooden tables, shielded from the rain by the dull plastic roof above the entrance to Victoria Coach Station. A few feet from him untidy groups of weary travellers walked past, pulling suitcases, before they turned the corner and were swallowed up into Europe's biggest city, their long journeys at an end. It was hard to imagine that Britain was an island state when buses arrived in a continuous stream from Paris, Brussels, Amsterdam, Zurich and towns further east: Split, Krakow, Sarajevo, dust-blown shitholes in Eastern Europe he'd never visited – and never would, if he was lucky. There was still the regular service clattering in from Cork, but the girls on that route were older now, richer, fatter and world-weary, their Catholic innocence groped away long ago.

The Eastern European girls were the ones he wanted to watch as he nursed his pint: the thin girls in the cheap clothes with plastic suitcases, grabbing for their first post-bus cigarettes. They were the ones he hunted with his eyes.

There were few who didn't fall into the arms of this person or that, weren't insulated by family or an address on a scrap of paper, but sometimes he would spot the rare one: a bag so small she could carry it on her skinny shoulder or, even better, no baggage at all, and no phone. Everyone has a phone, people said. It was the lazy comment that unthinking people threw out. You only needed a phone if you had someone to call. And he could spot the women who had nothing and no one. The women looking for rescue, thinking that where they were going would be better than where they were coming from. Their fear on arrival at their destination calmed him. They seemed stunned by the size of the task ahead of them, how hard it was to start over, a new town with new and unfriendly faces. These were the women who had bought into the cruel dreams of youth; the delusions of the army of the missing. And he would grip the pub table so hard that he would break his fingernails.

He felt the alarm vibrate on his phone – he'd been here half an hour. That was all he allowed himself, like a meth addict who needed a hit. He was still in control of his urges – just – and that made him feel triumphant and invincible. He knew that the security cameras covering the exit of the station actually worked, that the film was kept and filed. Life was a series of calculated risks, and following a young piece of meat as it left the station was one he was not prepared to take.

Even though he would never bump into anyone from work or his social life while having a drink here – they had long ago abandoned public transport for taxis and chauffeurs courtesy of the taxpayer – he might possibly one day bump into a friend's child slumming it to Europe. Although, even those pampered children mostly flew easyJet to the sun. The coach was for the truly desperate, and it was the truly desperate that he craved.

He got up from the table, yanked down the cuffs of his blue shirt and walked away. He was sweating; his desires would need to be sated soon. He turned on an old mobile he had bought earlier that day off a foldaway table on the Camberwell Road and made a call. 'I need product.'

There was a sigh of resignation from the man at the other

end of the line. 'There's a problem. I don't have anything, there's been a real squeeze lately.'

'What do you mean?'

'I'm sorry, I've got nothing.'

'Don't fuck me around!' He was frantic now, his voice low, as desperate as a drug addict pleading in an alleyway.

'You can harass me all you want. You'll have to go elsewhere. We're all feeling the pinch.' He hung up.

The man tried to contain his anger. He yanked on his blue cuffs again. Gert Becker usually had what he needed and it was a serious problem for him that he didn't.

16

Darren spent every one of his shifts braced for any opportunity to snatch a meeting with Olivia, but more practical problems were proliferating. He had only one uniform and was continually running the risk of his mum seeing the Roehampton logo that was emblazoned on the top when he washed it, so he had to go to see Kamal to get another set of clothes.

Kamal led him to the large cupboard outside his office, picked out a new top and trousers and handed it to him. 'The girls love a man in uniform, you'll be beating them off with a stick – or a mop!'

Darren tried to smile, hoping he could then slip away without spending any longer with Kamal, but his boss led him back into his office. 'Your DBS check, where is it? Get me the paperwork or you're out the door.'

'Um, OK, yeah . . .'

'And you haven't filled in the form with your bank details. Without those, you won't get paid. You want to work here for free?' He passed Darren a slip of paper and a pen.

Darren hadn't filled in the form because he was using the wrong surname. He had to stall Kamal. 'I don't know the numbers, I'll fill it in at the end of my shift.'

'Yes you will, you've wasted enough of my time already. Now get to work or I'll deduct you and you won't get paid!' Darren took his mop and bucket and waited by the door. Kamal appeared next to the group of cleaners and handed out the areas of the prison. 'You do Newman today,' he said to Darren as the door buzzed open.

Failure stalked Darren as he cleaned the corridors and worked his way to the rec room. He couldn't hold Kamal off on the paperwork forever; he was about to run out of time to achieve anything at Roehampton.

The inmates were there as he was buzzed in. Women leaned against the glass of the rec room doors or talked in low murmurs together. Olivia was sitting in a chair, alone. He had never seen her talk to any of the other inmates. She probably felt she was above them; there was probably a prison hierarchy and she had the hubris to think she sat at the top. His eye caught hers.

He pushed the bucket across the floor, working from the outside of the room towards the window. The willow outside danced in the wind.

He glanced around the room, at the two nurses by the door, the women moving lazily to and fro. Linda had her eyes open now and was watching them from her wheelchair, her mouth working slowly from side to side, like a cow enjoying a field of spring grass. Darren's mind was a whirl, calculating how best to use this precious opportunity. 'You were talking about the missing,' he said quietly.

She didn't answer. She didn't have to. He could see the fury like it was pulsing through her body. A vein pumped in her temple, her eyes were red and hard and mean.

'You think this is a joke? That I wouldn't notice who you were?' His sense of discomfort grew and he pushed the bucket away. 'You think I did what I did for my own pleasure? That I'm in here because I was stupid enough to get caught?'

Something was terribly wrong. 'I'm just working.' Darren turned and walked away, scared. He felt a movement behind him, but before he could even turn his head, the mop was grabbed from his hand. He flinched and spun, thinking she was about to strike him, but he heard instead the dull crack of the mop hitting Linda in the face. Linda's head snapped to the side, an arc of blood and spit arcing across the lino.

He tried to say something that sounded like 'no', but it died in his throat as he stumbled backwards.

Olivia lifted the mop and jammed the end of it into Linda's mouth. The wheels of the chair were on lock, carefully applied by a nurse earlier. The wheelchair toppled backwards under the force of the handle and Olivia began to pulverise Linda's face and throat with the end of the mop handle.

Darren jumped on Olivia and they tumbled to the floor, Linda's face a Rorschach inkblot in black and scarlet. A wailing siren exploded across the rec room as Olivia bucked and writhed beneath Darren like a lover. She lunged towards his neck and for a horrid moment he thought she was going to bite him, but she whispered in his ear instead.

'I know who you are, Darren Evans! I recognised you from a press conference your family gave!'

Darren felt strong hands pulling him off her as a team of six men armed with batons surrounded them. As soon as they were separated Olivia lay still on the floor, submitting without struggle to being carried away, one man taking each of her limbs, one supervising and one carrying a restraining jacket. She never took her eyes off Darren.

Someone turned the alarm off and silence rushed back in. The remaining women in the room were being hustled away by other staff.

A medical team was dealing with Linda, her pink slippers bobbing and jerking. Darren could hear wheezy breathing as she struggled to take in air. Something was broken. He saw a small grey object on the floor by the wheelchair and realised it was a tooth.

A nurse began to try to examine him too but Darren pushed him away.

'Don't look,' the man advised and turned Darren to the wall as he led him out to the door. Behind him Linda's gurgling and thrashing were becoming more desperate.

17

Kamal spooned another sugar into the cup of mint tea he was holding and handed it to Darren, who sat in a chair by Kamal's desk.

'Drink, the sugar helps the shock.'

As Darren raised it to his lips he could see the green water trembling as if a minor earthquake was occurring. Darren heard Kamal muttering something in Arabic.

The door opened and Helen McCabe came in. She looked flushed, as if she had been running. 'Come with me please.' Darren stood and followed her out of Kamal's office and up the stairs to a row of offices overlooking a courtyard he'd never seen before, Kamal bringing up the rear. This courtyard had no tree. He blinked away a tear. He'd never be able to see a willow again without hearing that sound of Linda choking.

Helen ushered him into a low armchair by a coffee table, shut the door and sat opposite him. Kamal sat next to her, hands on his knees, his eyes slits of hate.

'I understand that you've been examined by a nurse and you're not physically injured.'

'I'm fine,' Darren managed. He was still holding his mug of mint tea; he took a sip.

'This must be a very distressing incident for you—'

'Is Linda going to be OK?'

'You don't need to think about that now.'

'What do you mean? She was attacked right in front of me!'

Helen held up her hand to stop him. 'I want to concentrate on you.' She smiled again. 'Now, I've heard something of what happened, but I want to hear it from you, in your own words.'

'I was just cleaning the floor when Olivia grabbed the mop off me and . . .' He didn't dare say any more in case it got caught on a sob.

'That's OK, Darren. Did Linda say anything to Olivia before she was attacked?'

'Nothing that I remember.'

'Did she say anything to you?'

Helen's thick curtain of hair was catching the sun that shone through the window behind her. He took another sip of tea to give him time to think. There would be CCTV showing that they had been talking. The nurses in the room would have seen things too. 'Just how beautiful the willow tree was. And then she suddenly snapped.' He was fighting it, but still tears crested on his lower eyelids. 'She's dead, isn't she?'

'Yes she is.' Helen crossed her legs, never taking her eyes off him. 'Her oesophagus was crushed and partly ripped. She suffered a cardiac arrest from the trauma on the way to A and E.'

'Jesus.'

'I am head of psychiatric services at Roehampton. As such the patients here come under my care, as do the staff who interact with them. I want to reassure you that this type of event is extremely rare. In my thirteen years here I have never before seen this happen. The vast majority of all staff and patients never see or experience violence in all the time they are with us. We think of ourselves as a family here, staff and patients, and you are part of that family.'

He didn't understand what she was trying to say to him, so he sat mutely. Helen and Kamal both stared at him. There was a pause.

'We will be offering you counselling for what you experienced today, free of charge.'

'What . . . what's going to happen to Olivia?'

Her voice was even calmer. 'There will be a full investigation, and you will have to give a statement to the police. We can get that over with right after this meeting. We can help you with that. You are not to blame, Darren. There will only be a criminal trial if it's deemed to be in the public interest. Linda had no family left, so . . .' She swallowed, realising she'd steered the conversation in the wrong direction. 'Olivia will be placed in solitary confinement, she won't be able to mix socially with other inmates, her classes and outdoor time will be revoked.'

Darren's world was beginning to cave in on him. A police interview meant who he really was would be revealed. He had lied, which was a criminal act. He thought with horror of his parents, their shock and how they would react, how Orin Bukowski would hijack this incident for his own ends, how his family would be pulled through scandal and press intrusion all over again. His mum was ill; she wouldn't be able to take it. It could not be allowed to happen.

Olivia had well and truly fucked him over. That's why she had attacked Linda! Anger began to burn in him. He had been so unbelievably stupid and naïve. Silly sad-sack Darren with his murdered sister and his sick mum, thinking that the monster that had destroyed his family was opening up to him! Orin would demand to know how a victim's relative could have ever got near a serial killer with a deadly weapon in his hands. He had been able to get close because Kamal had cut corners, had not checked him out thoroughly enough, had not got all the ID that was required. His eyes slid to Kamal, who was sweating.

Darren had to fight back; it was all that was left to him. 'Counselling? I've just seen someone die. I'm just a cleaner.

It can't be right that I'm allowed in there with serial killers and psychos – she could have ripped my throat out! If I went to a union or a lawyer I could—'

Helen held her hand up to stop him. 'Let's talk this through.' She glanced down at a piece of paper in her hand. 'You've not worked here long, just a matter of weeks.' She was reading his CV. 'I see that you've got a degree from the London Institute. That level of qualification is unusual among our cleaning staff.' She looked at Kamal, indicating that he should agree. Kamal gave a pinched smile and went back to staring at Darren. 'Darren has been a good employee, punctual and hardworking?'

'Absolutely.'

'So even though he's new to the team, he's made a valuable contribution.'

'He's one of the best we have.' Kamal smiled. It looked to Darren like he'd slit his throat if Helen wasn't here.

They were trying to cover their arses. There had probably been a contravention of health and safety and if he took it any further they would all be tied up in paperwork for months, at huge expense. He looked at Kamal again. He could sense the panic in the system and he had to use that.

'With your skillset we can promote you to a Level Two,' Helen continued. 'It's a pay rise, and you'll get paid holiday. You would be employed by the hospital itself, not on a contract, so you effectively work for the NHS. This gives you pension rights, parental leave rights, benefits that are not available on lower levels. You are of course free to pursue whatever option you think is in your best interests. Facilities such as these do house challenging individuals and no job in this sector is risk-free.' She smiled. 'Have a think about it tonight and then we can proceed from there.' She stood. 'Do you require a taxi to take you home?'

Darren stood. 'I want to see her.'

He saw a look of panic cross Helen's face. 'Linda's body has been taken—'

'I want to see Olivia.'

Kamal stood now, the two of them facing him, but Darren wasn't going to back down. He had nothing to lose. He stared Kamal full in the face.

Helen turned to Kamal. 'I can take it from here, thank you.' Kamal grimaced and left the room.

'I want to talk to her. Alone.'

'That's impossible.'

'Otherwise there's no deal.'

Helen crossed her arms. 'I'm not here to bargain with.'

'Yes you are. I want a meeting with her, alone. If I don't get it, I walk out of here and call every paper I know. Bring the whole thing down on your head.'

Helen's lips became a narrow line but she remained calm. 'Why do you want to talk to her, Darren?'

'She killed a defenceless woman right in front of me. I want to ask her why.'

'That is a question you won't get an answer to. You need to know that. The families of the five people she killed never got an answer to that.'

'We'll see.' Darren took a step towards her. 'And I don't want to talk to the police.'

Helen opened her mouth and then closed it again. She moved the curtain of black hair slowly off her face and it settled down again, like a duvet deflating gently on a bed.

'I know you can do it, you can pull strings for your "family", so do it,' he said firmly.

18

Helen left Darren in the locker room while she went to sort things out. He had sunk down on a bench to try to collect his thoughts when the door opened and Kamal came in, advancing across the room towards him.

Darren got up and backed away, tensing for the balled fists that he thought were coming his way, but Kamal walked right by him to the toilet cubicles and checked to make sure they were really alone. Only then did he turn his attention to Darren.

'You, little fucker, are not going to lose me my job.' His finger was held high and pointing right at Darren's face. 'I've been here eight years. You know how many people I've employed in eight years? Thousands, too many for an idiot like you to count. You think I could do this job, stay in this country, pay that fortune for my visa, if I had to do the proper forms for all those idiots?' He was shouting, his voice reverberating off the metal lockers and the floor. Darren could see an artery pumping in his neck as the red in his face deepened.

'I've had to take care of little shits like you before, and I've taken care of you. You think I could get these corridors cleaned, get those shitters white, reach my targets if I had to wait for the Disclosure and Barring Service to pull their fingers out of their lazy arses? It's easier to rubber-stamp the form myself. And, against my better judgement, I've done that for you. And this is how it's going to work. You keep your gob shut, I'll do the same.'

Darren got it loud and clear. 'Mutual destruction.'

Kamal frowned and shook his head. 'No. Your head on a spike, not mine. You know why I know you're not going to be a problem for me? You know why I know you're going to put your head down and clean and keep your gob shut, even if really you're a fantasist who wants to meet Duvall so you can lick her cunt and say sorry, sorry sorry, for locking her up, for making her angry? You ride a fucking pushbike.' He opened the door, then turned back. 'Cut your fucking hair.'

He walked out, the door banging behind him, and Darren was left alone. He began to take off his cleaning uniform and noticed something stuck on the cuff. He recoiled when he realised it was blood. He was still washing his hands when Helen came to get him.

19

'We do it my way or no way.' Helen was standing close to Darren in a long white corridor outside a closed door. Her voice was low and calm, but there was an edge to it. He had pushed her as far as she was prepared to go. 'Olivia will be handcuffed, you will not touch her. I will be one of several people watching through the window. Anything we don't like, we come in. You get three minutes.' She walked away.

Darren took a deep breath and opened the door.

Olivia was sitting with her back to him, so he walked past her and sat down on the chair opposite her. Her hands were on the table in handcuffs, a chain running between her wrists to the floor.

'Are they recording in here?' Darren asked. He was amazed that his voice sounded normal.

'I meet my lawyer here. No tapes allowed.'

'You just beat an old woman to death. Why did you do that?'

'I'll tell you something about Linda.' Her face was contemptuous. 'Little, pathetic old Linda in her wheelchair sold her own daughter as a sex object to multiple men over the years, then when she was all used up forced her to drink drain cleaner.'

'People do terrible things, but Linda was judged insane, that's why—'

'I'll tell you about Linda's sentence.' Olivia spat the words out. 'She was judged insane for the drain cleaner, for pouring that acid down her daughter's throat, not what she made her child do before that. Not what she made her little girl do over and over again with many different men. She deserved to die.'

'Many would say the same about you.'

'I never asked for anyone's pity – or to meet you.'

'You have no remorse, do you?'

She didn't hesitate. 'No. And even if I could change what happened, I wouldn't.'

He put his hands in his lap and pushed his nails deep into his palms, trying to get the pain to distract him from the image of a thrashing Linda in the wheelchair, how Olivia had turned a mop into a deadly weapon in a second. *Play along,* he thought, *play along and see where it leads.* 'Where's my sister?' Her focus was gone; she was like a TV from the 1970s, picking up a signal and then fading away. She didn't respond. 'Tell me where Carly is.'

She yawned and a spike of defiance and anger shot through him. 'You don't like me being in here, do you? I remind you of Carly, of what happened. I don't think you like to be confronted with it.'

The focus was back, her voice low and quiet. 'I learned young and hard how a person suffers when power is held by another. It was a long journey to overcome my demons, to wrest that power back. Your sister, those other women, they helped me do that.'

'So if they helped you, help me. Give Carly back to me now. I demand it. Tell me where she is.'

'Never.'

'I'm going to find her – and those other girls.'

She almost smiled. 'You young men are so sure about the world and how it is. You are desperate to know what happened. But are you strong enough to cope with the truth? Strong enough to look into the darkness? You want to be a hero, but heroes have to suffer.'

'You have no idea how much I've suffered. No idea at all.'

She snorted. There was a pause as they stared at each other, then a strange expression flicked across her face just for a moment. She leaned forward and he could see the wetness on her tongue. 'Rollo is six foot two.'

'What?' Darren didn't understand. 'What did you say?'

She opened her mouth to say something, but it died on her lips. The door opened and a guard stood there.

'Time's up.'

'Just a minute – I need—' Darren began.

'Time's up. No extensions.' Darren stared at Olivia, but it was as if she had turned off every sense and her face was as blank and stony as an Easter Island statue. He stood and walked out of the room on shaking legs.

Helen watched the two of them closely through the one-way mirror. Watched as the serial killer and the cleaner talked, their lips moving too fast to interpret the words. Olivia was talking much more than she did in her therapy sessions. Helen felt outmanoeuvered. She didn't like to be proved wrong; her latest reports had reiterated that she felt the patient was making good progress and yet now Olivia had shown she was still exceptionally violent. It didn't fit with what she had observed.

She felt a headache beginning to drill through her frontal lobe. The routine here would be subject to press attention, victims' rights groups would be up in arms, there would be parliamentary scrutiny. She began to wonder about Darren Smith, the degree-educated cleaner, the laid-back hippy. He had proved pretty masterful in parlaying a cosy one-on-one with a serial killer. She'd met enough liars in her life to have her naïveté banished years ago – she had married a liar, after all.

She kept a strict watch on the time and sent a guard in after three minutes to take Olivia to solitary confinement. When Darren had left the premises Helen walked to security control and asked Sonny to replay the video of the attack in the rec room. She played it several times at normal speed and then in slow motion. She cursed silently. Darren was standing at such an angle that his dreadlocked hair hid Olivia's face. It was impossible to decipher anything more from their interaction here than it had been when she'd viewed them through the glass in the meeting room earlier.

But it was clear from his body language that Olivia's attack had taken him by surprise. Helen froze the camera on his face as he shrank back, fear clearly etched there.

She had felt earlier that she had handled a catastrophic incident with finesse. Darren was in shock but seemed to respond positively to offers of counselling. Numerous research studies showed that people who were willing to help themselves recovered more quickly from setbacks than others. Darren was showing all the signs of being a useful, reliable member of the team, too.

She picked up the phone. 'Kamal, Helen here. I need you to confirm that the paperwork for Darren's employment here is all in order.' She nodded at his reply. 'OK, good, thanks.' She put the phone down and walked out of security.

20

Darren cycled home, the heat shimmering off south London tarmac, pedestrians sweating in the sun, buses spewing fumes, drivers aggressive and bad-tempered.

He couldn't get Olivia's words out of his head. Who was Rollo? Why did how tall he was matter? Was Rollo even a person? He didn't understand why Olivia had said this to him. It could just have been distracting gibberish from a disordered mind.

He was also badly shaken, images of Linda helplessly thrashing in her wheelchair flashing through his mind, and Olivia's relating what Linda had done a lifetime ago. Was she even right? It was as if she had him in a vice from which he couldn't be released.

As he approached a junction he was badly cut up by an open-topped BMW. He had to brake hard and half tumbled off his bike into the gutter. The guy in sunglasses behind the wheel didn't even flinch. His girlfriend was chewing gum in the passenger seat. Darren rode up alongside. 'Look out, you made me come off the bike.'

The driver didn't even turn to look at him.

'Oi, I'm talking to you!'

The guy revved his engine, waiting for the lights to turn green. His girlfriend leaned back in her seat and closed her eyes.

A rage Darren had never felt before consumed him and he thumped the BMW's bonnet.

The effect was like an electrical shock on a stopped heart. 'What the fuck!' exploded the driver. The guy was barrelling out of his car door a moment later, big shoulders squared in a tight white T-shirt, dark blue jeans straining against heavy thighs. 'Don't you dare touch my wheels, man!'

Darren got off his bike and threw it down in the road in front of the car, blocking the lane. The lights turned green and car horns blared.

'Worried I laid a hand on your two tons of metal?' He took a step towards the guy. 'Don't you dare knock me off that bike and then pretend you didn't even see me.'

'I'm going to fucking deck you!' The guy balled his fists, aggression oozing from every pore.

'Come on then, let's see if you really got the guts. Cos I got nothing to lose.' He took a step towards the man, his eyes never leaving his face.

'You little punk-ass cunt—' The guy took a step towards Darren.

Darren could feel an explosion of great violence brimming inside him. His house keys were gripped in his fist and he brandished them menacingly. 'Get back in that penis extension before I blind you.' Darren saw the man hesitate just a fraction and knew he'd won. 'Now! And if I ever see you do that to a cyclist again, I'm coming for you.'

The man turned and got back in the car, showering expletives. Darren stood full in the lane, legs and arms outstretched, so the guy had to reverse awkwardly and manoeuvre into the other lane before roaring away from the lights with a bad-tempered squeal of rubber.

Darren picked up his bike and walked to the pavement, horns and shouts of abuse following him to the kerb. His legs had turned to jelly, but it had felt good to hold the power. Really good.

21

The management team at Roehampton didn't get all the interested parties to an emergency meeting until seven that evening. The governor's secretary had laid out Hobnobs on a plate like a fan and got some water in, but Helen suspected that what they all really wanted was a proper drink.

'So, bad day at the coalface, ladies and gentlemen.' The governor was considered a rising star in the prison service, youngish, black, with designer glasses and a bright tie. 'This is the first fatality we've had in more than fifteen years. Indeed, I'm not suggesting we don't have a near exemplary record in the care of our patients and staff.' He put his hands over the fronts of his chair arms. It struck Helen that it looked like he was sitting in an electric chair. 'But considering the patient involved, I need to know that every T is crossed, every I dotted on this.'

Back-covering. They were all up to it, Helen knew, but no way was she taking the fall for this incident. Of that she was completely confident.

'Shall I start?' Helen offered. 'It is the extremely unusual reaction from Olivia Duvall that has me puzzled, I have to admit. There was no relationship between Linda Biggs and Olivia, no point of disagreement, even. Olivia's always been a model patient and had built up a large degree of autonomy in here. In 2005 she helped separate two patients who had started fighting, at some considerable risk to herself.' She ran a finger down a report. 'Then in 2009 that rogue guard tried to attack her with a Stanley knife but she didn't retaliate. And then there was the time she reported that she believed Tracey Wilshaw was suicidal and Tracey's later attempt on her life was thwarted.'

The governor was nodding, forefinger tapping on his lips. 'There was that unsavoury incident at Rampton with the guard, though.'

'No violence occurred,' Helen replied.

He nodded. 'From what I understand, as soon as she had attacked Linda she became calm again. When she was being carried to solitary she asked several times about the state of nurse Vince Bayer's back. She was worried he'd put it out as he carried her.' The governor paused. 'The woman's all heart.' He stopped tapping his lips and began to scratch his scalp. 'And how in hell, excuse my French, did she manage to attack another patient from a standing start and kill her if she's got a heart murmur?'

All heads turned to Dr Vivek Chowdray, whose eyes couldn't be seen behind the light reflection in his glasses. 'I'm afraid it's entirely possible,' Vivek said. 'A heart murmur doesn't restrict a patient's ability to endure vigorous bouts of exercise, it just means that they have a greatly increased risk of a heart attack or collapse.'

The governor went back to lip-tapping. 'I think we're more vulnerable on the employees mixing with patients—'

Helen interrupted him. 'This was discussed at the meeting in April this year. We have implemented cuts of 12.5 per cent in the cleaning budget. If the cleaners weren't sometimes in the common areas with patients the facility would fail its hygiene inspections. I remind you that cuts of a further five per cent are coming next year.'

'And four and a half per cent the year after,' Kamal added.

'Darren Smith was not harmed?' the governor asked.

'No,' Helen said. 'Olivia attacked Linda, not him. He was certainly suffering from shock when I talked to him after the incident. It seems to be coincidence that he was there, although obviously none of us realised how quickly a mop handle can become a deadly weapon.'

There was silence in the room as they absorbed the uncomfortable implications of allowing cleaners to mix with patients.

Helen cleared her throat and continued. 'He has since accepted an offer of promotion to a Level Two cleaner as of tomorrow and he is open to the idea of counselling. But obviously there is the potential for a post-traumatic stress claim from him, and there is the issue of him going to the press.'

'So we need to be braced for negative publicity,' the PR added.

The governor sighed and nodded. 'I'll try and smooth things with the CPS. Can you liaise with building services about the funeral?' The PR scribbled a note. 'Poor woman.' He paused; he wasn't without feeling. 'I'll attend.'

'So will I,' Helen said.

The PR nodded again.

There was nothing sadder than a coffin being lowered with nobody there to see it off. Most of their patients were interred like that in the hospital graveyard – seen off for the final time by the men and women who had kept them locked up.

'Olivia's recreational classes and outside access have been withdrawn, I understand?' the governor asked.

'Olivia is in solitary and will remain there, pending an updated behavioural and emotional assessment,' replied Helen.

'OK, let's leave it there,' the governor said, standing and pulling his files towards him.

There was a knock at the door.

Martyn the nurse came in, shuffling and looking embarrassed. 'Sorry, sir, but Olivia Duvall insists she wants to talk to you,' he said.

'Me?' the governor said, looking astonished. 'No can do. Her privileges have been revoked.'

'She said she wants to speak to you and that it's very important.'

The governor shook his head, as did a few other people in the room. They were constantly dealing with the demands of those under their care. 'It's a bit too late for sorry.'

'She said it's about the missing women.'

The governor was a cool customer, Helen thought, as he didn't react immediately but instead looked at Helen as if to ask what she thought. Helen threw it back into his court. 'It's your call.'

The governor sighed. 'I'll meet her, because it'll make the guards happier if they think I've done what I can to calm her. But if she wastes my time, I'm extending her punishment.'

22

By the time Darren got home he was a nervous wreck – he couldn't eat, his legs were like jelly and his mind a disordered mess. He expected the doorbell to ring at any second and the police to be silhouetted against the front door – Olivia could at any point reveal who he was. He sat on his bed with his head in his hands. He had been the reason Olivia had murdered an old and defenceless woman. Whatever her crimes in the past, she hadn't deserved that. He also realised the hideous danger he had put himself in, unthinking and naïvely – Olivia could just as easily have murdered him. That risk, even for a one-on-one meeting with Carly's killer, seemed too high a price to pay.

He wouldn't be able to see her again, of that he was sure. Their snatched conversations were over; she would be in an isolation ward or cell, out of the reach of people she could harm. But even locked up and impotent, with drugs pumping through her veins or trussed up in a straightjacket, she still held all the power. Despite her being mad and bad, he had been closer to Carly when talking to her than at any time over the last ten years. He felt the frustration of having got close; he needed to get closer still.

His phone beeped with texts from his mate CJ asking if he wanted to sink a few beers. Darren dodged them. He couldn't see his friends now, couldn't pretend that life was still normal.

Instead he pulled a piece of paper towards him and began to draw.

He must have fallen asleep eventually because he woke to find Dad shaking him awake. The pale light of early morning was coming through his undrawn curtains, and he was still in his clothes on top of his bed.

'You need to come and see something right away. I haven't woken your mum. It's on the news.'

Darren yawned and stretched, scratching his sides. 'What time is it?'

'Six thirty. You know I never sleep in the summer.'

Darren looked down at his dishevelled clothes, at the joint butts in the wooden cannon, his messy room. He scratched his head, rubbed sleep from his eyes and followed his dad down the stairs.

The TV news was on in the living room, one story rolling on and on.

They had found one of the Five.

Darren felt the strength go in his legs and sank down on the sofa. The news reported that there had been an incident at Roehampton High-Security Hospital that had resulted in Olivia Duvall killing a fellow inmate. Apparently, in a rush of contrition following this event, she had confessed to the prison governor where the body of Molly Peters, last seen in Brighton in 2004, aged fourteen, had been buried.

Police had begun digging that evening by a stile on the South Downs, and a few hours later they had found bones, which were still being examined.

'When your mum wakes up, there's going to be hell,' Dad said. 'We need to be prepared.'

Darren's legs had drained of blood and he couldn't speak. 'I worry about her emotional state, Darren, she's weak and vulnerable. The timing couldn't be worse.'

The anger was building inside Darren like water behind a dam. He knew what Olivia was doing. She was dangling the promise of resolution in front of him, tantalising him with it. She had given one of them up, but not Carly. The price she would exact for *her* would be high indeed.

And Melanie wanted Carly alive; she lived for the moment when Carly would come back. The discovery of Molly's bones was further evidence that Carly never would. The extinguishing of hope was a cruel thing. And Olivia knew that too.

The TV news flipped back to the studio. Orin Bukowski was in a chair, in a sports jacket and a pink shirt. His American accent was loud and uncompromising. 'I don't know what regime they run at Roehampton, but that this child killer was allowed to murder another patient is a sick joke. The government should have enacted the true justice that the people of this country overwhelmingly desire and got rid of this hideous creature years ago. Why is the governor still in post this morning? Why does he still have a job? Why was this evil woman allowed out in a recreation room with other people? She is bargaining her way out of the punishment that is her due. Time and time again we see killers laughing at the justice system, laughing at the families of those they've murdered.'

'But Mr Bukowski, surely this proves that the capital punishment you and your organisation seeks is the wrong solution. If Duvall had been killed by the state she could never have revealed where these girls are—'

'I have said that she should be force-fed truth drugs. We should be treating criminals such as her, who are an aberration, who cause great damage to society and individuals, the same way we treat terrorists. They are a threat to our way of life—'

Darren switched off the TV.

'That man is all we need,' his dad muttered. 'No one else gets to have their say with him around.' He froze. The toilet was flushing upstairs. His mum was awake. 'I'll get her tea,' Dad said.

Darren trailed his dad into the kitchen and waited while the kettle boiled. 'Do you remember, Darren, when you were little, you had a toy called Billy and his Seven Barrels? They were brightly coloured plastic barrels, one inside the other, like a Russian doll. You open up each barrel and inside is a smaller barrel, until right at the centre there's a tiny little one, and you open that and it's empty.' He ran a hand through his hair, staring at the floor. 'I used to sit you on my knee and we'd open the barrels up one by one, and then you used to ask me, what's inside the last one?'

Darren finished the anecdote. 'And you'd say, nothing. The endless void, the big nothing.'

Dad nodded. 'I didn't believe in anything. The afterlife, or heaven, God, the devil, karma, ESP, Wicca . . .' He tailed off and looked at the ceiling, where they could hear the creak of Melanie's tread. 'But she did. She believed in everything. She's clung to those things for ten years to get her through.'

'What do you think now?'

Darren's Dad looked at him and it was as if a bomb had exploded behind his features somewhere and rearranged them in a way he had never seen before. 'Now it's just too late. We are so very tired and it's too late.' He poured a splash of milk into the cup and took a deep breath. 'Are you going to tell her, or am I?'

'We'll go together,' Darren said. And they walked up the stairs.

Melanie took the cup of tea that Andy gave her and stared at them hovering round her bed. 'Why are you both staring at me like that?'

She wasn't as clairvoyant as she claimed she was, otherwise she would have known, Darren thought.

'They've found Molly Peters's body on the South Downs,' Dad said. 'Olivia told them where it was last night.' Melanie put the tea down on the bedside table. 'They are widening the search to see if any other bodies—'

'Carly's not there. I can feel it.'

'Melanie—'

'She's not there!' She swung her arm out with a cry and sent the tea hurtling across the room, spraying Andy with hot liquid. 'Just get out! Just get out!'

'Jesus, Melanie, look at yourself!' Dad was pulling down his trousers, hopping round the bedroom to get the heat away from his skin. 'Why is this my fault? Why is it always my fault?'

'She's not dead!'

'She was my daughter too!'

Melanie was out of the bed then, a look of pure hatred on her face. 'You can believe what you want. I'll never believe she's dead. Get out, get out before I throw you out.'

Murder didn't bring the grieving together, Darren thought; it forced them away from each other. Grief had made his mum so tall that she towered over Dad and demoted him to a place where he couldn't reach her. Darren retreated down the stairs, his parents' argument rebounding with increasing intensity above his head. At that moment Carly had never seemed so far away, the hole she left behind so distorted and unfillable. He had brought this about. His poorly thought-through actions had placed this grenade at the heart of his family and he had pulled out the pin.

But there was something even worse. He wanted to see Olivia again. He was desperate to see her – to listen to her lies, to listen to every bit of rubbish that spewed from her mouth. And if he couldn't see her, he could get close to her psychiatrist. He had to get back to Roehampton.

He was taking his bike from the garden through into the kitchen when he noticed the flat tyre.

He shouted up the stairs. 'Mum, I need the car.'

When their argument didn't stop he picked up the key and left.

23

Traffic was bad, seemingly snarled up all over south London. Darren ended up in a long queue on the road that ran to the prison, shunting forward one car at a time, first gear, second gear. An ambulance passed him at speed, a jangle of noise bearing down on the gates of Roehampton.

He saw the TV vans and the crowd of reporters when he was eight cars away from the gates; the hatchbacks of the journalists parked up high on the opposite verge. They were reporting on Olivia, filling in the wait for police confirmation on the South Downs bones with speculation and gruesome rehashing of the events of ten years ago. The queue inched forward. Ten years fell away as he remembered the reporters who were often outside his house in Brighton back then, swarming forward as Dad parked the car. Darren had moved past their large bellies and recording equipment then, sometimes with his face squashed next to his mother's skirt, at other times his hand gripped like a vice by his nan. Later some of them came in the house as his mum gave interviews, the strange smell of their aftershave and cigarettes lingering in the hall.

The crowd here was large, thirty people at least. Panic enveloped him. Some of those men and women would be the same ones as ten years ago – back on a case that was never solved, the ones who wrote the books, who sold his family's pain for money. And they would recognise him as he drove slowly through the gates. It was their job to question and to enquire and they would know who he was, and they would wonder what the hell was happening.

Darren slammed the car into reverse and backed up to the bumper behind him. He signalled to turn out of the queue, hoping he was still too far away from the gates for anyone to see him. A car two in front of him was doing the same, hurriedly reversing to do an awkward five-point turn in the street and head away. Darren watched until the old Ford Fiesta was clear so he could complete his manoeuvre. The Fiesta's driver was the young befriender who had been waiting to visit Olivia. Darren watched as he drove away at speed. He didn't want to be seen by the reporters, just as Darren didn't.

A car far back in the queue honked. The traffic was speeding up, the obstruction further ahead cleared. Darren put up an 'indulge me' hand and did a three-point turn in the road, seeing the heads of the reporters turning his way. As he accelerated away he saw Helen, three cars back, staring at him as he went past.

24

Helen leaned forward in her seat, trying to get her armpit in the air conditioning stream. She had started sweating more lately, waves of it attacking her like some foreign invasion. As if being forty-four wasn't demeaning enough, her body had to start protesting at her driving to work. Whenever she thought about her bastard husband Joel the sweats would come on, flights of anger and scorn rising up in her. Her old university friend Liz counselled her to not be bitter and so she woke every morning saying it to herself like a mantra. But it didn't work, it did not work. Joel, aged forty-five, her husband of twelve years, had left her for a 25-year-old who 'really understood him'.

The queue shunted forward and she saw the press corps and the BBC vans and Sky and all the rest of them. She had known they would be here, of course; Olivia had pulled a pretty spectacular stunt yesterday. This interested her. Why that, why now? She pulled down the visor to check herself in the mirror. One day she'd probably be rumbled as the doctor, a woman no less, who treated Olivia. It could be today and she didn't want to look anything less than professional.

She watched a couple of cars do the aggressive leave-the-queue manoeuvre. They were always men, throwing their hunks of metal around self-importantly and holding everyone up, as if they all didn't have places to go, things they had to do. Any other route was much longer and they already knew that; they just liked to temporarily hog two lanes of traffic. She knew she shouldn't generalise about the sexes, but as she got older she was thinking more and more that clichés existed because they were true.

The first man roared away. The next car to come past was Darren's. He had the window down on an old blue hatchback and his tanned arm on the window ledge, a thin band of hippy string round the tattoos on his wrist. He was a strange one, Darren – bent and haunted, yet surprisingly articulate and with a strength of character. The way he'd handled her in the chaos post-Linda had been masterful, in fact. She wondered idly how long he'd stay here; the cleaning staff were always moving on to other, usually also low-paid jobs. Not long, she reasoned, as he seemed to be shirking his shift on this hot day. Probably getting out of town and going to the beach to get high. She realised she didn't know what people his age actually did – she'd read somewhere that they no longer drank. Could that be true? That they didn't get plastered? They had no money, she knew, and according to the press were all living with their parents, wanking to online porn twenty-four hours a day, piercings everywhere. His abs would be rock-hard. A pleasing change from Joel's middle-aged sag.

She watched the news crews do their thing. The hang 'em flog 'em brigade would be frothing over this latest development. One of the bodies recovered, one family with closure at last. Oh how she would love to be on a talk show, pitted against Orin Bukowski, and run his arguments into the ground! They would never understand her job and how valuable it was, what amazing results could be achieved. Helen felt her bitterness recede. God she loved her job. It had been the great revelation of her life, that she enjoyed work as much as she did, especially now that Joel had done the dirty and left.

It was a bloody outrage that he could pull a woman so young, a woman who by rights should be with someone Darren's age. Women accepted such low standards while subjecting themselves to such high ones. It was always men foghorning their bad breath at you while they pontificated about something every woman in the room already knew.

Helen was at the gates now and pulled in past the press chaos. Work was her saviour, work was what brought self-respect and economic power. She thought of Becky, her sister, mired in faux complaints about her kids and her husband. Becks needed to get up off the sofa, duck the coffee mornings and get to work.

Helen was angry, that was why she was sweating, she knew. She'd been angry for days, weeks, maybe even years. Becky was coming on a sympathy visit at the weekend with the girls. They were going to make her feel better by baking cupcakes. Her world had fallen apart and cupcakes were supposed to mend it. Those sickly-sweet portions of goo in paper with horrible icing made her more angry than her husband's infidelity. It was aiming so low that angered Helen. Why couldn't her nieces cook paella, won tons, spicy prawns, cheese fucking straws? *Jesus, women,* she thought, *rise up against the tyranny of the candy-coloured cupcake!* Joel's researcher probably liked cupcakes. Then again, considering the size of the knickers she'd found crushed between the mattress and their sleigh bed – which was what had precipitated this crisis – the girl was probably just throwing them back up down the pan, the barely digested contents of her stomach still pink as they splattered the sides of the bowl.

Helen had been entrusted with important work by the state, and she was doing that work well. Her professional success trumped her tawdry domestic mess. She swung round the car park, trying to find two spaces together so she could pull in easily. She began to sweat again at the thought of all those journalists watching her bad parking. She cranked the gears tensely, the anger swarming in her again. Going into the tight space facing forward had been a mistake, she realised, and her angles were all wrong. Fuck it, she thought, as she gave up trying to straighten the car and climbed out of the passenger seat, she wasn't going to be hard on herself. No one was perfect. Least of all Joel.

25

Sonny breathed in and out again, counting a one-minute in-breath and trying for an out-breath of a minute and a half. He prided himself on being able to sit still for hours, retreat into his own mind, watch the images on the screen flowing by. In another life Sonny felt that he would like to have been a yogi on an Indian hillside, wearing white baggy clothes, the faint thrum of drums in the distance.

But today Corey was ruining his bliss, insisting on having talk radio on, everyone getting heated about what Olivia had revealed. 'It's cause and effect,' Corey was saying. 'She killed Linda and then the guilt made her give up one of the girls. Saying that, I'm glad she did that to Linda, the girl's more important than her.'

'What you saying?' Sonny countered. 'You don't want anyone to die, surely. Duvall only using the girl to get out of solitary for what she did.'

'Well, since no one here telling us a damn thing about what's happening, we can only speculate.'

'You see that chaos on the front gate this morning? That kind of thing upsets everybody.'

'True dat,' Corey replied. They paused to watch Dr Vivek Chowdray drive his Volvo through the gates and park. 'We're powerless, know what I'm sayin',' Corey added.

'Yet we have to see it!' They had both watched the attack on Linda on the cameras.

'Him, people like the governor, Helen, they all got the

inside track. Think of Darren, man, she could have killed him!'

'A terrible thing.' Sonny shook his head. He was only two years away from retirement and he craved the quiet, regular life.

'We can take some of that power back, you know,' Corey said. 'With those.' He tapped one of the screens in front of them.

'How's that?' asked Sonny.

'See Vivek there? We can find out where he lives by his licence plate.'

'Or we could simply go up to him and ask him. Sometimes the old-fashioned ways are the best.'

Corey tapped the side of his head, as if Sonny were an idiot. 'Where's the fun in that? I have a cuz at the DVLA. You just give him the plate, and they can tell you all sorts of things – what other cars are registered at his address, where he lives, how long he's been there.'

Sonny was nonplussed. 'You been drinking the Kool-Aid. Why we need to know that?'

'It's the information age, yeah? James Bond or the CIA.'

Sonny gave Corey a long look. 'Let me repeat. You're like James Bond?' Sonny burst out laughing as Corey tried to backtrack. 'Bwoy, that's the funniest thing you ever say. James Bond.'

Corey got indignant. 'Maybe he's having an affair. It's always them quiet ones.'

'Like Darren.' Sonny thought of his lanky body and hunched shoulders. 'He's nice enough. It's a tough break when you just trying to earn a crust.'

Corey didn't look like he agreed. 'The man tougher than he look with that hair – don't be fooled by him. You can scoff, but when I find some juice, you gonna wanna hear it. You gonna pay to hear it!' Corey stopped talking to watch Helen arrive. 'Oh man, here we go.'

They both watched Helen try to drive into the tight space bonnet-first. Her angle was all wrong and she was in danger of clipping the brake light of the car one along. She reversed in a movement that looked angry even from this far away and tried to come in again. She ended up abandoning her car half in the space and clambering out of the passenger side.

'Man, that woman can't drive for shit,' Corey said.

Sonny watched Helen get out of the car, looking harassed, scraping her hair back off her face and dismissively beeping the door locked as she walked away. He wanted to give her some driving tips, explain how you reversed in, lined up rear lights and edges and then it was all smooth and easy, but he worried she would label him sexist and not take his advice in the manner in which he gave it. He couldn't imagine how she parallel-parked. He hoped she was rich enough to afford a drive outside her house. Then again, with her separation, that was unlikely.

'I can find out about Helen—'

Sonny threw his hands up. 'Bwoy, we know she been dumped, don't need no computer for that!'

26

Darren tailed the Fiesta to the first set of lights. He stared in his rear-view mirror, fully expecting a TV van to be following. But it wasn't. He looked at the Fiesta. This befriender didn't want to see reporters either. The lights changed and the line of cars began to draw away. At the next junction Darren needed to turn right for Streatham – he had abandoned his parents' argument to try and see Olivia and should go back to his mum, support her on this difficult day. But the Fiesta carried on straight ahead and Darren followed.

He turned the radio on and found that dental records had confirmed that the bones on the South Downs were Molly Peters's. He switched the radio off when Orin Bukowski's voice came on. His parents didn't like Orin. He had never been sure why, but the feelings were strong, even after all this time.

The white Fiesta was still two cars in front, and Darren just kept on following until it reached Clapham Park Road near Clapham Common and pulled round the back of a big corner pub that looked as if it had once been a bank.

Darren coasted to a halt further along and used his rear-view mirror to see what happened next.

The man appeared a few minutes later, crossed the street and let himself into a door next to a tired-looking charity shop. Darren got out of the car and approached the door. Just one bell, no name. There were two storeys above the shop, a flat-fronted Victorian building gone to seed, dirty windows that looked like they were never opened, grey nets over the windows. Darren got back in his car and waited five minutes but the man didn't come back out. He turned into the car park behind the pub and saw the Fiesta in a corner on the loose gravel.

He pulled up near it, got out and looked around. No one was about this early in the morning, the pub still closed. He peered through the car window. A mess of papers was shoved between the seats, along with a half-eaten Yorkie bar. He took a photo of the licence plate with his phone and walked back to the charity shop.

He opened the door and a bell dinged. By the counter were two plastic bags of clothing and a young woman. She had jet black hair and was skinny, with tattoos and a pierced nose. The shop smelled of old clothes and mothballs.

'How do I post something next door? There's no letterbox.'

'The post comes here, the flat is connected to the shop.'

'The guy who lives there, what's his name?'

The girl shrugged. An old woman came out of the back of the shop, a pair of patent black shoes in one hand. 'Can I help?'

'I've got something for the guy next door.'

'John Sears? We can take it in here. He has a key, the shop and the flat go together.'

'OK great, let me just go and get it from my car.'

'Here, take a leaflet.' She handed him something in a bright colour that talked about refugees in Bosnia and Kosovo and Darren left, the bell jangling as he went.

He walked to the Common, his mood dark, and phoned Kamal from a lying-down position on the grass. As the answerphone clicked in he hovered his legs two inches above the grass, so that when he finally got to leave a message about being too ill to come in to work he sounded like he was gasping his last.

He hadn't eaten, so he found a small café and ordered a fry-up. The TV news droned on a set in a ceiling corner of the room. He was tucking in to his food when Olivia's picture filled the screen, the stock image from ten years ago, with the swollen eye and the bad hair. Then the screen filled with pictures of the five victims. They always used Carly's school photo, her dark hair falling into one eye. Her teeth looked too big for her mouth to Darren now.

There were shots of the site where Molly had been found. In the glory of a June summer day the South Downs looked so beautiful it made Darren's scarred heart ache anew. He missed the sea, he missed the countryside, shut up as he was in south London. He had no appetite left; he pushed his plate away.

The girls and women ranged in age from fourteen to eighteen. They weren't alike particularly; some were blonde, others brunette, Rajinder's family were originally from Pakistan. Carly and Isla were friends from Brighton, Molly had lived in Hove, Heather was from Eastbourne and Rajinder was from Burgess Hill. The investigation into their disappearances had been slow to start and there had already been one inquiry into why. No one had realised at first that the disappearance of Heather, the first victim, was suspicious; she was a troubled girl who'd run away multiple times from a children's home, she'd had problems with drink and drugs and had been arrested for soliciting. The last known sighting of her was on Brighton Pier in 2001. She had been fifteen.

Rajinder came from a strict Muslim family and had rebelled against her arranged marriage to a cousin from Lahore. When her family reported the bright eighteen-year-old missing in 2002 the police had initially suspected the family, causing uproar in the local community. That Rajinder had fallen into Olivia's clutches was only discovered when Olivia was arrested and her house searched.

Fourteen-year-old Molly Peters never came back from a trip to Preston Park in 2002. The lack of urgency in the case was later criticised in an official report, but the investigation had been complicated by Molly's chaotic life – her mum was a drug user with multiple boyfriends and the family were known to social services. Molly had written a note to say she was running away.

Carly Evans and Isla Bukowski, fourteen-year-old friends, disappeared on a late-afternoon shopping trip in November 2003. Happy and contented girls from secure families, their disappearance launched one of East Sussex's largest police investigations.

Slowly, meticulously, the police investigated every avenue. It wasn't a dramatic breakthrough that solved the case, it was dogged, methodical police work where every little bit of information built on previous information to complete a solid picture. Finally Olivia cracked under the weight of the evidence put before her.

The police had a problem gaining much information from the runaways and drug addicts who had been Heather's friends. They all distrusted the police and were reluctant to get involved. One girl, ranting in the back of a police car, said that the only person who had been nice to Heather had been her social worker – she'd hung out at her house sometimes. This titbit of information led the police to pay their first visit to Olivia, hoping she may be able to shed some light on her disappearance. Olivia didn't reveal much but did give them some dates. Shortly afterwards, it was discovered that Olivia Duvall had for a few weeks been assigned as caseworker to Molly Peters. This time two senior police officers paid Olivia a visit and looked round the house; they noted the heavy lock on the door to the basement and the rings set in the beams that ran along one wall.

The police began to look into the life of the solitary

Brighton social worker, at this stage looking for men who might be connected to her. At the same time CCTV footage of central Brighton was being combed to try to find the last movements of Carly and Isla. The police had them walking past a security camera at 4.15 p.m. near the city centre; a week later one of the hundreds of cars that the police were processing from near that spot, a white Renault Clio, turned out to belong to Olivia Duvall. The police couldn't examine her car, though, because she had sent it to be scrapped days before.

They began a thorough search of her house, concentrating on the cellar, but found nothing. Behind a radiator in the hallway, however, they found a hairband with Molly's hair in it.

And then the team got the breakthrough – the scrapped Renault Clio had been sold on in parts. They traced the seats to a garage in Worthing, and deep down in the crack of the front passenger seat they found a sequin from Isla Bukowski's bag.

Olivia was arrested and the police went to work on her house, finding that household bleach had been used to clean almost every surface in the basement and the rest of the house, destroying fingerprints and DNA. On the second day the police began spraying Luminol and discovered that the wooden floor in the living room had once had a large arc of blood splattered across it. On the inside leg of an armchair in the same room they found a fingerprint that belonged to Heather. She must have been lying on the floor, reaching out for something to hold.

In the basement they found three blue threads from Carly's pants, caught on a nail. The police got an extension to keep Olivia detained for longer. The investigation was in a frenzy, public horror and disgust at fever pitch. Then they discovered that the blood on the floor matched Molly's. And then they began testing the soil in the secluded garden, screened by tall firs, and found high levels of components from human blood and several human bone fragments. The bones had lain in the soil for at least two years, and were impossible to identify.

On the third day Olivia made a statement, in which she admitted to killing five missing girls: Isla, Molly, Heather, Rajinder and Carly. She offered no defence, and never revealed where their bodies were.

She was assessed as having an acute personality disorder, tried and sent to a secure facility.

Olivia had broken all the rules. Serial killers were not usually women. If they killed at all they tended to kill men who had been violent and abusive to them, not young women and girls. Serial killers usually murdered within their ethnic group – Rajinder's fate threw that rule out the window. These types of killers were normally opportunists: long-distance lorry drivers, men who used prostitutes, men who worked at fairgrounds. But in Olivia Duvall something new and horrible had been revealed. Women who killed children nearly always had a man influencing them, a man in control. They looked hard, the police told his family, for a man behind the scenes. Olivia had lived for a while with one Eric Cox, who had a history of violent outbursts and drunken fights, but at the time that Molly and Heather went missing he was serving time in jail for fencing stolen cars, and was eliminated as a suspect. She was a lone operator, a freak of nature.

The trial and conviction had been unsatisfactory to many people – with none of the bodies recovered, a lot of questions had remained unanswered. Olivia was an opportunist in the sense that she had chosen vulnerable girls uncoupled from the safety net of family – until she had targeted Isla and Carly, that was. But why she had killed any of them, and how, remained a mystery.

Darren pushed his plate away, sickness flooding him. Now the TV was showing the grassy area where Olivia's house had been demolished and her garden dug over, the Brighton corner where the house had once stood and which was now a council garden. Less than a fifteen-minute walk from his old home, his former life.

Darren ordered a cup of tea and watched a mother come in to the café with a buggy and a girl aged about twelve. The girl was sullen, her trainers scuffed, hands in the pockets of her pink top. The baby started fussing and the mother tried to rock it into quietness. The girl sat down and stared at Darren. He looked back at her. She was still staring, chewing a sweet. How easy would it be to abduct this girl? How had Olivia done it? He leaned forward towards the girl and smiled. She smiled back.

He stood up abruptly and walked out of the café. Olivia had planted that thought in him. She was a master manipulator and he was shaken to the core. It was as if she had reached out of that prison and was pulling him about on invisible strings. That he had even imagined how you might take a child, even in an abstract way, made him feel ill.

He needed to go home; he wanted his mum. Love repaired the evil in the world, not chasing a serial killer's befriender in his car through south London.

27

Darren drove home, stopping at the end of the street and peering round the corner from the driver's seat, worried there might be some journalists hanging about who knew where they lived. But the road looked deserted. He pulled up outside the house.

Mum was lying on the sofa when he came in, the radio on, her eyes red and her face blotchy. She looked exhausted.

'Where's Dad?'

'He went to work. He said he needed to get away from me.'

He sat down next to her. 'He doesn't mean that.'

She smiled sadly. 'But he does, Darren. He does.'

Darren ran upstairs and came back down with his Roehampton uniform. He shoved it in the washing machine and came back to sit with his mum.

'Why aren't you at work?'

Darren looked away. 'I wanted to make sure you were OK.'

Mum struggled to sit upright. 'I saw where she had left Molly on the TV. It was a very pretty spot.'

'Mum, don't.'

'I know Carly's not there. She's just not.'

Hope still sat so strong in her and he saw that it was the crutch that kept her going. Maybe he had it all wrong. Maybe it wasn't for her that he needed to find Carly, but for himself.

Mum scowled as Orin Bukowski's deep voice carried over from the radio. 'Turn it off will you? I can't stand him.'

Darren turned the radio off and sat back. 'Why do you hate him so much? I've never understood what he did wrong.'

'In the beginning, when Carly and Isla first went missing, he was great at generating publicity, making sure the police were doing everything they could. He's passionate, committed to what he believes, a force of nature I suppose. But when the Witch was found, it all fell apart. We felt he got in the way of the police doing their job – he was getting special treatment from them before the trial, finding out things the rest of us had a right to know too.'

'Like what?'

'Details about what they had found. Stuff from the investigation was being leaked to him, it became an us and him situation.'

Darren watched his mum's face carefully. She was turned away, staring out of the window. 'There's something else. What aren't you telling me?'

She patted his hand, not looking him in the eye. 'Andy doesn't agree, but I felt it became all about Isla, not the others. Not Carly or those other poor girls. We withdrew from Orin's group. It was a difficult time. He's a man of very strong convictions and if other people disagree with him he finds that difficult.'

Darren sat still, considering. 'Was Isla like her father? What were Carly and her like together?'

She sat back. 'Inseparable. Carly adored Isla.'

'What do you mean?'

'Isla seemed much older than Carly. She was like her father, opinionated, willful.'

'You sound like you thought she was a bad influence.'

She shook her head. 'Not at all. I don't mean to sound negative. Isla was great fun, the life and soul of the party, so to speak. She was very bright, very focused, not into boys at all. She was – I don't know how to say it – political isn't the right word, but she was angry. Rebelling against her father, his money, his success. She was contemptuous of it. It was as if she wanted a different kind of life. She was a romantic, an idealist. She hated anything run of the mill. I thought I was lucky, lucky that Carly had found a friend who was above the usual boys and make-up trivia. That's why I let them go off on their own a lot, they were growing up.'

'Where were they going all the time?'

She smiled sadly. 'To the skate park, the pier, Isla's house, the usual places fourteen-year-olds go. Carly was always back on time, her homework was always done. She was never any bother to me. She was a good girl.' She paused, staring out of the window, and sighed. 'I really believe she loved Isla. Teenage friendships can be as strong a bond as women ever know.'

She reached forward and picked up a letter from the coffee table, obviously keen to change the subject. 'I've got a date for my mastectomy. It's next Wednesday at St George's Hospital.'

Darren reached over and hugged her. 'Dad and I will both be there, don't worry.'

She rubbed her hands together. 'Assuming he hasn't left me by then.' It was a weak joke and neither of them could raise a smile.

'I'll make you a tea, Mum.'

She followed him into the kitchen.

'What's that knocking sound in there?' Mum was staring at the washing machine. Darren stood in front of it, scared the Roehampton logo might twist into view.

'Something of CJ's that he wanted cleaned.'

'Something he doesn't want his mum to see,' she tutted. 'Why's it on boil?'

'Oh, yeah, silly me.'

'Honestly, Darren, you'll shrink it.'

Darren stood in front of the machine, feeling the heat burn through his trousers. He didn't move away but stayed with the pain. This was how it felt having seen Olivia, as though he was out of his depth and he was going to get burned.

'Where's the car key? I have to go out later.'

The knocking sound got louder.

Mum saw his stricken face.

'Tell me it's not in the washing machine, Darren!'

Later that evening Darren repaired his bike puncture and then looked up John Sears on the internet. There were hundreds of people called that on Facebook and Twitter, and after a long search he had still found no one who matched this befriender. Google turned up nothing useful either. The charity premises John lived above helped refugees in London fleeing the former Yugoslavia. Even twenty years after the civil war, the upheaval was still being felt, communities still shattered, money still needed. He read about befrienders; they were part of organisations that helped offenders adapt to release back into the community, a sounding board for long-term prisoners or lifers to talk about their problems. Their meetings with offenders were one-on-one.

Next Darren went to work on the spot where Molly had been buried. He printed out a map of the site and cross-referenced it with every detail he could find or knew about Olivia's former life. He marked Olivia's house at the top corner. Molly had been buried less than ten miles from where she grew up. He looked at the roads snaking away across the Downs, traced a finger along the most obvious route from her house in Brighton.

Why did she bury Molly there? If he could answer that, he was nearer to finding where the other girls were. Were they nearby?

What his mum had said about Orin Bukowski came back

to him. Orin knows more than anyone. He knows as much as the police, if not more. Darren needed to meet Orin Bukowski, and he needed to go back to Roehampton. He gazed again at the map. After only a few visits he had unlocked this much of the case; he would continue to go to Roehampton until he was chased from the place by the threat of imminent discovery.

28

Hounslow, West London

The man was parked behind a Renault 16 estate in a street with concreted-over gardens, weeds straining up through the cement desert. He was in the hinterland near Heathrow, planes punctuating the milky sky every four and a half minutes. Old habits were hard to break; he'd started counting the intervals between them as soon as he'd stopped the car.

It had been a strange day; the body of a young girl had been found and his speculations about the case had brought on the itch, the crazy itch that stopped him sleeping and sent him mad. The itch had got so bad he couldn't contain it any longer.

Gert Becker had fobbed him off and he had been driven to other sources, which he had to check out thoroughly. The house had blinds that looked as if they were permanently drawn, upstairs and down. He had checked the licence plates of the cars parked outside already, having driven past here earlier in the day in a different vehicle. There was nothing flagged up on them in the computer system at work.

He had done the usual scan of the road and the house – checking for cameras, marks on concrete or the sides of buildings that showed where things had been moved, vans that didn't look right – and had driven away.

He had come back at ten thirty, in a different car, wearing

a baseball cap. He walked up between the cars, rang the bell, saw the dark shadow pass in front of the spyhole. The door opened a crack, a chain hanging under the Bulgarian's face like a noose round a neck. Every cultural group had a speciality in something, and the Bulgarians were cornering the market in this type of fresh produce.

The Bulgarian didn't talk, just scanned the street, and he was let in.

He was in a shabby suburban semi with a narrow hall table covered in fast food leaflets, a stained carpet on the stairs, gold strips of something cheap from one celebration or another hanging in a living room that was crowded with a grey leather sofa and recliner.

The Bulgarian made him take off his shoes before he led him up the stairs. Being a stickler for dirt was ironic considering the smell from the bathroom and the faint tang of something sweet, heroin probably, that hung around the top corridor.

The Bulgarian opened the door to the main bedroom at the front of the house. There were five products sat on the bed, all in sparkly miniskirts, their bare arms and legs sticking out at awkward and defeated angles.

The Bulgarian shouted something sharp and they looked up, allowing him to see the glazed and vacant eyes on two of them. A third had a livid bruise on half of her face; someone's fist had cost the Bulgarian a lot of money or two more weeks in this bedroom to get it to heal.

There was one at the end of the bed, her dark eyes huge in the dim light, her hair long and dark. He walked over and took a cursory glance at her forearms. She flinched with fear, which he liked. He picked up her foot, pulled her toes apart to check for hidden track marks. She was clean. 'This one.'

The Bulgarian smiled. 'It's very good. We've turned down

many offers for it. Been here three weeks. We wait for the right price.'

'How old is it?'

'Fourteen,' he said proudly.

The Bulgarian was a liar of course, but it was a lie that missed by only a couple of years. 'I'll give you three and a half thousand.'

The Bulgarian made a scoffing noise. 'You're way out of line.'

He shrugged and turned his back, began to leave the room. Buying and selling was the same the world over, and had changed little over the centuries. A slave trader in ancient Rome would have immediately understood the haggling going on in Hounslow.

The Bulgarian called after him. 'Four thousand and it's yours.'

He had him now, keen to have the cash rather than the responsibility. Food and drugs were a cost they were always trying to cut back. 'Three-six is my final offer.'

'Done.'

He pulled the pack of notes out of his back pocket and handed them over. The Bulgarian flicked through the thick wad in a practised way, nodded and pulled the product up by her thin arm. She was shaking with fear but compliant; by the time they reached this place, both geographical and mental, they had learned to be.

They walked out of the bedroom. The remaining products on the bed either looked away or gazed at the floor.

She followed him in her bare feet down the stairs. Those feet were beginning to bother him. 'You have something to cover those?' he asked.

The Bulgarian barked into the kitchen at the back. A small boy came running out and saw the problem. He disappeared into the back again, emerging a few moments later with a pair of wellington boots.

The man frowned, causing the Bulgarian to shrug defensively. 'It never came with packaging.' The boy dropped the boots to the carpet and the girl put them on.

The Bulgarian opened the door and the man and the girl walked across the weedy front yard to the man's car. He opened the passenger door for her and she got in. He walked round to the driver's seat, got in and locked the doors. He took a careful look up and down the street as he adjusted the cuffs on his blue shirt. Then he drove his new toy away.

29

When Darren arrived at Roehampton the next morning he felt scared, more scared than he would have thought possible. What had happened to Linda in here couldn't be undone: the building appeared forbidding and ripe with danger. The lockers in the changing room seemed to clang extra loudly, the wheels on the creaking cleaning trolleys squeaked more intensely. Lining up with the assembled cleaners by the first security door he had an attack of claustrophobia, and wondered if he could cope with being shut up in there all day. It was only when Yassir patted him on the shoulder and said how sorry he was about what had happened, shaking his head in disbelief and resignation, that Darren felt better.

The promotion that Helen had given him at first seemed to mean little, but then Kamal took pity on him and gave him the offices on the first floor to clean. He took the cleaning trolley up in the lift and poked his head into the security room, but Sonny was on the phone and Corey had been replaced today by a man Darren didn't recognise, so he began to dust the windowsills.

He cleaned in and out of several empty offices, shut up and stale as if no one ever worked there. Helen's door was partly open and he walked in, but she was at her desk, pen in hand. She looked up and saw him and put the pen down. 'Darren, come in, come in. I'm so glad you've decided to come back and to carry on. How are you feeling today?'

He nodded sheepishly, not sure what to say.

'You might feel a little strange for a couple of days, that's entirely normal.' She smiled warmly. 'Has the counselling service phoned you yet?' He nodded. 'Good. They can help you a lot, there's a really good team there.'

Darren realised this was his opportunity to gain some information. 'What did Linda do to be in here?'

Helen sat back in her chair, holding the silver pen. She remained silent, weighing her options. She put the pen carefully back on the table. 'Linda forced drain cleaner down her daughter's throat until she died.' She swallowed. 'You see the dark side of life in here, Darren. You can't get away from that, I'm afraid.'

'Did Linda do anything else?'

Helen stared at him. 'Are you referring to the sexual abuse rumours concerning Linda and her daughter?' Darren shrugged. Helen's voice was calm and even. 'Did Olivia refer to these allegations during your meeting?' Darren said nothing, unsure how to proceed. 'I hope I don't need to remind you that Olivia Duvall is a very clever, manipulative individual with an inflated sense of her own self-worth. She cannot accept responsibility for what she has done and this manifests itself in all sorts of ways here at Roehampton.'

'But is it true?'

Helen sat back. 'You're very persistent, Darren Smith.' She said it like she was impressed. 'Nothing was ever proved in court. We are professionals, and we can't get distracted by innuendo and rumour.'

Darren had the uncomfortable sensation that Olivia had been telling the truth. He pressed on. 'It was pretty amazing that Olivia revealed where that girl's body was. Does that mean . . . I mean, is she likely to say where any of the others are?'

'That's impossible to predict. Clear-cut successes are rare, however much we would like it to be otherwise. My job is to treat my patients, not speculate.' She was unforthcoming, but she was being kind, he thought. She had the self-awareness to know that after what had happened he was entitled to ask these questions. She smiled. 'Come back in a little while to clean, I won't be here long.'

Darren was about to leave when a woman appeared behind him in the doorway.

'Helen? I hoped you'd be here.'

'Milly! How wonderful to see you!' Helen got out of her chair and came out into the corridor.

'I was here doing an assessment and I heard you were in. I wanted to come and catch up . . .' They walked off up the corridor together.

'Shall I just do your office quickly?' Darren called after Helen.

She turned back, distracted. 'Yes, fine.'

There was a neat pile of files on Helen's desk, and two coffee cups, both half drained. He picked up the cups and put them outside the door to take to the kitchen down the hall. The women were still further up the corridor, whispering now, Helen probably relaying the pain of a relationship lost.

Darren picked up the dustcloth and moved across to the desk. He glanced through the files; they were as he had hoped – patient records – but Olivia's wasn't there. He wiped the top of the lamp, sending a faint smell of burning dust across the room.

'Such a cliché!' Milly shrieked at something Helen said. Their voices were raised now, their conversation at an end. 'We should have a drink, Helen, have a proper catch-up.'

Darren turned and saw a key stuck in the lock at the top right-hand corner of the filing cabinet.

He was across the room and pulling it out as he heard the door squeak behind him. He ran the cloth across the filing cabinet, pulling the key with it.

He turned slowly, dread filling him. Helen was no fool. She was standing just in the doorway, looking at his hand where he was holding the cloth. He had to do something fast.

'Are you—'

'Will you come out for a drink with me? I think you're gorgeous.'

He took a step across the office, giving her his best lover-on-heat face.

She looked alarmed and took a step back. 'Now hold your horses, for goodness' sake.' She frowned but it was chased away by a smile. 'That's sweet, but really, it's not going to happen.' She smoothed her hair and pushed out her breasts.

Darren blushed to the roots of his hair, the key feeling as big as a football in his hand. He shuffled out of the door, embarrassed. He couldn't believe he'd actually done that, but it had felt good. Rejection wasn't so bad – and he had the key.

30

'I think the press have largely gone now,' the governor said, looking around at the group assembled in the conference room for the afternoon emergency meeting. 'Andrew, they stayed beyond the perimeter that we established?'

Andrew Casey-Jones, the head of security, nodded emphatically. He was a Welsh former rugby player with ham hands and a neck thicker than his head.

'And we're still waiting to hear from the CPS regarding whether they are taking this matter with Linda Biggs any further – they move at a glacial pace, as we all know.' Everyone nodded. The governor's secretary took notes diligently.

'But I understand Darren Smith is back at work and is using the counselling service?' The governor looked at Helen.

'He's back, and I can confirm that he's contacted the service.'

The governor nodded. 'We had a lot of negative press over Linda's death and we need to be sure all our systems are as robust as possible. So, Andrew, the security review?'

'It's going to be completed in four weeks and covers all aspects: interactions between patients and staff, outside agencies, vetting.'

'Can I make a suggestion?' Helen said. 'I think we need new filing cabinets in the offices. Maybe a combination system would feel more secure.'

'Data protection is obviously paramount,' the governor said.

'There's a new budget allocation for data protection,' the head of finance added. 'The cabinets could come under that category.'

Helen nodded, pleased. Her lost filing cabinet key could be subsumed within this refit. She felt she was an organised, efficient person, but her divorce had frayed her normally precise workings like a thread unravelling in an otherwise perfect cashmere sweater. She'd put her spare on her keyring now.

'We need to address Orin Bukowski,' the PR said.

'What's he done now?' the governor muttered, wiping a hand across his forehead.

'He has filed a petition of a hundred thousand names to you –' the PR dumped the large printout on the desk '– personally, asking for a permanent withdrawal of outside access for Olivia Duvall.'

Feet shuffled and bums moved on seats. 'Has he never heard of the Court of Human Rights?' Helen snapped.

'He's challenging their jurisdiction as we speak.'

'We want to avoid getting into any conversation with him if at all possible,' the governor replied. 'We have the government on our side over this, they hate having their boats rocked too. We'll ignore it for the moment, refer it to the Justice Secretary.'

'And he wants to visit Olivia,' the PR added.

'He needs to get in line,' the governor said.

'It's her right to refuse to see him,' Helen added.

'Don't I know it.' The governor paused. 'Which brings me on to the next topic.' He turned to Dr Vivek Chowdray. 'Her hospital admission.'

Vivek nodded and cleared his throat. He picked up a sheet of paper and began to read. 'Her conditions are heart arrhythmia and bradycardia, her symptoms are dizziness, chest pain and blackouts. She's being treated with 200 milligrams of Bepridil Hydrochloride daily. She needs a pacemaker, or she could to go into cardiac arrest. The fitting of a pacemaker requires a minimum of one overnight stay in hospital.'

'Over to you, Andrew,' the governor said.

Andrew laced his thick fingers together. 'She will be taken in an unmarked prison ambulance to St George's, Tooting. Two guards go with her in the van. She is restrained in the ambulance. Post-operative recovery will take place in a secure suite where she will be handcuffed to the bed frame. The nurses will be security checked before they can go in. Two guards are stationed at all times outside the room, others at a wider perimeter.'

'Which floor is the room on?' asked the governor.

'Second. Straight drop to the cement car park. A woman of her weight, age and fitness is eighty per cent likely to break a leg or back if they fall that distance onto concrete.'

'She will be weak after the operation too,' Vivek added.

'There's a media blackout, obviously,' Andrew said.

There was a small pause as the group in the room digested this information. 'Anyone have any questions, issues they want to raise?' The governor looked around. They all shook their heads. 'So, on Friday, assuming no post-operative complications, she's back in the prison van, and back here. Full of heart.'

They gathered up their reports, assessments and evaluations and pushed their chairs back.

31

Nathan was manning the security checkpoint as Darren left the building at the end of his shift. 'You coming for a drink tonight, Darren?' he asked. 'We'll be at the Rose and Crown, it's the first pub on the left as you leave, you can't miss it.' Darren shook his head. 'Come on,' Nathan said, flashing Darren his most sympathetic smile. 'I'm clocking off in an hour, I'll see you there. You need a drink after what happened the other day.'

Nathan was right. It was important to try to relax and put that awful episode with Linda behind him. He had spoken to no one for nearly four hours and the day was hot, the evening promising to be long and beautiful. A beer would go down well, he decided.

A little while later he pulled up by the pub on his bike and saw Sonny at a table outside in the sun. Sonny stood up and spread his arms wide, welcoming Darren in. 'Let me buy you a drink. It's good you came back, terrible what happened to you, real terrible.'

Darren felt the sweat beginning to pool on his back. Sonny was nice and he felt bad misleading them about who he was. He thought it would be better just to go home after all, but then he saw Chloe and a very large woman coming out from the bar with red drinks with parasols bobbing in them. Darren sat down, willing Chloe to sit next to him.

'Hi Darren,' Chloe said. She sat down beside him. 'This is Berenice, she works in the kitchens too.'

'Are you OK after what happened? You had only just started, I heard,' Berenice said.

'It's not your fault what Duvall did,' Chloe said. 'You tried to help, that's the main thing.' Her lovely hand was on his arm.

'I've been here seven years,' Berenice said. 'It can seem like a pretty gruesome place to work but it's OK really.' She shook her head. 'I've never heard of anything like that before.' She paused. 'Be careful.' Darren felt a little spike of alarm. 'You think this is just temporary, right? But you can end up here longer than you thought. Before you know it, you'll be twenty-five.'

'If we're not all killed by the inmates before then,' Chloe added, shuddering. 'You're lucky you're not full-time, Berenice.'

Berenice squared her fleshy shoulders. 'No one's attacking me, for sure.'

'Would be a terrible tragedy,' Sonny said. 'Imagine a world without Berenice's cakes.'

Berenice turned to Darren to explain. 'When I'm not working in the kitchens I make cakes at Borough Market and sell them, but it's hard, you know. Margins are small.'

Darren was impressed. Borough was the biggest farmers' market in London and snaked south from the river near Blackfriars and London Bridge stations.

'Berenice does retro classics. Pineapple upside-down cake, Victoria sponge, Eccles cakes . . .' Chloe sipped the red drink through a straw. 'Thursdays and Fridays she's out of this hellhole and baking away under the train lines.'

'If you're lucky you'll get to taste them, I bring them in to work sometimes. Loss leaders, I think they're called,' Berenice said.

Sonny put his hand up and called out to Helen, who had just come out of the pub. She carried her glass of wine over.

'Budge, Darren.' Helen squeezed herself on at the end of the row. The table fell silent, cagey at a more senior member of staff arriving.

'Don't let me stop you,' Helen said invitingly.

Chloe was the first to break. 'We're talking about what Olivia did and whether it means she's about to harm us.'

There were nods and murmurs round the table.

Helen leaned back. 'Well, I'm glad I came to see you guys. You'll all be receiving a letter about a security review tomorrow. We're sure all our procedures are safe, but a review is not a bad thing to have anyway. Olivia won't be interacting with staff or patients until we're sure she poses no threat to anyone's safety.'

'What's a security review?' Darren asked.

'Just routine. A check that people are who they say they are, that security procedures for getting in and out of the building are robust, online issues, the whole thing really.'

Darren took a long glug of beer. He was running out of time to achieve anything before he'd have to leave.

'Those poor families,' Chloe said. 'I wash her plate every day. I used to ladle for her when she was in the dining room. Eugh, she's horrible.'

There were murmurs of disgust all round.

Darren seized on what Chloe had said. 'Did she ever talk to you?'

'She told me my green beans weren't to her liking.'

Darren's heart fell. He had been hoping for something more useful. 'Weird.'

'God she is so weird!' Her teeth were lovely, bright and even in her pouty mouth.

'This is when Helen spends the next two years analysing why Olivia doesn't eat her green beans!' said Sonny.

'That'll be a hundred and fifty quid a session, thank you very much!' said Berenice.

'When the real reason is that Chloe can't cook them properly!'

'They're the most expensive and over-researched green beans in NHS history!'

Helen took their ribbing in good spirit.

'Why don't you torture the riddle of those girls' whereabouts out of her?' Berenice asked. 'Like that guy Orin what's-his-name keeps asking for. They waterboard terrorists, why's this less important? Just saying.'

Helen scoffed. 'Plenty would queue up to do that – that's why justice is dispensed by the state, not the families for instance. Would you really want to work for a place that tortured people?'

'My job seems like torture already!' Berenice joked and they laughed.

'Joking apart, Olivia is no threat to any of you. The security review is to ensure you – we – all stay safe.'

'So she can never escape or anything?'

Helen smiled and looked at Chloe indulgently. 'I can guarantee you that Olivia Duvall is never escaping from Roehampton.'

32

The next day was one of Darren's free days and he cycled to the South Bank and Orin Bukowski's office. Orin Bukowski was originally from Tennessee, had met and fallen in love with a woman from Brighton, had moved to England's south coast, made a fortune in industrial packaging, sold his company after his wife died in a car smash and, now he no longer had to work, devoted his copious time and energy to making criminals pay. The man had hardly been off the TV or radio in the last seventy-two hours. His office was in a building on the south side of the Thames and as Darren came through into the reception area, he could see the dome of St Paul's Cathedral bathed in sun and soaring skywards across the river.

'Nice view,' he said to the secretary, who smiled thinly.

'I wanted to see Mr Bukowski.'

'Do you have an appointment?'

Darren shook his head.

'Mr Bukowski's extremely busy,' the secretary said, shaking her head at the impossibility of the task of squeezing Darren in. 'He really doesn't have a moment all day.' She looked at something on her iPad. 'Can you make Tuesday next week at 4.45? He has ten minutes then.'

'I really need to see him now. It's about the missing girls. I'm family of the Five.'

She didn't react, just picked up the phone. 'Your name?'

'Darren Evans.'

She said the name into the phone, and listened. She put the phone down and pointed at a door across the reception area. 'You may go in.'

Orin was a big, clean-shaven man in a checked shirt and chinos, with a red face and small, quick eyes. He came from behind a huge desk to shake Darren's hand. He did it so vigorously Darren had to work hard not to wince.

'Darren Evans, it's good to meet you, have a seat.'

The office had the same view as the reception, but was bigger. A light-reflecting photographic umbrella was standing open in one corner and there was a video camera set up. The pale walls carried a series of large photos of stark rooms with a chair in the centre of each one. They looked like images from dentists' waiting rooms. 'How are your parents?' Orin asked.

Darren stumbled on his words. 'Not great, to be honest. Mum's got breast cancer, she's having treatment at the moment. She has to have an operation.'

He was nodding vigorously. 'I heard she was sick. I'll pray for her.'

Darren was taken aback. 'I didn't know that you knew—'

Orin snorted, causing Darren to falter. He held up his hand. 'I won't deny it, I heard that she went to see prisoner number 1072B.'

So it was true what his parents had said about him having insider information from Roehampton. 'That hasn't helped,' Darren added.

Orin shook his head. 'That a sick and grieving mother can be humiliated by a creature such as that is a national disgrace.' Darren rubbed his hands down his trousers, unsure how to proceed. 'That monster can't take a shit without me knowing, not going to apologise for that.'

Orin got up from his swivel chair and went to stand with his back to Darren, staring out of the window, hands in his chino pockets. 'And then she murders another patient. The regime at Roehampton is a joke.' He turned back from the window. 'But my job is to try and right the wrongs I see. How can I be of service, Darren?'

'Well, I, the thing is . . .' Darren scratched his hair, 'I want to know more about what happened back then, when Carly and the others were taken. I was only eleven, I didn't go to the trial, and I think it would help me to understand more, it would help my mum now she's sick—'

'Understand?'

'Well I . . .'

Orin began to pace in front of the window. 'I don't think you got the right word there, young gun. It's simple, don't try and make it complicated. Duvall's evil. Period. She can't be bargained with, or reasoned with, she doesn't feel pity or remorse or pain. She's not human in the sense you and I know it. There's no understanding to be done.'

'But I heard that you can get hold of information that others can't.'

'What information?'

'Police reports; what the police have found out about Molly's bones.'

Orin gave him a piercing look. 'Now that would be favouritism, that's something I've campaigned against all my life. This country is mired in secrets and that's not right. I've spent ten years opening files, smashing through ministerial oak, making the dust blanketing the English legal system swirl. Hell, I've only just got started.'

He was mesmerising when he spoke, Darren had to admit. His voice was low and deep and he had a magnetism that made everything he said seem somehow sensible. 'You say you know a lot about the regime at Roehampton, what things precisely? I want to know more about her,' he said.

'So do I. I've applied for court orders to see what she

blathers to her psychiatrist, that your taxes and mine are paying for. I'll win that in the end, I have no doubt.'

Darren seized on this. 'So everything she says to her therapist is recorded?'

Orin snorted. 'Every little thing! But she doesn't need to talk to her psychiatrist, she needs to talk to *me*. Sodium thiopental. Ring any bells? It's the truth drug. That's how we're going to find them, Darren. One day I'm going to stand over her as it's pumped into her veins by legal decree and she is going to tell me where my daughter is. Where your sister is. Stand with me, and we're one step nearer.'

Orin was certainly compelling and hard to ignore. What he was saying made a sort of twisted sense to Darren. He glanced at the photos on the wall again and found an uncomfortable recognition dawning. 'Are those electric chairs?'

'Sure are. I'll campaign till the day I die to see her sit in one and fry – once she's given up her secrets.'

'So you don't think she's mad.'

Orin's answer surprised Darren. 'Of course she is! She's insane, no question. Disturbances of the brain, chemical imbalances, are common, I believe. But just because you're mad doesn't mean you can't be smart. Doesn't mean you can't lie and cheat and do your best to try and evade true justice.' Orin reached down for a plastic bag behind the desk and pulled out a shirt still in its wrapper. He opened it and shook it out, began to unbutton the one he was wearing. 'CNN are coming in ten,' he added by way of explanation.

The tiny gold cross round Orin's thick neck made his hairy chest, flecked with grey hairs, look enormous. Darren looked away. When he looked back, Orin was still staring at him.

'I heard she sees a befriender?'

A look of disgust crossed Orin's face. 'You want to become a befriender, young gun? Spend your time giving a prisoner such as a rapist or a murderer the pleasure of your company, of your humanity?' He buttoned his cuffs. 'They are a security breach of the first order. Remember, that monster Duvall is a burrower. Killers like her, they have a perverse power that people underestimate. She can burrow into your psyche, make wrong seem right. Before you know it, you're sleeping with the enemy.'

His eyes hadn't left Darren's face. 'Heard about that prison guard a few years back?' Darren swallowed. 'The man was having an affair with her, professed to love her. That's what I'm talking about. John Sears, her befriender, is an apologist for violence and pain.'

Orin began buttoning up his new shirt, poking the collar skywards as he reached for a tie from the drawer. 'You have got it bad! These heinous crimes reverberate down the generations. Do you have survivor's guilt, Darren? It's a common psychological condition among those close to people who were taken or killed; the why not me, the why did I survive pain. It can turn a man's head, make them obsessed.'

Darren sat still, rubbing his hand down his trousers. What Orin was saying was true; real.

Orin pulled his collar back down and ran a hand down the front of his shirt, watching him. There was silence in the room, the faint thrum of barges on the river. 'I'm sorry.' His voice was soft now and full of sympathy. 'The pain you feel at your loss is something I understand. I wish it wasn't so.'

Darren swallowed. 'Mr Bukowski, I want to know why she buried Molly there, where she may have left the others. I want to find my sister. For my mother's sake, I really need to find her.' And then he was in a rush, years of doing nothing transformed into a desperate urgency as he pulled out the map of where Molly was buried. He stood up and laid it on Orin's desk and began to explain the things that appeared on it, but Orin interrupted him.

'Wait here.' He stood up and left the office for a few

moments before returning with a much larger scale map than Darren's, mounted on card. He laid it on the desk and began pointing with a stubby finger. 'This is her house where she grew up.' His finger hovered over the green expanses and rolling hills of the Downs. 'This is Brighton, where she killed them.' His finger moved south to the blue of the English Channel. 'This is where she buried her. She didn't go far, did she?' His finger moved to a small building near Molly's burial site. 'She rode at this stables when she was a teenager. Her sister owned a horse called Peanut.' He tapped the map again. 'Right here.'

Darren leaned in, drinking in this new information. 'So she knew the spot well?'

'The police searched the stables at the time, but they found nothing.' Orin sat down in his chair and steepled his fingers. 'Do you know that only ten per cent of murder victims are buried? You know why that is? Because it's difficult. Getting deep enough so that the body isn't uncovered by animals or discovered is harder still. But that's not the hardest part. Do you know how difficult it is to carry a dead body by yourself, to dig a hole, all alone in the dark, to get the body in a car boot or a van . . .' He tailed off.

'But there was no trace of any of the girls in the boot of Duvall's car—'

'In that Renault Clio, no.'

'Are you saying that you think there was somebody else who helped her?'

'I don't know, young gun, I don't know.' Orin smiled and even his very white and even teeth couldn't hide the sadness in it. 'Come with me.' He pushed back his chair and led Darren out of his office and across the lobby to a windowless room filled with filing cabinets, a humming computer and a map table. There was low-level lighting and a couple of chairs. 'I call this the nerve centre. I have researchers who come and sift through the evidence I've collected. I have all this, but nothing would beat hearing from Duvall herself. Somewhere in the tangled mess of her insanity lies the truth about where our loved ones are.' He banged his hand in frustration on the table. 'If I could just talk to her!'

She talks to me, Darren thought, *she talks to me*.

'This is all yours, if you join my campaign, become a signed-up member of The Missing.' Orin shut the door, barring the prizes from sight. 'Come and stand next to me at events, lobby MPs for what we want. We stand together as the bereaved fighting for the rights of the missing.'

Darren liked the idea, but considering what he was doing at Roehampton, it was impossible. And there was another problem. 'My parents wouldn't like it.'

'I forgive them, but you're an adult now. Make your own decision.'

'With respect, none of the other families are with you.'

Orin stuck a fat finger into the gap between collar and neck and ran it round. 'Grief doesn't curtail ambition, Darren. A group thrown together only because their loved ones were murdered will always have its differences. But you're a new generation, a fresh start.'

Darren nodded, thinking about Olivia in that small room after she had murdered Linda. 'Does the name Rollo mean anything to you?'

'Rollo?' Orin shook his head. 'No. We're holding a televised rally in Hyde Park on Thursday – come and stand next to me on the podium. Every scrap of information, every file I have, is all yours after that.'

Darren looked with regret back at the room full of files. 'I have to have a think about it.'

'Don't think too long. No good ever came of it.' Orin walked back into his office, Darren following. 'I've never hidden my private wealth. I can dedicate it to getting justice, others aren't so lucky.' He gave Darren the bone-crushing handshake again. 'Thursday. Think about it.'

Darren nodded and began to walk out of the lobby. 'I will.'

'God be with you,' Orin called as he left the room.

33

O rin waited for the sound of the lift to tell him that Darren had left the building. He checked his watch, took another look at the view, made sure his office door was shut and opened the locked drawer in his huge desk. He took out the washbag and walked into the en suite bathroom. He had searched all over the capital for the right building, he hadn't cared if there was a view, an iconic London location, or something TV-presentable. He had needed only a bathroom with a window that opened, wide, and that no one could see from surrounding offices.

He locked the door and took out the crack pipe, spent a few minutes getting prepared. He plugged in the blow heater that he kept under the sink and that would help push the fumes out of the window.

Everything he'd said to Darren was true. Grief twisted people into shapes they wouldn't recognise, made them do things they could never have imagined. The discovery of Molly's remains had thrown him off course, had forced him to travel down the dark alleys of horror all over again. He was drowning and the pipe helped him float in the froth at the top for a little while.

He had contacts in the Sussex police, of course he did, he was Orin Bukowski, whose daughter had been central to the biggest missing persons hunt of recent years. What he had been tipped off about just this morning, in confidence, because confirmation was still needed, would make the most hardened man quake.

He took a big lungful and waited for the hit. Public life was a gruelling performance, mental jousting and entertainment rolled into one. He would give the TV networks a show in ten minutes that would keep his daughter front and centre. That was his life's work: to keep her name alive. She no longer was, but her name would live on for ever. His money and his hard work and his determination and his outrage would make it so.

Darren had fallen unexpectedly into his lap. He was a relative. Relatives were table stakes in the political influence game, and he had no others. His forthright methods had scared all the other families away a long time ago. There was a terrible passivity to the Brits that he hated. Put up and shut up was their credo; he could do that in the grave.

He needed Darren, even though the bombed-out hippy image would be tough to PR. What he couldn't work out was what Darren needed from him.

He cleaned the pipe, put the heater away, left the window open and came back into his office. He felt invincible, chemicals racing through his brain and his heart, synapses crackling. He opened his door and called to his secretary. 'Can you copy the contents of the summary file and send it to Darren Evans. His parents' details are in their file.'

34

Nathan was on duty as Darren queued to get through the security checkpoint to enter Roehampton, and for that Darren gave a silent prayer. He believed he was getting somewhere; he potentially had a powerful new ally in Orin Bukowski, someone who shared his obsession with uncovering the truth. What he discovered in here, allied with what Orin had in his office, could be the break he was so desperate for.

He was sweating with fear. He had gone far beyond what he thought he was capable of just a few weeks ago; his audacious rule-breaking now tipping into outright criminality. Helen's key was deep in the matted twists and locks of his hair near the back of his neck. It had survived a cycle ride from Streatham across south London, and he thought it was secure enough to get him through the metal detectors. He knew only too well that if he were found with anything suspicious he would be arrested.

He passed through the metal detector and beeped. Nathan smiled and beckoned him over. Darren began to panic; he didn't want Nathan to have to find him out. He wanted to run, turn tail and sprint away, but Nathan's gym-pumped arms were already at his shoulder. Yassir the cleaner was behind him in the queue and he called out to Nathan: 'You, you Bradley Cooper?'

Nathan grinned and Darren laughed. It was a little bit of luck and it made Darren sure that he would be OK. He held his breath as Nathan felt behind his neck and down his back. 'On you go. You have a good day now.'

'You too, Bradley,' Darren said and passed inside.

He was put on office cleaning duty and he realised this must be tied to his promotion to a Level Two cleaner. He wasn't going to complain. He pushed the cleaning trolley into security control and watched the monitors to try to calm himself down. He said hello to Sonny and Corey and began to hoover the corridor, inching towards Helen's office. He noticed with relief that only a couple of the offices were occupied today; Helen's was empty. He needed to act fast. He opened Helen's office door and turned on the light. There was no bag by the desk, or jacket on the hook so she could be away for the day – or just about to arrive. He kept the door partly open and picked up the dustcloth.

He took a deep breath, moved into the room, walked to the large grey cabinet and pulled the key from his hair, inserted it in the lock and turned.

It opened easily, but it screeched on its rails to an alarming degree. He ran back to the door and looked out, but the corridor was empty. A moment later he was back with the files, working at a frenzied pace. The first drawer contained files labelled A-C. He pulled open the middle drawer. D contained five files, none of them Olivia's. He found O. It wasn't there either.

He forced himself to listen for noise in the corridor, then opened the bottom drawer. There were a selection of unlabelled files, but none of them were hers.

He shut the cabinet and locked it. He put the key back in his hair. He wanted to scream with frustration.

He cleaned the rest of the room, then did two more offices. He put the 'cleaning in progress' sign up outside the women's toilets and began to push the trolley through the swing door. He saw Helen walking towards him from the end of the corridor. She looked serious and didn't acknowledge him.

He turned away, full of resentment about the key, as if the missing file was her fault. She didn't move along.

'Can you come in here for a moment please?' She opened the door to the women's toilets and disappeared inside.

Darren looked up and down the corridor, a dull panic beginning to throb in his jaw. Had he been found out, was she about to confront him? He wondered wildly for a moment whether the filing cabinet had been alarmed and he was about to be unmasked, whether he could run for the exit, but knew it was hopeless. He followed her in like a man approaching the gallows.

She was leaning against the sinks it was his job to wipe. 'Shall we go for that drink after all?'

'Eh?'

She made a little movement of her head that made her hair fall over an eye. 'Don't be embarrassed, Darren, you made your feelings clear a few days ago.' She smiled, but there was a tension cutting through the edges.

Darren grinned broadly with relief. He wasn't about to be caught at all. He let out a large breath of air, freed to fight another day. But now he was caught in another net. He needed to let her down gently, not antagonise her. She would be a formidable enemy to make. He looked around, hoping the right words would magically be conjured from white floor tiles and strip lighting. He saw her red briefcase by her feet, the edge of a brown file like the ones in the cabinet in her office just visible inside.

Maybe Olivia's file was in there, or at her house. 'Er, yeah. OK.'

She gave a small laugh. 'Guys your age are so articulate.'

'Say what?'

'It doesn't matter.' Her voice was light and playful. 'So where would you like to go?' Darren's mind was a complete blank. Where did you take a woman old enough to be your mother? She smiled again, humouring him. 'We could meet in Barnes, there's a pub near the river. We're unlikely to bump into anyone we know there. How does tonight sound?' He nodded. 'I'll meet you in the Prince Albert, 8.30 p.m.,' she went on.

There was silence, Darren just staring at her because he didn't know what to say.

She moved past him to the door. 'Don't be late. I find that annoying.' And then she was gone.

35

The pub in Barnes was big and done up in a style that tried to suggest quirky country house but in fact made it look like every boozer in the Home Counties. It was very, very expensive. Darren had travelled there on the bus after wolfing down a leftover meal of cold chicken and oven chips, but Helen insisted on taking a table and having a steak that cost £18, so he drank and watched her eat and drink. She drank a lot – and talked even more – but seemed to stay sober all night. He could see where the line of her wedding ring had left a pale imprint on her finger.

It was a lot of fun talking to her. She was so refreshing after the usual girls he took out – not that there were very many of them – and she asked lots of questions about his course and what he wanted to do with his life. Normally the girls he dated talked about themselves all the time. She insisted on paying and he didn't stop her. 'Let me spend my money my way,' she said, brandishing a black credit card.

They came out of the pub and he wondered what was going to happen now. She hailed a black cab. 'Come back to mine, I want to show you my etchings. I'm being serious, I really do have etchings.'

Darren was up for anything and as the taxi coasted to a stop he gallantly pulled the door open for her. 'Hey, this door opens backwards.'

She stopped for a second and smiled. 'Darren, is this your first time in a black cab?'

He shrugged, feeling a little ashamed. 'You know what they used to say, no taxis ever went south of the river.' She watched indulgently as he spent the next few minutes playing with all the buttons inside the cab.

Helen lived in a block of flats so modern there was suede lining the walls by the lift. 'You can run your hands over it, it feels nice,' she said. He did, and his fingers left a tracery of lines in the surface, as if a ghost had passed this way. When she unlocked the door to her flat he saw that the living area had floor-to-ceiling windows and a view of the river.

'Wow, this is cool.' He jumped across the back of a corner sofa and landed on the cushions.

'We've been here years. Couldn't possibly afford to buy it now of course.'

He lay back and stared out at a balcony with pot plants and a wooden table and chairs, the lights on the river winking in the tide. How he'd love to light a big fat joint and sit here with CJ watching the boats slide by. 'It's gone up about a gazillion times. Darren?'

'Mmm?'

'Sorry, am I boring you?'

Darren got off the sofa – fast. 'It's amazing. Can I have a look around?'

She smiled and waved at him to go ahead as she pulled glasses from a cupboard and bent down for something. 'What about a drink?' she called as he headed for the rooms off the living area. 'What do you want?'

'I dunno. Beer?'

Her bedroom had piles of colour-coordinated cushions on a bed shaped like a sleigh and yards of fitted wardrobes with dustless, flat fronts. It was so different from his mum's junk-yard rail where her dresses and blouses and shoes lay piled up and disorganised.

There was an en suite wet room and in another part of

the flat a bathroom with a sunken bath with a river view; and next to that the prize – a study. He hunted on the desk for files, but it was all immaculate and ordered. He spotted a filing cabinet.

He came back into the kitchen-cum-living room and took the beer she had poured into a glass for him. 'Do you like that piece?' She indicated a large modernist artwork hanging above a fake fire.

Darren felt the burden of having studied art – it meant everyone wanted your opinion on what they had bought, like a French person always being asked to recommend a wine.

'It's great,' he ventured cautiously. To him it was bland, uninteresting work from the 1980s. There was a pause. She was expecting something more incisive than that, he realised. 'There's really great movement in it,' he added, then to stop being asked to comment further he walked over to the window and stared down at the river. 'Life must seem so different here from what you do at work.'

'The job's challenging, that's for sure.'

'So what do you do to get away from it all?'

She came towards him, a glass of wine in her hand. 'I can certainly think of something.'

He grinned at her and she grinned back. 'Well, this is very Mrs Robinson,' she said slowly.

'What?'

She gave a small laugh and sighed, enjoying herself. 'Dustin Hoffman, Anne Bancroft?' He frowned and shrugged. But he liked the way she was standing, arm round her stomach. He took a long slug of beer. He wanted to touch her, smell her.

He put her glass of wine down on the floor and reached out and kissed her. She smelled of expensive cream and her hair was glossy and smooth. She was a great kisser.

She broke off, flustered. 'You seemed so shy and timid

when you started at Roehampton, but now I see you're not at all like that.'

He put his hands under her thighs, carried her across the room and shoved her up against the kitchen island. 'Hello,' she said.

He started to pull her shirt over her head, to feel her body. 'You look great,' he said, pulling back to appreciate her.

'I must do more exercise,' she muttered. He kissed her neck, feeling her skin. His fingers felt nice running over the bumps of the moles and sunspots on her back.

They eventually fell backwards over the corner sofa. She writhed beneath him as she pulled off his T-shirt. 'God, look at that,' she giggled as she laid her palms on his abs. Darren looked down, nonplussed. 'You have no idea how refreshing that is.' She looked like she was touching something she shouldn't. She was enjoying herself and he loved her for that and they tussled and play-fought on the sofa and then on the floor as they shed their clothes.

She began giving him a blow job and pleasure exploded across his body. It was true what CJ said about older women: the head they gave was ultimate. The river distorted into a beautiful mirage of lights outside the windows as he gave in to the sensations, but she stopped and grabbed his hand and they staggered through into her bedroom. Her bush was as big as a salad plate. She pulled him into her and soon she was coming, loudly and lustily and without being coy.

Darren lay back, Helen lying in his armpit as he stroked her hair. 'God, that was great.'

'I needed that.' She giggled.

Darren smiled. It was great here with Helen, like he'd been transported to a movie set. He could be someone else, step out of his usual life. He wanted to pull out a joint and smoke it with her, in this ridiculously large and comfy bed. Maybe she'd make him eggs in the morning.

But now she was sitting upright, slapping him on the knee. 'Chop chop, I have work I need to do.'

'What, now?'

She stood and stretched, energised and invigorated. 'Get dressed, you can catch a late bus back south.'

He struggled to his elbows. 'Can't I stay here? We can splash in that tub.'

She looked at him indulgently. 'Fun's over, for now.'

She headed across the room to the bathroom and he heard the shower start.

A volley of rain hit the plate glass window. He was downcast, his zenned-out mood evaporating. He got up, scratching, his mind beginning to drag itself from pleasure towards why he had come here in the first place. She was a product woman; he'd noticed that the bathroom was loaded with lotions, potions, scrubs and masks. Her shower would take time.

Guilt momentarily rooted him to the spot. He'd had a great night and it felt wrong to be abusing her trust by poking about in her private things; but then he heard his parents shouting at each other, the pain of loss permanently etched on his mum's face, and he ran through into her office.

Her filing cabinet wasn't locked. The drawers opened silently and he began to rifle through a series of hanging files. They were labelled: insurance, car, flat, employment, stuff belonging to Joel. It was all in order but it was Helen's life, not the lives of her patients.

He checked the desk drawers but found nothing useful, hunted for her briefcase, which was sitting on top of the kitchen island, but the brown file he'd seen earlier that day contained only copies of a medical journal. He was frustrated at drawing such a blank. He stepped back into the bedroom and heard the shower go off; he jumped back on to the bed as she came out of the bathroom, a towel with tassels wrapped round her head. 'You look lovely.'

'Thanks. Come on, clothes on.'

He got up and reluctantly pulled on his pants. 'What work do you have to do now? Isn't it all at Roehampton?'

'There's simply not enough time to complete everything there, not that the powers that be think that. So I catch up on paperwork here.'

'Isn't that a security risk? If the files get lost or something?'

She gave a defensive movement. 'I keep them in a safe, it's all strictly controlled, totally above board. Now, run along you little animal.' She came over and traced her finger down his chest. 'Gorgeous, simply gorgeous.' She started tickling him but her nails felt sharp and he didn't like it.

She saw him out and he took a last lingering look at the view and at her. She kissed him on the cheek and then she shut the door.

It was raining harder by the time he got through the lobby and out into the windswept courtyard. It took him an hour and a half on two night buses to get home.

36

Darren cycled to Roehampton the next morning feeling cloaked in failure. He was getting nowhere fast. His bad mood intensified when Kamal caught sight of him and hustled him into the locker room. When his boss was sure they were alone, he let rip. 'You, fucker, need to be gone by the end of the week. Resign. The security review they're doing in the wake of your love-fuck with Duvall makes it too risky for you and for me. Leave, or I'll make you.'

Darren was exhausted and frustrated by his failure to find anything at Helen's and was in no mood to be shoved about. 'I'm a Level Two.' Darren tapped his chest. 'I have a sub team to organise.' This in reality involved nothing more than ticking a box on a sheet of paper, but that wasn't going to stop him trying to pull rank on Kamal.

Kamal muttered something in Arabic, then said, 'You are so out of order—'

'Don't hassle me again, I'll tell the governor I don't have the correct forms – I'll be sacked, yeah, but you'll be on a boat back to Tangiers.'

Kamal narrowed his eyes. Darren sensed that this was war, and there could be no prisoners. 'You're on Newman ward,' Kamal said as he walked away.

Darren's anger grew. Another day with no opportunity to see Olivia, Helen or the secrets in Helen's office.

He was buzzed into the facility and began to clean down the long, isolated corridors. He no longer thought about what

colours he would paint the walls if he had the chance, he
didn't draw surf on the floor to pass the time. He ran over
everything Olivia had ever said to him, schemed about how
he could be more proactive, glean more slivers of information.
Eventually he was buzzed into the dayroom where he had
first met Olivia. There was a group of inmates there but as
he feared there was no Olivia, she would be sitting in a locked
room somewhere far away from here.

He felt deflated. He knew there was very little chance he
would ever see Olivia again. He felt keenly that he hadn't
made enough of the golden opportunity she had handed him
just a few days ago. One on one, in a private conversation!

He began to mop the floor, noting that there was an extra
member of staff here: the security review was changing prac-
tices, he was running out of time and taking a reckless risk
of being discovered. Murmured conversation from some of
the women filled the room. Others were reading newspapers;
a small pile of papers sat on a table by the window. The top
page of the paper fluttered slightly as he whisked his mop
past it.

He mopped the floor where Linda had been attacked. There
was no trace of the incident having ever occurred, except in
his memory, but Olivia's presence was all around him. Her
words came back to him: *I learned young and hard how a person
suffers when power is held by another.*

He looked up at the security camera in the corner, his
actions being recorded by Sonny and Corey. He would have
to try harder. Make more effort to get to the truth. Take more
risks.

At the end of his shift Darren was pleased to find that Kamal
wasn't in his office and he was able to slip out of the changing
rooms to the exit without having to see him. As he was
queuing to leave, Nathan took one look at him and went so

far as to put his hand on his shoulder. 'Mate, you look like death.'

'Got to get out of this job, man.'

Nathan grinned. 'I'm sorry to hear that. I've some news though, I've got a casting next week.'

'That's great.' He really was happy for Nathan, a nice guy who deserved his break.

'Cheer up, look, here's Chloe, the finest-looking girl in Croydon.'

Chloe, in the queue ahead of Darren, turned round to look at Nathan. 'Hi Nathan.' She appraised Darren. 'He looks tired, don't you think?' she said to Nathan.

'He's lovesick,' Nathan said. Darren shot him a look. 'He's trying to get up the courage to ask you out.'

Chloe smiled, handed Nathan her bag for him to check and passed through the metal detector.

'You fancy going for a drink with him?' Nathan pressed.

Chloe was putting her bag strap over her head and across her body as she looked at Darren. He felt the deep blush of complete idiocy travelling up to his face. It was the final humiliation of his whole psychotic experience at Roehampton.

'Yeah, I'll go out with him, he's cute.' She turned with a flounce, shaking her curly hair, and looked back as she headed for her car.

'I'll meet you at Croydon clock tower, seven-thirty Friday,' he managed to shout.

She held up her hand to wave and didn't look back again.

Darren grinned, his feelings about the world doing a one-hundred-and-eighty-degree spin.

Nathan gave Darren his catalogue-man smile. 'See how it all works out?'

Darren gave him a fist-bump. 'Thanks, Bradley.'

37

Mayfair, Central London

The man walked round the room and listened to the sharp crackle of the tarpaulin beneath his feet. He was naked and could feel its slippery, cool surface under his toes. He had draped it over the few pieces of furniture in the room, including the sofa bed so that its bright blue hues undulated like waves. He adored the sound as he moved as much as he loved this grace and favour flat, a workplace benefit the department had graciously bestowed.

The one-room studio was in a mews with attractive cobbles and tasteful window boxes brimming with summer blooms, but that wasn't why he loved it. When he had been shown around a few years ago by a departmental secretary she had apologised for its size; bijou, she had muttered, with an embarrassed laugh. He, though, had been astounded at his immense good luck: the flat was on the first floor and had an entrance that led straight up from the back of the garage directly underneath.

That occasional work functions or department dinners kept him in town and meant he had to stay here didn't bother his wife – she rarely had any desire to leave the vicarage in the country. He alone liked the city and all the distractions it had to offer.

The lights were off and the curtains drawn, his car in the garage below. He stood for a moment by the window, scanning the street, checking methodically for lights in windows or unusual movement. But this was central London at the weekend; it felt like a city subjected to a prolonged bombing campaign that had forced all able-bodied residents to flee for their lives. Nothing stirred. He let the curtain drop and turned back to the bed, careful to step over the rope.

The flat had a tiny kitchen area in one corner with a small fridge and cooker, and a breakfast bar from where one of two tatty kitchen stools had been removed. A tiny, fully tiled bathroom had a toilet and shower. The living area housed a wardrobe in which he had hung his suit and a selection of the blue shirts he always wore. His socks, pants and shoes were also in there on top of a fresh roll of tarpaulin, the door firmly closed. He had once had the problem of disposing of a suit that had got splattered.

He used the toilet, flushed. He would wash his hands later. The windows were firmly shut even though the evening was hot, but he had an air conditioning unit running – it helped with the smells and the whimpering that came from the bed.

One of the stools was jammed between the wardrobe and the window and a length of rope was tied round one of its struts, the other end pulling tight on the thin wrist of the girl on the bed. The old armchair had been pulled to the window and a second rope was secured round one of its legs and the girl's other wrist.

He heard church bells ringing, mournful in the night-time stillness, and mused that God was the only thing that could help her now. He picked up his phone and took some photos of her. He was careful to include the oversize wellingtons she was still wearing; they made her look younger than she was.

At moments like these every sensation was beautiful to him: the bells outside, the rushing of blood through his head, her wide eyes. He had been livid with Gert Becker earlier in the week for putting a hurdle in the way of his desires, but now he felt generous towards the entire world. He typed Becker's number, but before he clicked send he paused. Nine hours ago he had wanted to punish Becker for the extra risk he had been exposed to, but now he was feeling sated and generous. He wrote some text before he sent the image. 'Love tarpaulin.'

He unpacked the video camera.

38

Sonny was two hours into his shift. The morning was hot and only going to get hotter. 'One day, just one day, me like to push the big red button,' Sonny said to Corey.

'When the time comes, fool, *my* hand's gonna be slamming the big red button,' Corey replied.

Sonny shook his head and shifted in his chair. 'Time come, me race you.'

'You don't stand a chance, cuz,' Corey said, licking his lips.

The big red button was Lockdown, Armageddon, Point Zero, the End of the World. They all sounded like Hollywood films to Sonny. A security breach could mean one of only two things: an escape attempt or, since 2001, a terrorist attack.

The big red button sat high on the wall of the security room behind a thin film of safety glass and connected straight to the local police station. Once the glass was broken and the button pressed, an emergency alarm sounded throughout the hospital. All staff had been drilled in procedures should Sonny's big hand ever make contact with that red shiny button. All interior and exterior gates and doors would automatically shut. A full police complement would be onsite in seven minutes.

In Sonny's nineteen years at Roehampton, he had never slammed his palm down on that red button. 'Me telling you, even if it never happen, when I retire, me still be dreaming 'bout it.'

'Yo cuz,' Corey said as Darren came into the room.

'No nightmares from what happened with Linda I hope?' Sonny asked.

Darren shook his head.

'I'm glad to hear it, Darren, really glad to hear it.'

There was a companionable silence as all three of them watched the moving images of the car park on the monitors.

'So many people drive here,' Darren said, looking at the rows and rows of vehicles.

'People like to take the easiest option,' Sonny replied.

Corey shook his head. 'People take the stylish option.' He pointed at the screen. 'That's the governor's Audi.'

'The man has a nice set of wheels,' Sonny agreed.

Darren caught Corey looking slyly at Sonny. 'We could do his car.'

Sonny made a scoffing noise.

'What are you doing?' Darren asked, intrigued. He watched the cameras trained on the car park, saw Berenice from the kitchens step out of a white Ford Transit van.

Sonny leaned back, his face full of disapproval. 'Corey here has a way of finding out things about people that they would prefer to keep private. He's part of the internet generation, he thinks privacy is outdated.'

'How so?'

'Got a cuz at the DVLA.' Corey looked proud.

'Jesus, you guys are bored,' Darren said.

Sonny took exception. 'I'm never bored. Got my eye on the cameras twenty-four seven.'

'You could always phone up about my pushbike.'

Sonny and Darren laughed at Corey's expense, but as Darren looked at the car park on the monitors he remembered that John Sears always drove here to meet Olivia. Could Corey help him find out more about him? Corey was glaring at Darren, miffed that he had been the butt of their joke. Darren realised he had made a mistake laughing at Corey;

he had alienated him at just the moment he wanted to ask him for a big favour.

'I need a leak.' Sonny got up from his seat, stretched and headed out of the room and down the corridor.

Asking Corey to check the licence plate of a car that parked where he could potentially see it on the cameras was risky, but it was a risk Darren was prepared to take. He wouldn't be at Roehampton for much longer anyway.

'What you want, bro?' Corey was staring at him aggressively.

'Can you find the details of a licence plate I give you?'

Corey's lip curled in distaste. 'Why would I do that for you?'

Why indeed. Darren had to conjure something that Corey cared about, something that would outrage him enough that he would go out of his way to help him. 'It's not for me. It's for my mum.' Corey didn't respond. 'Some toerag dented her car, swore at her, gave her the finger, then drove away. She got the licence plate but she's hopeless with cars, hasn't got a clue what make or model it was. Without that info the DVLA won't help and the insurance people are washing their hands of the whole thing and she's out of pocket. I want his name and address.'

Corey sat very still for a long moment, his face stony. Darren's heart sank. He wasn't going to buy it. Corey liked wielding power; being asked for favours by someone who he didn't respect didn't interest him. 'Gotta get my mum's back, one way or another, especially when she's ill.'

Corey raised an eyebrow. 'You think you gotta get your mum's back.'

'Too right. It's a son's job, look after your mum. One way or another, gotta put it right.' At that moment Darren felt like crying as he thought about her and how she was suffering.

Corey began to nod, impressed. 'You don't mess, do you?'

Darren shook his head. 'No. This is the plate, write it down.'

Darren could hear Sonny singing as he made his way back from the toilet. Corey picked up a pen, slowly pulled a scrap of paper towards him. Darren was desperate for him to hurry up. He read out the licence plate of John Sears' car just before Sonny came back into the room.

Corey became defensive with his boss there. 'I'll see what I can do. I'm not promising anything.' He turned away and tuned back in to his job.

'Yeah, OK,' Darren said, and left the room to continue cleaning. He moved down the corridor with the hoover and passed Helen's door, intending to enter the next office, but Helen was there.

'Come in, Darren.'

'I can come back later, I didn't want to disturb you.'

'No no, now is fine.' She got up and pushed her chair back. He ran the vacuum cleaner quickly under the desk and round the outer edges.

'Close the door.'

'What?'

'Close the door.'

'The cord on the hoover . . .'

'Just do it.'

She went over to the venetian blinds that covered the bank of windows next to the door and slowly tilted them closed.

He shut the door.

She sat on the edge of her desk, her skirt riding high up her thighs as she crossed her legs. 'I've missed you, Darren.'

'Helen, I don't think this is a good idea. This is where you work, it's not—'

'Let's do it, Darren, NOW.'

There was a look in her eyes that wasn't to be ignored. He thought helplessly about Chloe, about how he wanted to have sex with her, not Helen. His evening with Helen in the pub seemed like a lifetime ago. He had already moved on.

'I don't have all day.' She had got off the table and was pulling her black pants off. He could see the pale flesh at the top of her hold-ups under her skirt. 'Fuck me like you mean it.'

Darren felt himself withering away under his uniform. No one liked to be trapped, and he was beginning to see how fruitless his attempts at using her to get to Olivia had been. She wouldn't take rejection well.

She pulled him to her and began to kiss him. 'I put these shoes on hoping I'd see you today. They're killing me.'

She was grinding against him, getting frustrated. 'Come on, use the danger, Darren. I want this to be as hard as your pecs.' She unzipped his trousers, grabbed his dick and held it tight before sliding to her knees.

Darren felt fear and pleasure rolled into one – this brief moment of release could well be the highlight of a tortuous eight-hour cleaning shift, or it could be the end of all his efforts to find Carly if someone opened the door. Helen began to suck and his knees buckled from the sensation. His hands touched the keyboard on the desk behind Helen and the screen jumped to life.

Words jumped and swam in his vision, lists of medicines and conditions he didn't understand. It was a patient's file. Darren pressed the page down key and the top of a new page appeared. Olivia's name was at the top of the file. Transfixed, he kept his finger on the key, watching Olivia's life at Roehampton spool in front of him. The file onscreen was going back in date order; he was near the back of the file now, back at the beginning of Olivia's life inside.

Helen came up for air and put her bum back on the desk. 'That's better.' She pulled him towards her, one leg round his back. She was gasping quietly as he banged her against the desk. Helen was thrusting harder against him now, pressing her mouth into his shoulder to stop herself crying out. Now her head was lolling backwards, her hair touching his hands as he jabbed at the page down key. 'Don't stop, don't stop,' she whispered.

He was beginning to panic, his erection sliding away from him as he tried to concentrate on what he was reading. She was bucking more energetically, more desperately against him. She looked at him, forcing him to abandon the screen behind her for a moment. 'Tell me what to do for you,' she murmured, grabbing his bum.

He was desperately trying to attach his mind to something to bring back the hardness; he could see the frustration in Helen's eyes as they swam in and out of focus.

'I'm a good person,' he mumbled.

She stopped grinding and grabbed his head with both hands. 'You're a good person, a very good person,' she sighed, so close to his ear he could feel the hot breath on it.

He rammed into Helen so hard the desk shunted against the wall. All the blood in his body rushed to the right place as if he had been jabbed with a cattle prod. He felt huge, he felt white hot, omnipotent, as he held Helen against him and read the screen over her shoulder.

Olivia had a son. Born May first, 1992. Put under the care of East Sussex social services aged eighteen months and placed for adoption.

He read the paragraph below. 'Numerous attempts have been made to get Olivia to talk about her son and his adoption. Whenever subject is raised, Olivia "shuts down", and becomes uncommunicative. It should be noted that all attempts to allow patient to talk about this issue have failed. The significance of this event for the patient's psychological condition is—'

Helen's arms were flailing around above her head now; she

was transported somewhere else entirely, little grunting noises beginning to rise to a scream. He clapped his hand over her mouth as she fell backwards on to the desk, pulling him with her. He lost his balance and the keyboard slid off the desk. He half picked Helen up and lowered her and himself to the floor, where she lay still, all the strength gone from her body as it flooded with ecstasy.

A few moments later Darren got off the floor, picked up the keyboard and tidied the disorder on Helen's desk. He adjusted the blinds and stripes of white sunlight filled the room. He opened the door and pushed the hoover out into the corridor.

The corridor was empty. Helen sat with her back against the desk, eyes half closed, a flush across her chest and cheeks.

'Darren Smith. You maniac.'

He pushed his trolley along to the lift at the far end of the hall, steadying himself for the long dull hours of cleaning ahead.

39

Olivia was gazing from across the desk at the honey tones of the skin on Helen's cheek, the way the small shards of light from the window high up in the room shaped a shadow under her cheekbone. Her mascara had made a slight smudge under her right eye. Olivia imagined running her tongue along that dark line, tasting the salt and feeling the little spikes of clumpy product. She tipped her head to the same angle that Helen held hers. She loved mirroring what Helen did; her movements seemed delicate yet strong, like a gymnast or a dancer. Helen used both hands to smooth down her glorious hair. Olivia tried to raise hers to copy her, but the clank of her wrist restraints brought her back to earth. She felt the itchy inner fabric of the metal scrape against her ankles.

Helen was talking now. She loved listening to Helen's voice, though she never gave the slightest indication she did so. Helen was clever and often amusing and, in the mind-numbing boredom of incarceration, Olivia's sessions with her were a welcome break. Plus, she liked the walk down the long corridors to this room, although she had missed out on that today as she had been trussed up and pushed here in a wheelchair. This would be the new regime post-Linda, until she impressed Helen sufficiently for security to soften. She had to take her pleasures where she could get them.

Olivia watched how the light caught on the fuzz of Helen's navy sweater. Cashmere, she judged. Her eyes roamed across

Helen's shoulder, and her eyes lost their soft-edged blur and came sharply back into focus. A thin white line of something wound up and around Helen's shoulder, caught in the down of her sweater. Olivia looked harder. It was a long hair. Not white, but blond.

Olivia sat very still and stared, first at Helen then at the watch that poked out from beneath the three-quarter-length sleeves. Olivia had been kept waiting in this bare room, strapped into the wheelchair, because Helen had arrived late. Flustered. She studied the outline of Helen's face, noted the flush still on her cheek, the pen that she held loosely between two fingers. Olivia bent down to scratch her ankle and looked at Helen's shoes with the higher-than-usual heel, the seven deniers, the legs wound tightly round each other. Tightly wound to stop Darren's passion and desire from spilling out, a failed attempt to keep her rutting a secret.

Helen stopped talking and they looked at each other in silence.

'Having a good day, Dr McCabe?'

Olivia watched the smile spread far across Helen's face. 'We're here to talk about your day, Olivia.'

She felt a tremor of something new: respect and anticipation. Darren was proving himself more adept than she had dreamed at lying and conniving.

She looked at the laptop on the desk next to Helen. As she gazed during their talks at her intent mouth, leaned forward to catch a drift of her perfume, Helen would type away furiously on that keyboard. It probably had Darren's fingerprints on it.

'You seem to be amused by something, do you want to tell me about that?'

Olivia smiled and shook her head.

40

'Did Olivia ever have a kid?'

Darren saw Dad freeze with his forkful of food an inch from his mouth. They were eating dinner, chips and fish fingers and peas. Mum's pills were killing her appetite and so she sat and watched the two men eating. Darren took a swig of beer from the can.

'Don't bring her up now,' Dad said hurriedly.

Melanie looked at him for a tense moment. 'The Witch never spawned a kid.'

'I'm sorry I brought it up.'

Melanie took a sip of water to wash down the two pills that had been lying on the table by her plate. 'Imagine her having a child. God what a thought.' She shuddered, and Darren wasn't sure if it was the pills, the cancer or the thought of Olivia having a child that had done it. 'Imagine it walking around, living a life. Touching people.'

Darren reached over and held his mum's hand. 'I'm sorry I mentioned it.'

'But more to the point, the police have told us nothing about Molly's body. Nothing at all!'

'I think the tests take time, they don't want to say something if it's not certain—'

Mum interrupted Dad with a huff. 'That's not true is it though? There's a hierarchy to suffering, and we sit at the bottom. I bet Orin's being briefed by some snitch in the department—'

'Melanie—'

'Mum, you've got to take it easy, don't get stressed about this,' Darren broke in.

She got up from the table, anger in her movements. 'Talking of snitches, what have you been up to?'

She pointed a finger at Darren and he was alarmed. She had rumbled him, had discovered where he was working. He braced himself for what was coming next.

She walked to the counter where a pile of household detritus sat in a teetering pile. She threw an A4 envelope across the table at him. 'This came for you today. By courier. Nothing about that man is subtle.'

The envelope was addressed to him. Across the top was the logo of The Missing charity with the strapline 'Get angry, get justice, get results.' A chain of hands encircled the logo. Sitting on top of the circle, like a bauble on a ring, was an angel. It was the combination of hard-hitting and emotional that had proved wildly successful with the public.

His heart sank.

'Did you go and see him?' Dad asked.

Darren pushed his plate away. 'Yes. I wanted to understand more about what had happened back then when Carly went missing.'

His parents looked at each other.

'You could have just asked us,' his dad said quietly.

'You never talk about it. It's too painful for you.'

'We want you to live your life, not think about that period,' Dad said.

His mum sat opposite him, arms folded. She was less forgiving. 'You could hardly have done worse if you'd gone and seen the Witch herself.'

'*You* went to see her!'

'It was a mistake. I wish I'd never done it. She's just evil.

But don't be seduced by Orin. There are lots of people who want to hang on your grief, who want to profit from it. As if losing Carly wasn't enough, you become a magnet for other people's agendas. You can't even trust your friends any more.'

Darren put his finger in some spilled salt on the table and drew an abstract pattern with it. He knew what his mum meant. Having a sister who had been murdered by a serial killer had given him an unwanted celebrity status at school that he had only managed to shake off once he'd gone to art school. 'Why do you dislike him so much?'

'Every time I see him on TV or in the newspapers, he tells me there is no hope left, that there is only hatred and pain. But hope is all I have.'

'Mum, you've never talked about the logical extension of your belief that she's still alive, which is—'

'Darren!' Dad was warning him off, but it wasn't going to work this time.

'Which is that if she's still alive someone is keeping her captive.'

'God alive, Darren, how can you even imagine—'

But he pushed home the point. 'Who is that supposed to be?'

His mum was silent for a moment. 'I can't give you that answer, can I? All I can tell you is that a mother's intuition tells me she's not gone. Until I have a body, I can't believe anything else.'

Dad muttered something under his breath and pushed his plate away, leaving the room. Mum didn't follow him.

Darren picked up some of the grains of salt and threw them over his shoulder. His nan had once told him you did it to ward off the devil, but he chose to visit the devil's lair every day.

He wasn't sure now that he was strong enough to cope with it.

41

After dinner Darren hurried to his room and took the papers out of Orin's envelope. There was a folder containing newspaper reports and neatly typed profiles. A lot of the information he had never seen before and he read it all avidly.

It was certainly interesting reading. Olivia's life read like a checklist of upper-middle-class privilege – a big country house on the beautiful Sussex Downs, a tennis court, a horse, a mother who didn't have to work and a father who commuted to London and was a big noise locally. The large parties at their country house were written about in the local paper. Olivia and her younger sister Lauren were educated at private school. When Olivia was away in her first year at university, though, their sun-dappled existence came to an abrupt end. Lauren had been a quiet, shy girl who, when she hit fifteen, suddenly changed: she started playing truant, taking drugs, hanging out with the wrong crowd and self-harming. There was a report in the file on her arrest for shoplifting. Darren saw a sullen teenager with a large nose ring staring out of the police photo. He stared at it a while longer and finally realised that Lauren had shaved her eyebrows off.

A local news report explained that Lauren hanged herself when she was sixteen, from a tree in the garden of the family house. Darren read further and discovered that after Lauren's death Olivia must have dropped out of university. She was living in Hastings when she was arrested for being drunk and disorderly, and was later charged with affray when she attacked a man in a bar with a broken beer bottle. She got a suspended sentence. She lived with a man called Eric Cox for two years – he later got a prison sentence for fencing stolen cars.

But she had obviously managed to turn her life around, because she resurfaced a few years later in Brighton, where she began studying to be a social worker. Lauren's suicide must have sent a shockwave through her family: the report showed that her parents separated soon after and her mother moved to Melbourne. Her father had died two years before Olivia was arrested.

There was nothing in Orin's notes about a baby. That didn't mean he didn't know about it, though; Orin was a wily operator and had sent this stuff to woo Darren. He would be keeping information to himself if it suited him, and maybe there was a reason he wasn't revealing it to him.

Darren got out his laptop and typed Olivia's name into the search engine. After two hours of searching and reading, he closed the lid. There was no mention of a child anywhere. Fleet Street's finest tabloid reporters, the courts – none of them had noted anything. He dropped to the floor and did thirty press-ups, sat on the floor in a yoga position to stretch his legs. So Olivia had a secret. He didn't know how she felt about this child, but its existence was information he wasn't supposed to have. And that meant he had something he could use.

He thought for a moment about this son. He would be about Darren's own age. Did he know who his mother was? That would be a shock to discover. Darren thought with shame about what he himself had done – tried to track down his birth parents without telling his mum and dad. He'd done it in his first year at college, the freedom of living away from home stirring a new sense of independence in him, a curiosity to know what a life without the pain of Carly's disappearance could have made him into. The agency was neutral but helpful, the systems all in place to help the thousands of children separated from their biological families for one reason or another.

At the last moment he had backed away. The file was there if he wanted to look, he had been told. But he didn't have the courage. It had felt too disrespectful to his parents, to Carly. He wouldn't have been able to contain the emotions that would have sprung up had he taken that step – finding a new family, maybe biologically connected brothers and sisters, when his own sister was gone. He had been a coward, he believed now, to duck the opportunity.

Darren got back up, itching to do something he'd been thinking about for a while. He picked up the drawing he had started a few days ago and examined it again. It was perfect.

He cycled to Streatham High Road and locked his bike up outside the tattoo parlour. Once inside, he sat in the old barber-shop chair next to a console with needles attached to containers of ink. He stared at his face in the mirror. It was as if he didn't know himself.

'You look miles away, mate, on another fucking planet!' An Aussie tattooist in a tight T-shirt was standing behind him, both arms green and black with tattoos. But Darren barely noticed those, because right across the man's face was etched a spider web. 'What can I do you for today?'

Darren handed him the design.

'Cool mate. Where d'you want it?'

Darren tapped the back of his neck, under his mane of hair.

The man made a wincing sound. 'On a bone there, it'll be more painful.'

'Good.'

The man grinned as he pulled a piece of tracing paper

towards him, piercings in his ears and nose jangling as he moved. 'Pain is part of the process, man. Nothing is created without the pain of birth. Now nose to the floor and let's get this baby started.'

42

Darren saw Chloe walking across the park and waved, pushing himself off the bench he was leaning against. She was in jeans with a rip across the knee and a tight T-shirt, with a small bag hanging diagonally across her body.

She came up to him and he bent down to kiss her on the cheek. She smiled at him, weight shifting from one small foot to the next. 'So . . . where you taking me?' Her lips were dripping something pink and glossy.

'Dunno. This is your manor.'

She shrugged, looking vacantly about. 'I don't mind. We can do whatever you want.'

They paused, neither feeling the need to actually head anywhere. 'Fancy a horror movie?' Darren asked. 'There's one on nearby, I checked.'

'I love horror movies.'

'Great. That's what we'll do.'

Neither of them moved. The evening was warm and sultry and they lingered on the grass by the flower beds chatting about nothing at all, until Chloe realised they were going to be late for the film. They ran down pavements and across roads to get to the cinema on time.

The place was almost deserted; the guy selling popcorn gave them extra and the woman checking tickets told them they could sit anywhere. They sat back in their seats as the adverts screamed out their slogans on the screen.

'I can't believe you agreed to go out with me,' Darren said.

'You didn't even ask me!'

'Well, you know what I mean. What happened to the Audi guy?'

She shrugged again and rolled her eyes. 'Let's not talk about him.'

'So tell me what you really want to be doing with your life.'

'Well, I hate cooking. Who could like it after the people I've cooked for? I'm only doing that job for money before my course starts in October. I want to be a midwife.'

'You certainly love hospitals. Maybe the smell of disinfectant is addictive.'

'I've got to get more money first. Mum wants rent off me, I've got to get some savings.' She took a long slurp of cola. 'I heard you went to college already.'

'I did an art degree.'

'How was that?'

He picked up some popcorn. 'Great. I loved it. Bit of a crash back to earth now, living at home, all that.'

'Don't you like home?'

'No, it's fine. Though, there's Mum and Dad and there was Chester, our dog, but he just died. And my mum's ill. She's got cancer.' He felt his chin wobble as he confided in her. It was so nice to sit close to her and talk things through.

'I'm so sorry.'

He changed the subject, not wanting to get maudlin. 'What about your family?'

'Just me and Mum, but she spends a lot of time at her new boyfriend's in Thornton Heath.'

He was mesmerised by her face, the dimples that appeared and disappeared in her cheeks as she munched her popcorn. He reached over and put his hand on her face, drew her gently to him and kissed her. She smelt of peaches and cola and she was soft and lovely and full of promise.

When the film ended he took her hand and they wandered out of the cinema and into a loud crush of people in a bar. There were just the two of them, insulated in a bubble from the noise and movement around them.

'Did you meet nice people at college?' she asked him.

'Yes, loads.'

'Any nice girls?' she asked flirtatiously.

'I went out with a girl called Amy. A mate got us together because her brother was dead. He died in a climbing accident in the Alps.'

She frowned. 'Why would that make him get you together?'

The bubble burst. He was back in a raucous Croydon boozer, about to tell lies to a girl he knew he could love. The most defining thing about him had to be hidden from her.

He couldn't remember what he'd told other people at the hospital. Would she know that he had a sister? The confusion of keeping all the lies straight made his head spin.

'Darren?'

'My sister died when I was young, that's why.'

'Oh Darren, I'm so sorry.'

He changed the subject fast. 'But after a year and a half, Amy and I broke up.' He took a long drink. It was partly true. He felt bad lying to Chloe; she deserved better.

'Did she leave you?'

He shrugged. 'Yeah, I guess so.'

She looked up at him through thick eyelashes. 'Maybe you're bad news, Darren Smith, one to avoid.'

He winced as she used his fake name. It felt wrong. 'Don't say that.'

'Maybe I'll just have to get closer to find out. Do you want to come back to mine?'

Darren watched her as she slept, snuggled next to her in the single bed in her tiny bedroom. There was something about her that he found compelling: her energy, her joy at simple things, her acceptance of the world the way it was.

And the same feeling came to him that he had had when he first got together with Amy. Carly had never had the chance to fall in love, to be as happy as life could possibly make you. This was just another of the many things that had been stolen from her.

And so his night with Chloe, so rich with promise and excitement, ended with him lying awake, twisting and turning in his new girlfriend's spongy bed, thinking of Olivia.

'You sleep like a baby.'

Darren opened his eyes to find Chloe stroking the side of his face. He stretched, his ankles hanging off the edge of her bed. She was sitting in a pair of knickers and a vest, holding out a cup of tea.

He sat up on his elbows. A weak sun was coming through the curtains, holding the promise of a beautiful summer day.

'You're lovely,' he said.

She smiled and climbed back into bed and he snuggled down next to her, wrapping his long arms round her, pressing his erection against her.

'Your hair is amazing. The colour is mega,' she said. He grinned at her, Roehampton seeming like a bad dream from another century. 'What's that tattoo on the back of your neck?' she asked. 'I was looking at it earlier while you were sleeping. Are those initials?'

His happiness drained away. The initials C.E. that he'd forgotten about, entwined round each other and emblazoned in black ink on his neck. The closer he got to Chloe, the more tangled in his lies he would become. But he couldn't stop himself, because he just wanted to spend time with her. 'It's my mum's initials.'

'Oh, that's lovely.'

One lie was no better or worse than another, he thought; he was telling her so many. He pulled her down close to him and looked at her face, her high cheekbones, the clear blue eyes, her hair's lovely dark roots where they showed through the blonde curls. He had woken up next to her and hadn't felt the need to be away as quickly as possible, his desire spent and his attention on other things.

He knew deep down that she was a keeper, but he had no idea how to do that – keep her – when with every lie he told he sent her further from him.

'What are you doing this weekend?' she asked.

He looked at the sun again and wondered if there was a way to blast Roehampton from his brain, at least for a while. He picked up his phone and checked a weather chart. He grinned. 'Fancy coming surfing with me?'

43

The sun was a yellow disc in the sky, the music loud on the stereo. Chloe was beside him rolling joints as he threw his mum's car round the bends in the country lanes. Once they had decided to go west for the weekend, it was easy; he phoned Mum and pleaded for the car, Chloe threw some stuff in a bag, they tracked back to his house, threw his gear in the boot, strapped his surfboard to the roof and headed off. By mid-afternoon they were nearing the beach.

Darren roared round a corner and the beach appeared below them. 'Corduroy!' he shouted and pulled into the car park, executing a donut on the gravel that made Chloe squeal. 'Fuckin' a-mazing,' he sighed.

The waves were dark, even lines forming offshore and marching beachwards before crashing in white walls onto the sand. A northern, pale blue sky hung over the fields dotted with sheep. A warm wind blew straight from the Caribbean.

They carried their gear down to the beach. The surf was dotted with children, couples, boarders, kayakers and boogie-boarders in a joyous free-for-all in the miles of waves.

He liked teaching Chloe how to surf. She looked scared at the big waves, but he managed to get her on her knees on the board in the smaller breaking waves close to the beach, her perfect bottom skywards in her blue bikini bottoms. Chloe screamed and then laughed as she was toppled by a wave.

They sat in the shallows for a while giggling and canoo-dling. Darren could see large sets of waves further out to sea, their dark faces plunged into shadow when they rose to vertical. He strapped on his ankle tie and picked up his board. 'I'm going out. You OK hanging here for a while?'

'I'm loving it.' She smiled. 'I'm going to bodyboard. I'll watch for you.'

He kissed her; her mouth was fresh and salty. 'In Hawaii they know the surf's up because the pictures fall off the walls.' He imagined Chloe with a flower behind her ear and a grass skirt he could put his hand through. One day he'd go to Hawaii, try to surf the massive breakers of the North Shore with her by his side. He'd live his life, instead of waiting for it to start.

He pushed the board out into the water. He liked the idea of her watching him, driving him on, her simple devotion. He got on his stomach and began to swim out beyond the breaking waves.

The first waves smacked over his head and he struggled for the surface. He began to swim. Harder and faster, diving under the churning surf, gripping the board hard, breaking the surface and ploughing forwards as the next wave formed a mountain ahead. Darren was six feet tall on the beach, but when he lay on his board he was less than one.

The waves were six feet high, clean and even. He could see the next one breaking and dived under the wall of foam that smashed into him, gripping the sides of the board. He surfaced, spitting water, preparing for the next one, swimming hard. He saw a bigger, steeper wave approaching and swam hard to dive below it as it broke right over him. The next was easier and then suddenly, panting and exhausted, he was out beyond the breaking waves, the sea calm, the beach far away. He bobbed lazily up and down with the swell of the waves moving beneath him, one wetsuit-clad figure in a line of surfers.

He watched the waves forming beneath his board and

began to swim into the correct position to catch one. The water rose sharply behind him and he was lifted skywards, but he just missed the lip of the wave and didn't commit, sitting back up instead. A few minutes later he caught a wave but didn't manage to stand up. He bailed and swam back to the line-up.

The waves were increasing in size, the ocean shifting continually. He looked at the beach. He and Chloe could have a fire there later and watch the sun set, erect the tent in the campsite in the dark, wake to the gentle breezes of a British summer and a massive fry-up in the cafe.

He felt a shadow fall across his shoulder. A mountain of a wave had risen up behind him in the couple of moments he had been daydreaming. He scrambled to get flat, his arms propelling him through the water. The face of the wave formed beneath him, bigger and steeper than he had expected.

Waves are measured not in feet and inches, but in increments of fear. And on the fear scale this monster was a ten. He took off and whipped his legs underneath him in one movement as he swooped nearly vertically down the face of the wave, the water curling over him. He struggled for balance, his arms wide, his body low. He shot along the line of the wave as it curled over him and suddenly he was in its centre, the calm spot in a surging, boiling mass of water weighing many tons.

Time slowed to a stop; it was a moment of transcendental joy. And Carly came to him. She had been a better surfer than him; she had been magnificent. It was her love of surfing that had been the reason he had started; she was the reason he was here now, racing beachwards, suspended in the green room. She was here with him now, her wet hair flying free from her face, her lips tightly puckered in concentration, knees bent, one arm touching the side of her board.

The wave shifted and the face he was traversing grew too

vertical, the tunnel in front collapsing, tons of water coming down on his head. The wave changed into a monster and in the next instant that monster was Olivia. She was the devil that had risen from the deep, that had swamped his family and crushed their joy. He jerked backwards and was sent plunging to the ocean floor, slamming his head into something hard, the boiling mass of water collapsing down on top of him. He fought to get himself up, broke the surface disorientated and was immediately thumped down again by another wave. He felt his leg being yanked by the cord, his head spinning, vision turning white, the boiling water disorientating and endless. He started to panic, unsure which way was up and which down. He was tossed on to the beach like a piece of driftwood and lay panting on the sand.

Someone touched his shoulder. 'You OK, mate? Major wipeout you had there.'

Two surfers were standing over him as he nodded.

He lay on the sand, spent and exhausted. Chloe jogged across and leaned over him, the sun making her shadow into a blanket over him. 'You OK?' Her face was twisting between concern and happiness.

He coughed out salt water and lay back. 'Best surf I've ever seen. It nearly ate me up.'

She knelt down and kissed him. He lay back on the sand and closed his eyes and she lay down next to him. He let her soft contours and warm smell pull him to a safer place.

'I love you.' It was too soon to tell her this, she would think him desperate, but he couldn't stop himself. He felt a terrible fear that he needed to seize the moment because he was running out of time to spend with her.

She smiled and ran her hand across his face, grains of sand scouring his cheek as she pulled his face towards her. 'I love you too.'

They climbed the steps away from the beach to the car

park and put the surfboard on the roof. They sat smoking a joint and staring at the sea.

'There's something you need to know,' he said.

She had her bare feet on the dashboard, her bare legs radiating heat next to his arm. He stared at her as the sun sank low on the horizon. 'I'm going to leave Roehampton. On Monday I think.'

'Really?'

He nodded. 'A lot more things will become clear when I do that. It's time. I've got to stop.'

'Stop?'

'I mean leave.'

She nodded, not disagreeing. 'I'm not surprised. It's not the best place to work in south London.' They both smiled, staring out at the car park and the beach and surf beyond.

'The people are nice.'

'Shame about the inmates.' She took a drag on the joint and laid her head back. 'It's funny. White vans. I thought their spiritual home was our manor, south London – but in fact they're all here! White-van men and surfers go together as a tribe.'

'They're perfect for carting surfboards around.'

Chloe exhaled lazily, the smoke drifting round their heads. 'And bodies. You could have bodies in there and no one would be any the wiser.' She paused. 'I've always thought that.'

44

Lincolnshire

The countryside was vast, mile upon mile of fields stretching away on either side of the long straight road, interrupted only by a solitary barn or an ancient tree, silhouetted against the moon and thrown into relief by the man's headlights. He could finally relax out here, the suburbs of Peterborough far behind him, the urban sprawl of the south-east whipped away from him by the wind.

He was exhausted, struggling to keep his eyes open and focused on the road. He had had no sleep for thirty-six hours as his every whim, every impulse, had been indulged over and over and over, and the clean-up at the mews was always long and painstaking. Now that the manic impulses had been sated his military training kicked in, like a survival test on a winter mountain; he still had a lot to do, and limited time. He turned right on to a one-lane road with a stripe of grass down its middle. He passed a field of pick-your-own strawberries, then black fallow fields, before he hit the wheatfields stretching away on either side.

It was flat from here all the way to the Urals. Maybe that was where she had come from, heading west for something better, her pretty little head filled with girls' dreams. Instead she had fallen through the gap and become one of the missing.

He slowed, anticipating the gate, and stopped. He got out and listened to the emptiness for a moment. A sense of history always struck him here at this point and he thought of all the peoples who had been here before him: the old British tribes like the Corieltauvi, the Romans, Danes, Scandinavians and Normans, fighting and killing, raiding and raping for thousands of years, their blood and bones mulching down in this fertile soil just as hers would do. He put on wellies and opened the boot, pulling out a shovel and hoisting the long object in the blue plastic sheeting on to his back. He locked the car and headed into the huge wheatfield.

Lincolnshire produced more fresh produce than any other county in Britain, its grade-one soil supporting bumper crops of everything from sugar beet to cauliflowers, potatoes and organic wheat. He began to dig the fertile soil; no roots or stones or pipes to impede him going deep. The night was mild and he began to sweat. It took him two hours of hard work digging in the moonlight to have a trench deep and wide enough to put her well under. He never normally even glanced at them after, but the wellies she was wearing caught and jarred his eye. He stepped down into the grave and pulled them off. Covering her over and tamping down the fresh soil took forty minutes. Replanting the wheat stems took another hour, including trudging back to the car to get the gallon drum of water to make sure the plants took. When they came to harvest in September, the threshers would move over her in the swarms of dust of a million particles of wheat, the cycle of life on another revolution.

He walked out of the field, closed the gate and threw his wellies, her wellies and the spade in the boot. He pulled sharply on the cuffs of his blue shirt, had a long drink of water and drove away.

45

O n Monday morning Darren had thought long and hard about whether he would actually go back to Roehampton. He needed to come clean to Chloe, Olivia was detained somewhere where he would not be able to meet her, the security review meant he would soon be discovered and serious consequences would follow. But once he had got up and showered he had realised his desire to be back here was too great.

Now as he came out of the changing rooms to gather his cleaning materials for his shift, Kamal barrelled out of his office, waving a slip of paper. 'You,' he barked, waving it under Darren's nose. 'Fill this in and I'll forgive you.'

It was a form to show he no longer worked at Roehampton. Darren shook his head and turned away towards the security door. Kamal came and stood behind him and Darren tensed, but Kamal whispered in his ear. 'I'm giving you as many shitters to clean as I can this shift. You're doing the accommodation blocks.' Kamal walked away as the buzzer sounded and the security door slid open.

Kamal's revenge was prolonged. Darren mopped floors in an area with no windows or people and cleaned a toilet block devoid of windows or people. He was staring at another wasted day. A few hours later he arrived at the accommodation area and took small comfort in the fact that at least another person was here. A large female guard with sleepy eyes let him in to the cell area, a long featureless corridor with no natural light, a shiny lino floor, doors leading off on both sides and a locked door at the far end.

The guard walked with him along the corridor but didn't think it necessary to talk to him. She unlocked the first door. The room was small, with a stainless steel toilet in the corner with no seat or lid, the cistern hidden in the wall. A small square of towel hung from a stainless steel sink. There was a shelf that protruded from the wall and served as the bed. It was covered in a mattress and a small pillow. There was a desk, nailed to the floor, and a chair under a tiny window with bars across it, too high to see anything from but a small patch of sky.

Darren squirted bleach down the toilet and ran a brush round the pan. He put the brush back on his cart. He wiped down the sink and came out. He picked up a duster and ran it over the desk and a shelf. He mopped the floor. When he had finished the guard shut the door and opened the next one, where he repeated the process, and the next. The rooms were all identical; they only varied in where the women put the toilet paper – on the floor or on the desk – what pictures or photos clung to the walls – usually family snapshots taken a long time ago when presumably few could have imagined they would have fallen so far.

Darren had cleaned nearly all the cells when the guard began to talk into a radio, using codes and language Darren didn't understand. He came out of a cell to find the exit door at the end of the corridor opening and three nurses arriving, one pushing a wheelchair and another holding restraints in his hands. He was ordered to pull his trolley further back down the corridor as they entered the last cell on the right.

He backed away with his trolley and waited, the guard leaning against the corridor wall.

A few moments later the little group emerged from the cell, pushing the wheelchair. They backed it up against the exit door and stood beside it.

'You can go in and clean now,' the guard said.

Darren was standing about twenty feet away from Olivia. She sat staring at him from the wheelchair, her legs shackled with restraints and her hands bound together in her lap.

No one spoke. Darren began to push the trolley down the corridor towards Olivia, one wheel making a gentle squeaking noise as he went. Her face appeared blank, impossible to read. He stopped the trolley and paused. Now he was closer to her he could see her eyes flaring with flecks of gold. He picked up the toilet brush and entered her room.

Olivia watched Darren push the cleaning trolley towards her. She noted the width of his shoulders; he was tall and rangy, his wrists wiry but strong. His youth and health telegraphed out from him. No wonder Helen was fucking him.

Jealousy shot through her. Helen was hers, she felt. His being here, breaking the rules and running risks, rifling through what few possessions she had, gave her strange sensations. She understood there was no space for regret or pity; she had shown that pretty forcefully to his mother, to other mourners over the years. She didn't care. She didn't like most mothers, her own included. She felt the pull of the straps holding her arms in place, her emotions flickering between hate for this naïve young boy who was trying so pathetically to find his sister and regard for the fact that at least he was attempting something.

Darren re-emerged from her room, tiny drops of water falling from the toilet brush and reflecting like a chain of jewels in the harsh strip lights. *He's here to follow a trail that I can lay down*, she thought. *Like a child in an enchanted forest, he yearns to see where the trail leads him.* She felt her lip curl with disdain. *He is so young, and so naïve. In the centre of this wilderness there isn't a house made of sweets, but there is a cell and a wicked witch.*

And no one to save you.

Darren picked up the duster and returned to Olivia's room. He looked at the indentation in the mattress made by her slim body. He noted the hairbrush and a toothbrush in a plastic beaker; a book about ancient Greece and one about philosophy. The desk was stained with newspaper print that a water beaker had transferred to the table, but the papers were gone. He rubbed the stain away with his cloth. The walls were bare, except for one photo of a smiling teenage girl with blonde hair, her arm round the neck of a horse. Her likeness to Olivia was striking. It must be her sister Lauren. There was no photo of her son.

Darren cleaned and wiped and came back out into the corridor. Olivia was still staring at him, unreadable, the nurses waiting patiently on either side of her wheelchair.

Darren picked up the mop, dipped it in the water and twisted. He gripped the handle hard, flashes of what had happened to Linda about to overwhelm him. Poetic justice, revenge . . . He could just swing it right now and get her back. End it. Finish her. Olivia's eyes were widening, glittering. She was waiting, almost willing him on, pulling him towards the darkness.

If I don't leave here I'm going to go mad, he thought.

Darren thought he might faint. The corridor began to close in on him, the floor began to tip upright. He turned and with enormous effort re-entered her room. Tears stung his eyes. He wasn't nearer to Carly here – he felt further away from her than ever. He thought about Molly, lying in the ground, all alone for all those years. He began to mop. On the floor was the meal tray from lunch. Olivia had eaten little, but the plastic tumbler that held her pills was empty. He managed to pick up the tray without falling over and put it on the floor outside her cell.

When the room was done he came back out and the guard said, 'Can you take the tray back to the kitchens?'

Darren nodded and began to calm down. Maybe he'd see Chloe. He backed the trolley down the corridor and stood facing Olivia.

Olivia watched Darren, trembling as he held on to the trolley for dear life. Poor boy. He was out of his depth; groping in the dark, scanning her pathetic cell for any tiny clue – as if there was going to be anything left after all these years, as if it could be *solved*. He was seeing shadows and ghosts in every corner, meaning in the clouds, or tea leaves, or the mashed potato from her discarded meal.

He needs to leave here or he's going to go mad.

Her pills often fogged her brain, but today she felt strong. She ran her tongue around her lips, like she was eating him up, and she grinned. She lost sight of him when the nurse pushed the wheelchair back into her cell.

Darren pushed the trolley down a long corridor towards the kitchen. The further away from Olivia's cell the better he felt. When he turned a corner and light from an outside window shone on him, he felt better still. He stopped pushing as he looked at Olivia's meal tray. Her scoop of mashed potato was untouched, except where it looked like she had traced a heart in the top of the scoop.

He was wondering what it meant, if anything, when the door he was waiting by buzzed open and Helen came through from the other side.

She stopped when she saw him, looked flustered and glanced around to check they were alone. 'How are you?' she asked. 'Good weekend?'

He nodded grimly, itching to be gone.

Helen leaned back against a wall and smiled. 'Get up to anything fun?'

How could he tell Helen that he had been with a girl in Devon all weekend when he had been fucking her against her office desk just days before?

He shrugged.

She looked him up and down, her eyes lazily roaming over his body. 'I called you but you didn't answer.'

'Sorry, I never listen to messages. Text is the best way.' *Please don't text me*, he was silently begging her, *please don't text*. 'I really have to get this to the kitchens.'

She nodded and used the bunch of keys on her belt to open the door. She held it open for him to pass through. 'We should get together again some time, Darren Smith. You maniac.'

He nodded balefully as she walked away.

The door to the kitchens buzzed open and Darren was in. It was light and bright in here, sunlight slanting across the lino floor. Behind the counter the catering team were still clearing up from lunch.

He placed Olivia's tray on the metal countertop and waited as Berenice picked it up and cleared away the meal Olivia had barely touched.

'You did her room today?' Berenice asked. Darren nodded. Chloe saw him from the sink and came over.

'You didn't have to see her did you?' Chloe asked.

Darren shrugged. 'Only from a distance.'

'That's close enough,' Chloe said. 'You OK?'

'I guess.' He felt sweat break out down his spine.

She sighed. 'I guess she's going to be eating in that room for a long time after what she did. She used to line up here with everyone else.' She waved at the space around Darren. 'But now one of us has to take all her food to her room every day.'

'I like the walk,' Berenice said, patting her sides. 'Gotta try and keep it off somehow.' She looked at Darren. 'I hear you and Chloe have a rather more pleasurable way of keeping the weight down.' She winked.

Darren blushed.

Two lads in the kitchen behind Berenice began tossing ladles at each other in some kind of game. Daren was glad he was here, among normal people who had a laugh with each other, instead of stuck in the enclosed corridors and silent rooms.

A ladle clattered to the floor behind them and someone swore. Darren turned round and asked the guy, 'Did she talk to you much when she was in here?'

The dropped-ladle guy came nearer. 'Only to the women. She never talks to me. She's got a *real* thing about women.'

Chloe and Berenice rolled their eyes. Darren pressed on. 'In the dayroom one time she talked about Rollo being six foot two. What does that mean, I wonder?'

They all shrugged. Berenice wiped down the counter with a cloth. 'Who knows? She's mad remember.'

'The really mad ones often sing, you know,' ladle guy said.

'Better that they sing than that they scream,' Berenice added.

'Yeah,' Chloe said. 'That's the worst. The screaming.'

46

Kamal watched Darren Smith come through the security door from the facility. The little fucker had changed his name. Who knew what he was really called, what he was really trying to achieve turning up to this shithole every day?

It was hot in Kamal's office and he had already jumped enough hurdles to leave him exhausted for the rest of the afternoon. The security review was giving him sleepless nights. It was a pointless exercise in his view – not that anyone asked him for his view; *that* was a luxury someone from his part of the world never experienced.

The pompous Andrew Casey-Jones had been in here only this morning, ordering the employee files to be inspection ready. Kamal's assistant Roksandre had already complained that the printer was about to break under all the photocopying that was being done. The summer holidays were upon them; there was a blizzard of employees jacking in their jobs, or leaving for a break and not bothering to come back or send so much as a postcard. The governor had lost sight of the main point; no one had ever escaped from Roehampton and they weren't likely to do it anytime soon – but Darren out the door with his security pass revoked would mean one less problem on Kamal's desk.

He picked up the phone and made a call. It was time to give Darren whatever-the-fuck-his-name-was a taste of Tangiers – brutal, spicy and ugly.

Darren waited near Kamal's office to put the trolley back

in the cupboard. His shift was over, and he was desperate to get out in the fresh air but there was something he needed to do first. Before he changed into his own clothes he turned round and headed up the stairs to the first floor and security control.

Sonny and Corey were there, surprised to see him. 'Hi Darren, you not cleaning up here at this time of day are you?' Sonny asked.

'No, I just thought I'd come by and say hello. I've just finished.'

'Well, that's nice,' Sonny said. 'I wish we had something interesting to tell you, very quiet the days at the moment, eh Corey?'

Corey smiled, looking uncomfortable, giving Darren daggers behind Sonny's turned back.

'Let me take those,' Darren said, leaning over and picking up a couple of mugs from the desk. 'I'll put them in the kitchen for you.'

Sonny pushed his hand away. 'You work hard enough! Your shift is over for the day.' He stood. 'I have to stretch my bad back every opportunity I get, doctor's orders. You want another drink, Corey?'

Corey smiled and shook his head as Sonny walked out of the room.

'We should have another drink soon,' Darren called as Sonny walked away.

'A lovely idea,' Sonny said.

'What the fuck you coming up here for, man?' Corey hissed. 'People'll get suspicious.'

'Did you get his details yet?'

'No man! Jesus!' Corey got up and poked his head out of the door to check that Sonny wasn't close.

'I really need them—'

'Yeah, yeah, my cuz could lose his job.'

'If you get me the details I'll stop coming up. Take my number and text me.'

Corey scribbled the number down on a piece of paper. Darren patted him on the shoulder and left the room.

A few moments later he came out into the lobby and found Nathan on security. 'How you doing, Nathan?'

The perfect forehead pinched into a frown. 'Nightmare, Darren, nightmare.'

'What's the problem?' Darren put his possessions in the tray and walked through the barrier. He didn't beep.

'That.' Nathan pointed at a tiny red dot on his chin. 'It's the size of Krakatoa and I've got a casting.'

Darren had to squint to see it. 'Don't worry, you can't even see it.'

Nathan shook his head. 'Studio lights, HD TV, nightmare,' he muttered again. 'Life's so unfair.'

Darren was at that point thinking life was unfair to those who hadn't been blessed with Nathan's looks.

'I mustn't grumble, Darren, I know that other people are less fortunate, that in many ways I have been blessed.' Nathan put his hand on his heart. 'Others toil unseen.' It was an Oscar speech in the making.

Darren heard a voice behind him. Berenice was leaving, putting her handbag in the tray.

She passed through the barrier. 'You know, Nathan, you really look like someone, I can't remember their name – who is it?'

He gave her his catalogue-model smile. 'Bradley Cooper?'

Berenice looked startled. 'No. I was thinking of that Polish cleaner who started recently. Piotr, is it?' She picked up her bag, affronted at his arrogance, and walked hurriedly away.

47

When Darren got home his mum was packing her bag for her mastectomy. It was small, containing only what she really needed for her hospital stay. She was a practical, sensible woman in so many areas of her life, Darren thought – except one.

She was nervous, and he couldn't help her with that. But he wanted to do something to support her. He took the rubbish out and glanced back up at the house. She had been nagging him about the clapboard for so long now. He'd already booked a couple of days off work so that he could be with her in hospital while she recovered from her operation. He could spend the rest of the time stripping and painting the front of the house.

He got excited about his idea.

He went out to the shed and rooted around among the dried-up tins of paint and the stiff brushes no one had cleaned properly. He was searching for paint stripper, but he couldn't find any.

He was about to go shopping for supplies when his phone rang. It was Orin Bukowski.

'You got a TV, young gun? I suggest you put it on.'

'Just a minute.' Darren went into the living room and put the news on. Details of how Molly had died had been made public. Darren listened to a reporter reveal that she had been smashed across the skull with a heavy, blunt object. Her injury was severe enough to kill her instantly.

'What they will not tell you, and what I am going to announce in ten, is that for the angles to match with the height of prisoner 1072B Molly Peters would have had to be kneeling.' Orin paused for effect. 'You come join my campaign, we'll buy better justice.'

Darren shook his head. 'My mum's about to—'

'Go into hospital. I know. You want me to pay for a private room? You just have to ask.'

'Thanks, Orin, but let us get through this first. I'm sorry.'

'You're not the one who needs to be sorry.' Orin ended the call.

Darren sat down on the floor of the stuffy shed, warmed by the sun so the creosote in the wood released its musty, pleasant perfume. It was the smell of the summers of his childhood. Some of the paint supplies on the shelves had been here since Carly was still alive. Dust motes danced in the light through the ill-fitting slats. Darren felt the impotence and pain rise up in him again as he absorbed what had happened to Molly; tiny strips of light trying to illuminate a picture, but highlighting only horror. The only thing that stopped grief overwhelming him was his phone beeping. It was a text from Corey.

John de Luca, 91 Clapham Park Road, London SW4. U o me cuz.

Darren ran back into the house and upstairs to his computer. Number 91, the flat above the charity shop, was where John Sears lived. Were John de Luca and John Sears the same person? Why did anyone visiting a serial killer need two names? As he himself knew only too well, that would require a lot of fake ID.

48

Darren cycled to Clapham and parked round a corner from the charity shop near the Common. The tinkling door jarred his nerves; the musty smell evoked old men in dressing gowns. He noticed that there was a video camera in the corner, trained on the shop floor. He couldn't understand why a humble charity shop would need that level of security.

He was pleased to see that the woman who had helped him last time wasn't in today. Instead, there was a black woman at the counter. She looked up from the pages of a paperback. 'You dropping off, dear?' Darren shook his head. 'There's men's at the back there.'

He was unsure how to proceed, so he walked past a rack where pairs of creased and wrinkled shoes begged to be picked up, past belts on a rotating display and mismatched crockery struggling to find space on some narrow shelves.

'Where do you put all the stuff you can't sell?' He began to flick through a rail of tweedy trousers no one could possibly want to buy in the hottest June for years.

The woman put down her book. 'We get too much, that's for sure. Some too dirty, some too worn. We bag it up and ship it to the Third World. I think they push it through huge machines and shred it and make new stuff from it.'

Darren was interested in that. 'That sounds like a big industry.'

The woman smiled. 'I don't know, dear. But open that

door behind you and take a look.' Darren turned and saw through a partly open door a small storeroom piled to the ceiling with black bin bags brimming with clothes and bedding nobody wanted.

'World is full of too much stuff, eh?'

The woman nodded. 'Too much stuff around us, you know.'

The bell tinkled and the door opened. Two dark-haired women came in, both pulling suitcases. 'Maybe it's a bit like people, it feels like there are too many of them at times,' Darren said.

The woman was being friendly. 'Some of the people who come in here feel a little surplus to requirements, but we do what we can.'

Darren nodded, noticing a door to the right of the storeroom. It would lead to the stairs and the flat above.

Darren walked closer to the door and looked at some T-shirts on a rail. He was about to ask the woman about John when he heard the heavy tread of someone coming down the stairs from the flat upstairs. He grabbed a T-shirt off a rack and darted into the changing cubicle as the door to the flat opened and closed.

A man coughed.

The woman at the desk said hello, and whoever had come through the door murmured a greeting.

'Quiet today?' He had a south London accent.

'Like always,' she said. Darren heard a metallic creak. He looked down and saw under the bottom of the cubicle curtain the dusty work boots of Olivia's befriender. 'I haven't seen you around much lately, where you been?'

'Keeping out of trouble. By the way, I wanted to tell you, I think someone's been trying to tamper with my post – I had someone trying to take out a credit card in my name. No one suspicious has been in asking about me, my name, anything like that? My bank says I need to be extra vigilant.'

The woman made a clucking noise of disapproval. 'That's terrible. I've seen nothing like that, but I'll warn the others.' Daren heard more creaks and shuffles. 'You OK in there?' she called out to him suddenly.

'I'm fine,' Darren said, taking a step backwards towards the mirror. The boots were back outside the curtain, pointing towards him this time.

Darren held his breath. The boots moved away and he heard the door next to the changing room open and shut behind him.

Darren pulled back the curtain and came out into the shop, the T-shirt in his hands.

'That's three pound fifty dear.' The woman licked her finger and used it to open a plastic bag.

'I heard that man,' Darren said, shaking his head and pulling out the coins. 'Same thing happened to my mum last year. Someone took out a credit card in her name and ran up a bill of seven grand. You can never be too careful.'

The woman grimaced. 'They just want your personal information nowadays.'

'So true. John, isn't it? I had a chat with him a few weeks back when I came in. Has he recently moved in? If you've just moved it's much worse I've heard.'

'Oh, John's been here years.' She settled back in her seat and, just as Darren had hoped, looked ready for a long conversation. 'When I first started the shop was—'

'What are you doing?' One of the dark-haired women was right behind Darren.

'Excuse me?'

'Why are you asking about John?' Darren could see the women were sisters or twins. They were English, with flat south London accents. 'Who wants to know?'

'I'm not asking about anything—'

The woman took a step towards him. 'Don't play dumb

with us. Who's asking?' The other woman shut the door to the shop and flicked the Yale lock closed. The black woman pushed her chair back against the wall, watching.

'No one, I'm not asking anything.'

There was a very tense silence. 'You won't talk? I know who can make you.' The woman closest to him turned towards the door that John had disappeared through and Darren lunged for the exit.

One of the sisters screamed out John's name and Darren could hear heavy footsteps thundering down the stairs above his head. He grabbed at the shop door, twisting the Yale lock. The other woman tried to pull him back from the door. 'Who are you?' she shouted. 'You won't get away with it!'

Darren had to turn and shove her hard to get her off him so he could open the door. She stumbled backwards into a rack of clothes, which began to roll away from her, leaving her in a tumble of hangers and shirts on the floor.

The door to the flat at the back flew open and John Sears or de Luca came through it. Darren finally got through the front door and sprinted away down the street. He didn't stop running until he was nearly in Stockwell, when he realised he was still carrying the bag with the T-shirt in it. He was about to throw it away when he actually took a look at what he had purchased. It was a black T-shirt with a picture of a man smoking a massive reefer.

He waited an hour before he dared circle back to the Common and collect his bike. His pulse was still racing as he unlocked his chain. What had Orin called befrienders? *They are a security breach of the first order.* Who was this man, why had he changed his name and why were those women – his sisters, surely – so protective of him? He was still no nearer to an answer when he had cycled back to Streatham and bought the equipment he needed to start decorating the house.

49

In the morning Darren and his dad took his mum to St George's. Darren stood by the car as his mum got ready, watching Dad pick the smashed bodies of gnats off the car paintwork. Mum was always last out of the house, needing to check the door and windows were locked. A text beeped on her phone – a 'thinking of you' message from a friend, no doubt.

Darren picked up her hospital bag and put it in the boot of the car. He got in the back seat. Even now he was an adult, his position relative to his parents in the car hadn't changed. Dad drove carefully, leaving Darren to wonder if he was already over the limit for drink-driving.

At the hospital they watched Mum have her IV fitted and the nurses did a lot of kindly patting of forearms and making of light jokes designed to put the men at ease. Melanie would be in surgery for three hours and recuperating afterwards for a few days. She was wheeled away and the Evans men were left alone with their demons.

Dad told Darren to go home; he would wait in the hospital until she woke up.

Darren did what his dad wanted. He went home and decided to start on the front of the house. He was still badly shaken by what had happened in Clapham in the charity shop. The women were aggressive and protective, but what it all meant he couldn't fathom. He had to stay busy to stay on top of his panic about so many things: the threat of discovery at Roehampton, the fact that his face would be clearly visible on the security camera in the charity shop – and the darker fears, the horror of what had happened to Molly and what might have happened to Carly.

Darren planned his DIY in detail. He opened up his new cordless paint-stripper gun and plugged it in to charge. He dragged the ladder from the shed to the front of the house. He got his phone out and got some tracks playing. He took out a new scraper and stood back, examining the scale of the job. It looked big. He rolled a joint. The sun was hot and pleasant. He had a cup of tea.

He played around for a bit with the paint-stripper gun; it made a pleasing noise, like a jet engine passing overhead. He climbed the ladder and applied the jet of heat to the cracked and peeling paint. It began to come away in strips, falling to the paving below him. He used the scraper to get into the grooves between the splits of wood. He climbed down the ladder and moved it along a few inches. He became distracted by a beetle crawling across the paving slabs between the bubbled paint remains. He climbed the ladder again and pulled away more peeling paint.

He started to sweat. He got the munchies. He went back into the house and rummaged through a variety of cupboards for biscuits or cereal or chocolate, knocking over packets and leaving boxes on the table.

He smoked the joint.

By the time he texted Chloe to ask if he could come over he had been working on the house for three hours and had stripped a door-sized section back to the bare wood. He felt ridiculously pleased with himself. Dad phoned to say Mum was out of the operation and in recovery; it had gone as well as could be expected.

He had another joint.

He arranged to visit Chloe after he'd seen his mum.

He picked up his tools and took them into the kitchen, leaving them on the kitchen table. He didn't notice he'd tramped hundreds of flakes of burnt paint into the house. He tried to carry his bike through the house from the garden and tripped over the paint gun charger that was plugged in in the hall. He yanked the plug out of the wall and took the charger in to the kitchen. He began to pack a bag in case he stayed at Chloe's house later, then changed his mind; he needed to be with his dad.

He got confused. He remembered to put the joint in the bin, but put the stripper gun in his rucksack. He couldn't find his phone. He put his bike keys in his back pocket and the stripper in the kitchen drawer. He locked the house and cycled away, leaving the ladder propped up against the front of the house.

Mum looked so small and vulnerable in the hospital bed after her mastectomy that Darren stopped short and his eyes filled with tears. A nurse was moving about beside her, and she reassured him and Dad that she was OK.

They sat together for an hour and then Mum said she was tired and needed to sleep.

'Mum, I'm going to Chloe's house now,' Darren said.

He saw her give Dad a look. 'Who's Chloe?'

He shrugged. 'Just someone I met at work.'

She grinned. 'When do I get to meet this someone?'

He shrugged again. 'Someday.'

'Don't wait too long, my days might be numbered.'

He left to the sound of Andy shushing her and urging her to stay positive.

'I like your T-shirt,' Chloe said.

'Yeah, it's kinda cool.'

Darren was wearing the T-shirt he'd bought from the charity

shop as he lay on Chloe's sofa. He was trying to get up but Chloe kept pulling him back down.

'I tried to friend you on Facebook, but I couldn't find you.'

He froze. Here was yet another problem he hadn't thought through.

'I don't do social media.'

'Oh.' She frowned. 'Didn't you say in Devon that you did?'

He panicked. Trying to remember what he had and hadn't said to her was proving impossible. He was not naturally a liar and he hated doing it. He needed to never go back to Roehampton, come clean with Chloe and move on with his life.

'I've been thinking a lot about Duvall,' Darren said. 'How easy is it to keep a secret, do you think? I mean, if you did something really bad, like Olivia has done, could you never tell anyone?'

Chloe lay back on the sofa and thought about it for a while. 'I could keep a secret for ever. Easily.' He fancied she was staring right through him.

'Really? I'm surprised.'

'Yeah. If it was important enough. And it seems to be very important to Olivia to keep the secret about where those girls are.'

'So why did she reveal where Molly was?'

Chloe sighed. 'I don't know. Some at work are saying that she did it to get less time in solitary for killing Linda, but I don't think it's that. It's about power. Power over something we don't understand and maybe never will.'

'Mmm.'

'Or maybe it's all about you, Darren Smith.' She smiled and ran a finger down his nose. 'Maybe it's all about you.'

50

Olly felt cold, his skinny nine-year-old shoulders shivering, even in June. It felt like a gale was blowing off the North Sea. The water had merged with the sky, one massive slab of grey with just the bobbing boats to cut the monotony.

He scratched the wall with his fingernail, wore it down till it hurt the end of his finger. Beggs would be along in a minute, a football under his feet, and they would go and hoof it about on the playing fields. Beggs didn't understand why Olly liked to lean here and watch the boats, why he liked being alone. The harbour held riggers and outboard motors and grappling poles and lobster pots, and he just liked the colours of the boats, liked the way they bobbed and swung and moved in the water. He never told anybody this; Nan would call him a poof from her armchair before taking another drag on her Richmonds, and being called that was the worst thing in the world. So he watched the boats alone.

Fishermen, the blasted race, Nan called them. Most were solitary, or it was a family affair, dads and sons, coming back with their small catches and half-full nets. He didn't have a dad, otherwise maybe it would be him out on the water. Olly didn't know anyone here who actually ate fish; there was nothing a fisherman liked more than sausage or onion rings as far as Olly could tell. Neither of which came from the sea, Nan would have said, grinning at him.

The red boat was the one he liked the best. Most of the time it was sealed in its green tarpaulin, the sides running with rust. It was a largish boat, with a top of the range outboard and a roomy cabin. The owner didn't come very often. The harbour master had told him once that he was called Gert Becker. Olly had remembered the name because it sounded foreign and because he was rich. Of that Olly had no doubt. He always parked his dark green, late model hatchback behind the Spar, as close as he could get to the boats. Gert Becker liked rolls of tarpaulin. Brought one with him each time he came.

Olly liked watching boats and building shelters, and he liked building them with tarpaulin. It sounded like a sail when the wind blew, made a loud noise when the rains came, made him dream of adventure, and he liked its bright, cheerful colours: blue and green and white, the colour of the sea in the sun.

There was no sun today though. He watched Gert, dressed in the yellow plastic of the fisherman, chug out of the harbour in his red boat and out to the open sea in the drizzle. The guy was strange, but then that was no dealbreaker for Olly. Most people were strange and best left well alone. He had all the gear and no idea, as Nan would say, money to spend but his catches were no better than anyone else's. Olly had climbed aboard the red boat once when no one was around and seen the man's folly first hand: he had weights for the deep sea on the boat, but any local person could have told him that vessel didn't have the range to go out there.

And tarpaulin was expensive, and even though this guy had a lot of money, no one in the harbour ever wasted anything if they could help it, Nan said, and this guy never came back with his. The roll was always gone when he returned. Profligate, Nan would have said, if he had ever told her.

Beggs was late, as usual. The tide was already past the old black post that stuck up by the sea wall. Soon the water would turn and retreat, taking with it the secrets the sea never gave back. Olly licked his finger where a tiny line of blood had begun to show at the edge of his ragged nail. He turned and saw Beggs dribbling the ball along the windswept harbour road. He joined him and they ran and dribbled the ball away from the shore up the road to the field.

There was a woman standing on the other side of the road, going neither this way nor that, her blonde hair streaming outwards with the wind. She was watching him. She was so still, thin and unbending in the wind. For a moment he thought she was a ghost. He got over it and thought, another weirdo. He couldn't imagine how many there must be in Lowestoft if there were this many here.

He had an image of the seabed covered with rolls of tarpaulin, a vast dump no one ever visited, but then he saw the white crossbar of the goalpost and he raced Beggs towards it, the wind on their backs and squeals coming out of their mouths. When he turned round, the woman had vanished.

51

Olivia heard them before she saw them, the governor's hard soles clicking on the floor outside her cell. There was also the muffled chaos of lesser mortals scraping and bowing.

The door opened and they crowded in: the governor, Helen, Dr Chowdray, two guards and a third who worked the cell block. The governor was a dandy from head to toe, his tie good and bright, his suit designer.

'You ready, Olivia?' the governor asked.

'I'm ready.'

The dandy nodded. 'It'll be over soon. And then you'll feel much better.'

She held out her arms and spread her legs and the guard called Tracey frisked her thoroughly, soft hands running over her contours. She could smell her perfume on her hands and one of the other guards, Alan, a lover of pies and ale, hand-cuffed her wrists together. Tracey began a check of her toilet bag. Olivia watched her carefully. She was thorough: feeling the toothpaste tube, even the crimped metal end, shaking the face cream for a giveaway metallic rattle, breaking the soap into small chunks. She ran her fingers over the seams in the bag, checked the zip.

Dr Chowdray had the blood pressure cuff on her arm and Olivia could feel her pulse beating inside her body. She opened her mouth for him to check her teeth and gums and under her tongue with a small wooden spatula. She saw

Tracey watching and caught her eye. Olivia winked at her; she just couldn't help it. Tracey started and looked away, swallowing nervy saliva.

It was an entertainment of sorts.

Olivia looked at Helen. Her psychiatrist looked right back. 'You look tired, Helen,' Olivia said. 'It's important not to have too many disturbed nights.'

She didn't reply. Her expression didn't change. She was no fun at all.

And then they were off, down the long dirty white corridors of Roehampton, through the safety doors, through more doors, the security buzzers interspersed with the dandy's talk of his upcoming two weeks in Tuscany, Helen recounting a tale of pasta eaten in a vineyard. Lives lived without fear, self-indulgent and without struggle.

Another door opened and they were in a loading bay, a private ambulance waiting. Alan opened the back door and led Olivia up the steps. He handcuffed her feet to a low rail and Tracey got in beside her. The washbag sat on a shelf near the door. The driver up front revved the engine.

The dandy himself closed the back door and the van braked and swayed over speed bumps as it headed towards the gate.

52

D r Faisal Waheed looked down at the rectangle of white chest skin inches below the scalpel he held in his fingers. This was the third pacemaker he had inserted on this shift, and he had one more to do before close of play today. Patients tended to blur one into the next in this job; he saw them only when they were outside the theatre, already lying down on the bed, stripped of their usual clothes, apprehensive and compliant. Bovine, he usually thought. It was easy to put them at ease; the operation was after all quite straightforward.

But obviously this patient was rather different. He had seen the name at the top of the notes, had agreed to allowing the handcuffs that attached her to the bed frame. He should have been unmoved; he had operated on a former Wimbledon tennis champion, a famous actress and a member of parliament or two in his private practice, but that was not what he felt. As he had scrubbed up he had thought of his own daughter. Of course; it would be impossible not to – her charmed life, her privilege that his hard study was paying for. He remembered her at thirteen, in the grey prep school uniform, the violin case in her hand. He had tried to imagine life without her, what that would actually mean, and found he was shaking as he had turned off the tap with his elbow. He had berated himself for his sentimentality as the implement tray had been moved carefully to the other side of the room on instruction from the prison. They were to take no chances. This wasn't a debate at the Oxford Union. He had signed up to the Hippocratic oath; he was here to do his job and save a life, whatever that life had done to others.

Now Faisal was looking at the monitor where a 3D image of Olivia's pumping heart was displayed. He had the scalpel in his fingers, handed to him a moment before by the nurse. Below him was the white rectangle of skin in a sea of blue sterile paper where he was to make the first incision. The two assistants, faces half obscured by their masks, were staring too.

Pacemakers were fitted under local anaesthetic, so the patient was still awake, her face now obscured behind a wall of paper. Faisal wondered if she could sense his pause.

'Looks like an expanded and misshapen left ventricle,' Dr Mehmet Budak offered.

Faisal wondered whether the Turk was only one generation off the soil himself, whether the superstitions of the Levant were close to his own Pakistani peasant family's.

He felt ill. Was it too hot in here? He turned to the nurse, who dabbed his forehead as if she understood. Faisal tried to concentrate on the vessel leading into the heart chamber where he was to insert the tiny lead of the pacemaker, but all he could think was that his patient had a twisted heart.

He wanted to be out of here and back with his family more desperately than he had ever wanted anything. His father had slogged to escape from the soil of the Indian subcontinent, had worked like a dog to put his son through an English public school where he was imbued with the classics and turned into a westerner, and one look at the twisted heart of a serial killer and he was thrown back to tribal territory.

Faisal said a silent prayer; not in one language or another, this religion or that, but a personal prayer that his family be protected from witches such as this.

He took a deep breath and made the first incision.

53

Orin was standing in Hyde Park, central London, holding a bottle of water in one hand and trying to attach a microphone to his head with the other. The make-up artist was dabbing at his forehead as he tried to get the microphone in the right place.

'I'm feeling so hot today,' he said to the woman, who was holding three brushes in one hand. 'I've got a terrible case of the sweats.'

She smiled. 'I've got pancake here that can obliterate anything, babes.' She dabbed more powder on his nose.

A roadie was unbundling wires that ran across a podium like some impossible child's conundrum. They had brought in a bigger sound system and it was taking too long to assemble, the roadies bending and lugging equipment and swarming around the stage like ants. It was threatening to rain, and Orin cursed the heavens: he could control almost everything, but not the British weather.

Molly being found, and the discovery of the injuries she had sustained, had made Orin's rally soar up the news and political agenda and there were several TV interviews planned. He was also gratified to see that a larger than expected crowd had gathered already – and there was still half an hour until they started. It was fertile recruiting ground; the movement always needed new foot soldiers.

Darren Evans had dodged him – he had played the trump card of a sick mother and an operation. The young man was an opportunity Orin needed to incubate. He was teetering, Orin could sense it, and would probably be on board soon.

His secretary came over, holding up an iPad. 'You need to see this, Orin.'

He pulled off the darned microphone and looked at the screen. The news was out, in black and white in all its horror. The forensic investigators had made their report public. Molly Peters's bones had been examined and their details were different from what had been reported when she went missing in Brighton in 2002: her thigh bone was a centimetre longer, her shin bone point five of a centimetre. Her teeth also differed from her dental records. Molly Peters had grown three and a half centimetres and gained four new adult teeth in the time between going missing and being killed. There was only one explanation: she had been held captive for at least eighteen months.

In the hour between the first news reports and the start of Orin's rally, the details burst upon the media in a fury. The suffering of the teenager, the agony of her family, of the other four families, meant that by four o'clock a phone was picked up at Roehampton High-Security Hospital and someone with a sense of personal outrage and in an attempt to right the tremendous wrongs in the world had phoned Orin Bukowski and told him, anonymously and off the record, that Olivia wasn't even in the high-security psychiatric unit where the press were gathering again, but in hospital, her life being saved by the British taxpayer.

One thing got Orin hotter than injustice and suffering, and that was not being in the know. As he mounted the podium for his 'Rally for the Missing', the audience swollen by several thousand people because of the news breaking, Orin did something on a whim.

Behind him fluttered pennants carrying huge photos of the missing women and girls: the five secrets of England. He looked out at the huge crowd, at the thousands of people who had given up their precious time to show their support and their outrage. They were waiting for him to speak, for him to stir them up with his southern Baptist preacher style, his fire and brimstone rhetoric. He remained silent. The distant hum of the West End was all that could be heard.

And he started to cry. His sobs could be heard clearly through the microphone. His secretary came forward, full of concern, but he waved her away. The crowd were mesmerised and horrified. They felt his pain. He sniffed back his tears and he looked out over his followers. He raised his hands in a command. 'To St George's!' he cried, and the crowd screamed back their support.

54

Darren was sitting backwards on a chair, resting his chin on its hard edge, staring down at his mum as she dozed in the bed. He could smell the fug from his trainers, wafting up to his nose in the overheated hospital.

To make the time pass quicker before she was released he had kept her company, entertaining her with silly stories and progress on the front of the house; and while she slept he had roamed the building, walking the stairs, corridors and lobbies, checking out the shop and the charity stalls and the gardens and the chapel. He knew the names of the wards, marvelled at the departments with exotic names, examined the yellow X-ray symbols, the shabby chaos of the basements. He spent a lot of time chatting to volunteers and auxiliaries and he became a favourite of the nurses on his mum's ward, who treated him like a surrogate son. She was making good progress and should be out soon, maybe tomorrow or the next day.

He heard the chanting through the window by his mum's bed.

He leaned out, understanding in an instant who they were. The Rally for the Missing.

He went to the nurses' station to find a crowd at the window and tension in the air.

'What's going on?' he asked no one in particular.

People shook their heads, took photos on their phones.

Behind him Darren could hear a TV. He tuned in to it for a moment. Molly's face filled the screen.

'Can you imagine?' said a nurse behind Darren, shaking his head.

'Terrible,' agreed another.

Darren turned and stared at them, then back at the screen, which was now showing the spot in Sussex where Molly had been uncovered after lying so quietly for so long. He read the ticker tape flowing past the bottom of the screen. She had been held captive for eighteen months.

They were showing Orin's rally in Hyde Park: his tears, his big fist thumping down on a lectern, the crowd surging and shouting, the pictures of the women, including Darren's sister, fluttering in the breeze behind him, like pennants from a medieval pageant.

There was a disturbance in the huddle of people by the television. They could see a live feed of the crowd from the Rally for the Missing swarming in through the entrance of St George's itself, past the collecting boxes and the Friends table, passers-by gawping.

The worst serial killer of recent times was being operated on – right here in a normal hospital.

People got angry, and angry people do stupid things. A woman on the welcome desk began to block the crowd's path, trying to shoo them out with exhortations about respect for the sick and the elderly. A security guard was overwhelmed.

Olivia was having an operation, right here in the hospital where his mum lay resting! Images flashed across his mind: the fluid that dripped from his mum's damaged tissues into the bag by the side of her bed; Molly's head caved in with something hard; his own scarred heart beating. As he walked over to the nurses' station the vulnerability of those he loved and how endless suffering could be overwhelmed him. 'Do not tell her about this,' he ordered the nurses. 'Do not wake my mother.'

They all nodded, their eyes already back on the TV, their backs turning away.

Darren looked behind the station at the piles of notes, papers, pens, Post-its, a hairband, an empty cup of tea and a name badge with a barcode security strip at the bottom. He picked up the badge and walked away.

Then he broke into a run.

He was stupid, that was a given, but something had fallen into place. He had wandered the hospital for hours over the past few days, and he had a hunch he knew where they were taking her.

In the empty wing on the second floor the guards outside Olivia's room got a call. There had been a security breach: protestors were on their way and they were angry as hell.

Alan Brown had been a prison guard for fifteen years, Tracey Young had been one for twelve. They had worked at Roehampton together for five years, and they knew what to do. They swung into action immediately. Tracey called for backup while Alan entered the room and double-checked the prisoner, pulling at the handcuffs that held her to the bed frame to ensure they were secure.

'What's happening?' Olivia was awake and sitting upright.

Alan didn't bother to answer. 'Let's go.'

Tracey nodded.

'What's going on?' Olivia was leaning forward, asking louder this time.

The two prison guards left the room and shut the door.

The corridor outside Olivia's room had three exits. The first was a door at the far end that led to a staircase. Tracey ran over and tested it again. The door was locked, but that wouldn't prevent someone with the correct pass opening it from the other side. But there were guards stationed at the bottom of the staircase that led to that door and the protestors were coming from the other direction. Halfway along the corridor was an elevator large enough for beds to be transported to and from theatre. The lift had been programmed remotely so that it was stopped on this floor with the doors open. The weak point was the other door, a swing door at the other end of the corridor, round a right angle. It was the public way into the ward and was manned by two more guards and the attending nurses.

The noise of the protestors was growing louder, fast, and the guards at the swing door needed extra support, but that meant Olivia's room would be out of view to Tracey and Alan. They had prepared for her trying to escape, not for others trying to get in, and uncomfortable scenarios were beginning to yawn in front of them.

Alan drew his baton, dancing slightly from foot to foot, a sheen of sweat on his upper lip. He was listening on his radio. 'Five minutes away,' he said, referring to the police backup.

A panicked nurse came at pace round the corner, pointing. 'They're in the outer corridor.'

They both strode round the corner. Alan looked through the square of glass in the swing door and gritted his teeth. The two extra guards were out in the corridor facing down the crowd, batons at the ready, but the crowd was at least fifty strong, high on righteousness and the flouting of rules. The big American was in front, sweaty and glassy-eyed. Alan and Tracey took up positions by the swing doors.

'Be ready,' Alan commanded. Tracey nodded.

Darren took the stairs three at a time. He reached the second floor, ran to the door to the empty wing and looked through the small square of glass. The corridor was empty.

He swiped the security card across the door and it clicked open. He could hear the protestors nearby. He walked quickly past two rooms with their blinds down. The third door he came to had the blinds up. He opened the door. Olivia was in there, looking at him. He could see that her hands were chained to the rails running round her bed.

He was across the room to her in two strides. He saw himself putting the pillow over her face, stifling the voice that had set up home in his skull, that had destroyed the fragile peace he had built over the years since Carly had gone. It wasn't about finding Carly now; it wasn't even about saving himself.

Their relationship had shifted – he was now strong and she was weak and he was going to make the most of it – terrorise her into telling him the truth. He saw the fear in her eyes and the tables were finally turned: he would mete out to her the same treatment she had to his sister.

Steps sounded in the corridor, someone in a hurry to check and control. He couldn't get round the bed to the bathroom in time. He froze.

'Under the bed.' Her voice was low and urgent, like a command.

He did what she said just as a man burst through the door, radio crackling. He stepped towards the bed. 'We're clear,' he said into the radio. He walked to the bathroom and glanced inside.

'Tell me what's happening,' Olivia said.

He didn't reply and Darren saw part of the sheet that had lain across her body begin to unfurl over the side of the bed, helping to cover him.

More people arrived and Darren overheard urgent talk about procedure and safety protocols.

'There's a room in the basement, with only one way in or out.'

'What else is down there?'

'Storerooms. We only have to worry about the one door, we can shut off the lift.'

There was intense crackling from the radio and codes being repeated. 'Let's do it,' a man's voice said.

Darren could see nurse's shoes near the head of Olivia's bed, and the black and shiny boots of the guards moving back and forth. The bed rolled out of the room towards the elevator.

The sound of chants and jeers echoed from somewhere nearby. A mini stampede of black shoes came from the corridor to Darren's right and headed off towards the noise. 'Securing the corridor downstairs. Wait,' someone said into a radio.

There was a long wait outside the lift.

'Someone's going to fucking fry for this,' a man's voice said.

'Move!' The bed was wheeled into the elevator.

Darren was lying prone under the bed, a central column supporting the wheels between his legs, his feet jammed up under the mattress and his hands holding on near his head. His arms were trembling and he knew he couldn't hold on much longer. He counted six people in the lift.

'Corridor clear.' The bed bumped along uneven lino, round a corner and into another lift, down one floor and through a set of doors. 'Clear.'

The bed moved through another door and into a room where a light was switched on.

Three of the pairs of feet left the room.

'OK guys, good job,' a voice said, less urgent now.

Darren felt the sweat dripping down his temples. Tears squeezed from his eyes. The veins in his forearms stood proud like ropes.

'I'll reconnect you now,' the nurse was saying to Olivia. Crackle came through on the radio.

'Jesus, that was a close call,' someone muttered.

'There, your drip's back in.' There was the sound of pillows being puffed up and the nurse tried to adjust the sheet.

'No thank you, it's fine like that,' Olivia said.

'We're good to go,' the nurse said. 'I'll be back shortly to take your temperature, Olivia, OK?' Normality was returning.

The door opened. Everyone left, and it swung shut behind them.

Darren collapsed on to the floor under the bed, then scrabbled out and backed away to the wall.

55

The room was large, heating ducts criss-crossing the ceiling, collapsible tables stored in one corner and a stack of chairs; no windows or bathroom.

Darren looked around, desperate to find a hiding place. Could he move a table and construct something? His moment of madness when he had wanted to harm her had been overtaken by fear about how he was going to get out.

'You're in a pickle. One door in and out, guards everywhere.' Olivia lay unmoving in the bed, her face pale, her hair lank, the drip snaking away from the back of her hand.

'Why are you in this hospital, anyway?'

'I've got a weak heart. And now they say it's mended.' Her voice was quiet and croaky.

He walked towards the bed, which seemed like a grotesque shrine containing something small and frail and old.

'Under the bed's still your best bet if you want to stay out of jail.'

He tested her handcuffs, then pulled back the thin sheet that covered her hospital gown. He put his hand round her neck. She gasped slightly, straining under him. He could smell her, feel her skin, the way her bones and muscles moved. Here was his chance to ask all the questions he wanted. He would never get another. He stared down into her dark eyes. 'Where's my sister?'

'When your mind drifts off down long passageways and

into dark basements searching for her, you end up with me, don't you Darren? I've got you, in my hands.' She held up an arm until the handcuffs clinked. 'It's been ten years. There will be many more. We will grow older, together.' She paused. 'That's a tear, Darren. Just the one?'

'Why did you tell me about Rollo? Who is he? What is he?'

She didn't respond and he wondered if she couldn't remember now, whether her thoughts ebbed and flowed in no coherent order, whether most of what she said was the babblings of a madwoman. 'Carrick bend knots. They're such beautiful little trifles.'

Darren snatched his hand away as if her neck was scalding. 'What did you say?'

Her eyes focused on him, seemed to hold him tight. 'Carly told me about that time on the beach, that afternoon when you got lost. What was it she said to console you? This is me—'

'And this is you,' Darren finished. Olivia might be insane, but her ability to invade the memories he shared with his sister was unparalleled. It was as if she had pissed and shat inside his skull.

Carly used to make bracelets from strands of coloured string, ribbon or plastic. She would join two strands together with a Carrick bend knot, which when pulled tight formed a beautiful woven lattice of colours. One summer when he was young, probably no more than seven, he had got lost in the dunes behind a beach in Devon. Hot, thirsty and disorientated, he had wandered for what seemed like hours before he was finally reunited with his family. What he had felt, trudging up those mountains of sand, was a searing sense of abandonment. He had become convinced that his adopted family didn't really want him, because he was tainted and unlovable. When his parents finally found him he had cried inconsolably, and nothing they offered, from ice creams to beach balls, made him feel better. Until Carly had picked up two strands of seaweed, one a bluey purple, the other russet, and knotted them together in a Carrick bend. 'Look, Darren,' she had said, flipping the russet strand over and under, 'this is me,' and she looped the deep blue under and over, 'and this is you.' She had tied the ends of the two strands under his wrist. 'You know we're family. We can't ever be parted.'

Darren looked down at Olivia, felt hot and bitter tears in his throat. He put his hand round her neck again, tighter this time, and she gasped for air. 'I know about your son.'

She stiffened. He felt it under his hands. 'You think the clue to who I am lies with my son?'

'How did it feel, Olivia, when they took him away? Was it the worst pain you have ever known? When *you* lie alone in the dark, is it him who comes to you?'

Her eyes narrowed. 'I would have hoped that you could think beyond clichés. Extend yourself beyond conformist little boxes. The mother figure, her lost son, blah, blah. But then maybe you really are someone who believes that stuff. You're one of the good ones, aren't you? You've won your battle to stay on top of your basest desires. It's a shame so many fail even at that.'

'You never managed it.'

Her eyes narrowed more until they were almost slits. 'No. I didn't. It took me a long time to turn my desires into action.'

'Molly never did anything to deserve that.'

'Being deserving doesn't come into it—'

'It should!' He lifted her head by the neck and slammed it back down on the pillow. He had to whisper, afraid that his voice would be heard in the corridor.

Her eyes flared with anger. 'You think the world is as you see it, but you're wrong! People can drop through the wormholes, into a world of horror you can't even imagine—'

'I can imagine, and I have!'

'No—'

'Carly was a child! She was so young!' He grabbed her skull and slammed her head down on the pillow, the secret he was so desperate to know suspended in there. If he could pull it out with his bare hands he would. 'Just give her back, just tell me where she is. My sister didn't deserve it!'

'Neither did mine!'

Their eyes met. He dropped his hands from her head and she stared up at him. He fancied he saw alarm. 'What happened to your sister?'

Her Adam's apple danced as she swallowed. 'She died.'

'I know that. But what *really* happened to Lauren?'

She couldn't speak; a tear slid from her eye. Darren felt something was giving way, like an avalanche finally collapsing down a mountain to reveal what had lain buried for years. He pressed on. 'She killed herself and left you with so many what-ifs, with a feeling of impotence that lasts a lifetime. You loved Lauren, more deeply than you can ever express. You feel grief at her loss, a pain so acute you can't believe you can still breathe.' He put his fingers to the side of her face, caressed the soft skin on her cheek, his voice slow and calm. 'I know how that feels, Olivia. You're looking at one of the few people who *really* knows.' But I'll tell you something – there's a pain even worse than that unleashed by death. Missing is worse than dead. Olivia, find it in your heart to end this pain for me.'

He had said the wrong thing. Her emotions moved like quicksilver, and now her tears dried up and were replaced by hard, narrow eyes. Her voice came out in a low, bitter rasp. 'I have given up everything for Lauren. And I'll give up you.'

She screamed. Her voice was loud, full strength even after her operation. 'There's someone here!'

Darren was off the bed and at the door in two seconds. The corridor had two right angles, and he ran blindly round the right-hand one and saw three doors leading off the corridor, and a grey cement and brick wall straight ahead.

The first door was locked. He tried the second and it opened on to a storeroom full of boxes and chairs and obsolete medical equipment. He heard the sound of running feet behind him, the crackle of radios. 'Check the room,' someone called. 'You two, the corridor.'

He had less than a second to decide whether to try the third door. He raced for it and pushed it open, closing it behind him just as two policemen rounded the corner.

He was in the furnace room. To the left of the incinerator were large laundry hampers, to the right a desk with the control panel for the incinerator, a console covered in buttons and large metal bins with yellow symbols on them, and a chair. He raced for the laundry bins; dirty sheets lay at the bottom of one, the other was empty. He only had seconds before they opened the door. He got his arms on the metal rim of the bin and was about to hoist himself over and try to hide in the soiled mess at the bottom when he saw the door of the incinerator.

He raced towards it, pulled it open and crawled in.

When Alan and Tracey came through the door, Alan thought for a second that maybe one of the hampers was just spinning to a stop on the right-hand side of the room. Son of a bitch, thought Alan, maybe the witch in the bed was right. Tracey took the right-hand side of the room, Alan waited by the door. Tracey carefully pulled the hampers aside, nice and easy so no one would get a shock, and began poking the contents with her baton. She did all five. They were all empty.

They glanced at each other and walked over to the huge metal bins where hospital waste was kept before being burned.

Alan opened the large hatch. Tracey shone a torch in. The foul smell of old blood wafted up. The second hatch they approached in the same way.

'Maybe she's yanking our chain,' Tracey said. But they didn't stop. The door opened and they were joined by two more guards. 'Corridor and patient's room clear,' one of them said. Tracey and Alan nodded.

'Can you believe this bullshit?' said one, as they watched Alan reach in and prod the two yellow sacks in the last bin with a grappling pole he'd found in the corner of the room. No one was inside. All four of them moved to the incinerator door.

Darren could feel the still warm grate below him, cooling down from the day's burning. He stifled the urge to cough, ash and dust and something oily coating the inside of his nose and his throat. He moved as quietly as he could to the back of the furnace, feeling around him in the pitch black.

He could hear muffled voices in the room, could feel the cold sweat of fear on his back. Above him was the flue that took the fumes and smoke up and away. Darren was a big guy, rangy and long-limbed, and only back here he could unfold and actually stand up properly, his feet in the incinerator and his body in the pipe. Darren put his hands on the side of the flue and pulled himself up, anchoring his body with his trainers against the sides.

Tracey counted down from three silently on her fingers before opening the incinerator door, Alan standing ready with the baton and a torch. Alan shone the torch in. The space was small, blackened and scorched from a thousand sad things and redundant or poisoned body parts being seared within. Tracey and the others leaned over his shoulder and shook their heads.

Everyone relaxed a little. Alan shone the torch beneath the grate and around the small space again. He was about to stand up and close the door, put an end to this attention-seeking charade, when something made him stop. He squinted and frowned. At the back of the furnace something had caught in the light of the torch. Alan leaned in closer.

It was a shoelace, hanging down from the flue.

'Suspect in the furnace, come out now!'

Darren knew it was hopeless, that there was no way out, but he did the only thing he could do. He carried on, like they had done when Carly went missing. Every day then was like crawling through the darkest hole, the horror of what had gathered them up never-ending. He began to climb the flue, pushing outwards with his hands and feet to give him traction.

Alan didn't hesitate to crawl into the incinerator. In the torchlight he could see a figure making rapid progress away from him. But Alan did think twice about climbing after him; he was a big guy who liked his pies and his pints and he knew when he was beaten; when a big round object wouldn't fit. This guy was trapped like a badger in a hole, anyway. He scrambled back out and they began to organise.

Darren kept going blindly in the pitch dark, up, up, up, because going back was worse. The pipe turned a right angle and now it was easier to pull himself along horizontally, but soon the flue turned to vertical once again. He climbed on up, his thighs burning and his arms cramping. He was soon gasping for air, a foul burning sensation at the back of his throat. He lost his sense of time and direction, and his panic began to build. After what could have been minutes or hours he came to an obstruction and, after feeling around for a moment, realised that the flue divided into two. Left or right? He chose the left tube and crawled on. The space was smaller than that he had been climbing until now but he groped on, his shoulders straining and his legs screaming.

He hit his head on the roof of the tunnel and nearly fell back down the pipe he had so laboriously climbed.

He couldn't go on. The pipe was squeezing the very breath out of him; he would die and he would have failed his parents and Carly. Tears stung his eyes, something acrid and stinging draining into them.

He came to another twist in the pipe, scrambled round another corner and crawled along horizontally. He came to another right angle that bent upwards, but the angles were smaller here and he couldn't get round to stand up in it. The metal was clamping round his chest as he scrabbled for a way through. He started to scream. He was stuck in a pitch black tube, unable to go forward or back. Yawning chasms of terror overwhelmed him and he nearly blacked out.

He took a deep breath in, the air still acrid. He couldn't bend his body round the right angle of the tube, so wriggled round until he was lying face up and tried that way, slithering along on the oily residue. The pipe felt inches wider now, which to Darren seemed as large as a cave. He began to climb, pressing his palms and his knees against the sides of the pipe for traction, and felt the air change. He looked up and above him was a small circle of night sky.

A police team were in the car park strapping themselves into flak jackets and checking equipment, their leader on the phone to a maintenance manager.

'The furnace is a pyrolysis incinerator that is environmentally efficient—'

'Where does the flue go?' the sergeant demanded.

'Up through the walls of the hospital. About halfway up the flue splits into two. One returns the gases back to the incinerator and the other goes up to the roof.'

'Is it large enough for a human?'

'I doubt it. We never checked. No one's stupid enough to climb into an incinerator.' There was a pause. 'I thought.'

The sergeant sighed. 'The fool's more likely to get stuck in it. Where does it come out?'

'On the roof to the far left of the helicopter pad.'

'How many storeys in this building?'

'Three, but only in some parts. It varies.'

The policeman looked up at the jumble of levels, the new wings and departments added in different decades, floors jutting out further the closer to the ground one got, like an ugly tiered cake. 'You need a ladder. It's twenty feet off the ground,' the maintenance manager said.

'Go,' the sergeant commanded his team.

Darren pressed on, exhausted and panicked, the goal ahead of him tantalisingly close. The fresh air was so joyful he cried anew. He reached the top of the flue and pushed at the wire grate that covered the entrance. It wouldn't budge.

Three policemen used a variety of ladders near the helicopter pad to move across the roof of the building. It was slow work, negotiating maintenance ladders in the dark. They went in formation, keeping low in the shadows.

Darren pushed and punched again and again at the wire grate across the exit to the flue but it held fast. Even more worrying than being caught was his fear that he was going to fall, that his arms, strengthened though they were by his fitness regime, all his chin-ups, would eventually fail. He started shouting, banging on the top and sides of the flue, his hands bleeding, his nails ripping.

The moon came out from behind a cloud and gave him a little more light. The wire was attached to the metal flue by a rubber ring. He began clawing and pushing at the rubber and, instead of trying to push the wire, grabbed it and tried to pull it towards him while pushing outwards on the rubber. It moved. He yanked hard and managed to dislodge one side of the wire from the rubber. He got his hand on the edge of the flue and could rest his burning thighs for a blissful moment. Using brute force he pushed the wire cover with his head and climbed out, scraping his head, neck and shoulders as he passed.

He rested, his chest hanging over the side of the flue, miles of south London stretching away all around him. Then he realised he was twenty feet off the ground.

Now, instead of the relentless push outwards with arms and legs to climb the flue, he needed to grip tightly. He climbed out and down by hugging the sides of the flue tightly with his thighs and his arms. The contrary movement was a blessed release for his aching limbs. He fell the last ten feet and lay on the ground for a moment, stunned. Then he got up and ran to the right, away from the helicopter pad he could see in the distance.

The police fanned out across the roof, careful not to miss anyone who might be hiding in the shadows, and surrounded the flue. Two of the men kept on going across the roof; the other climbed the ladder.

Darren ran across the roof and down a ladder to a lower level, came to the edge of the roof and looked over. Squares of light from the windows on the floor below him lit up the roof felt. He used a drainpipe to climb down. The windows were in a corridor and two were open to the warm air. He pulled at one of them and slid through, closing it behind him.

He walked fast along the corridor and ducked into a toilet.

His face in the mirror was a shock. He was covered in black smears and his hands and head were bleeding and bruised. He ran the hot water and cleaned himself as best he could with paper towels and soap, ditching his shirt to reveal the T-shirt underneath and wash his arms. He stuck his face under the cold tap and let the water run colder and colder over him. Then he followed the signs for the exit.

The policeman climbed the ladder carefully, keen to avoid

a mishap. He looked carefully over the rim of the flue, tensed for a surprise. He saw the bent grate, sharp edges pointing starwards, and a collection of long blond hairs caught on the wires and drifting in the wind.

56

A senior police officer was interviewing Olivia, standing at the end of her bed in the basement. 'What did this person look like? I want as accurate a description as possible.'

Pronouns told a person a lot, Olivia decided. The policeman had used the word 'person' twice in two sentences, which meant to Olivia that they didn't know who they were searching for. Darren had got away. She was genuinely surprised. But then many things about Darren Evans were turning out to be surprising.

She had been careless. But he had got inside her Teflon shell and when she had screamed she had been prepared to give him up. After all, power was an illusion that was easy to puncture – she needed to keep it inflated.

She studied the policeman at the end of the bed. She had already been subjected to a body cavity search; she was damned if she was going to make their jobs easier.

'I was groggy, half asleep, the pills, the pain . . .' She was laying it on thick. I woke and wondered if I was still dreaming. It was a woman.'

Olivia saw the detective lean in, more animated now. 'Why do you say that?'

'The hair. I saw long hair.'

57

They would come for him. It was only a matter of time. Olivia had given him up. The worst thing was that it felt like betrayal, as if they had had an acknowledged connection that she had then cast aside, a code of behaviour and she had let the side down. Darren was delusional expecting such a thing from a despicable creature such as that.

He had committed a serious crime. He needed to man up, take responsibility and tell his dad what he had done before the police pulled up in the car with the flashing lights and he gave his parents a whole fresh level of pain. And his mum wasn't even out of her hospital bed.

But he was so tired, emotionally and physically, from his desperate battle to get out of the flue, that he was pulled back home. Like an animal returning to its burrow, it was the only place he could think of to go. He dragged his bike into the hallway and left it there, managed to get up the stairs and collapsed on his bed.

His sleep was as deep as the grave.

He was woken in the morning by the sun drilling into his eyeballs through the open curtains. Every cell in his body ached, every taste bud contaminated with something tangy and unpleasant, every inch of skin papery and sore.

He staggered downstairs in search of tea, and found his dad already there. He had that look on his face, Darren realised, that he had seen before: disappointment.

'So you left her without even saying goodbye for the night? She was waiting for you to come back from wherever you'd gone to.' He wiped a hand across his brow. 'After she found out who was there in the hospital . . .' He trailed off, not wanting to have to explain further. 'She was upset.'

'I'm sorry. I didn't feel well.'

'You came in so late. Where were you?'

'I walked home.'

'Walked? I had to move the bike out into the garden. You couldn't even be bothered to do that.'

'Shit.' Darren ran his hands over his hair. It felt greasy. 'It's Orin's fault.'

'You leaving her alone isn't his fault. Take some responsibility.' He gave a huff of frustration. 'She needs you to be reliable right now, Darren. Now of all times.' He reached into the fridge for a beer, not even pretending to hide what he was doing.

Guilt stole over Darren like a shroud. 'I'll go to see her again today.'

His dad looked away. 'That's not necessary. She's discharging herself and is coming home.'

'Is that wise?'

'No, but she wants to be away from all that. I can't persuade her otherwise.'

Darren felt responsible for this too. His worry increased in tandem with his guilt.

'You left this place in a right state. She needs to come back to somewhere clean. What are all these white bits all over the carpet? And the front of the house, what's happening with that? It looks worse now than it did before.'

'I'm sorry, I'm sorry.' He opened the fridge, took a look at the sorry contents within. Mum's absence had made the proportion of bottles to food change dramatically. He picked up a takeaway food carton and opened it. He was starving, hadn't eaten last night. 'This spicy?'

'Thai red curry.' He pulled a fork from a drawer as his dad slurped from his beer. Darren picked up a cold forkful and chewed the curry.

His dad winced. 'You don't want to heat that up?'

Darren shook his head. He needed Tabasco, though. He opened a cupboard and scanned its contents. He put a knee on the kitchen counter and hoiked himself up, pushing aside containers of dried herbs on the top shelf. He found the Tabasco and turned back to Dad, who was leaning back on the counter, staring up at him, his arms folded in a 'what the hell' gesture.

Darren froze.

'Jesus, do I really look that bad?' Dad asked defensively.

Darren put the Tabasco down. With his knees on the counter he was much taller than his dad, and he saw his tired and drawn face in a new light. And a thought came to him that changed everything.

He got slowly off the counter. 'No. I just looked at you from a different perspective.'

'You need to finish painting the house. You promised her.' Darren wasn't listening. His mind was a whirl of possibilities. 'Are you even listening?'

Darren focused on what Dad was saying. 'Yes, of course.'

'I can't take much more,' his dad said. 'All I can do is go to the hospital and sit there and hope she's going to be OK. You know what I thought yesterday, Darren? You know what I spent most of the day at the hospital thinking? That I was lucky.' He took a long sip of beer.

'What do you mean?'

'That I have a wife who is seriously ill with cancer, and I was lucky. Because I wouldn't have to spend my time thinking about what might have happened to my murdered daughter.' Dad looked at the ceiling as if waiting to find an answer there in the cracks. 'Maybe she was right. Maybe I'm guilty.'

'Of what?'

'Of giving up too soon. Maybe if I had tried harder we could have found her—'

'Dad, stop that right now.'

'But it's true isn't it?' He turned to Darren now, anger and pain and regret at work on his face, deepening the lines, obviously gnawing at him like an animal. 'Carly was being held somewhere, wasn't she, maybe for a long time, and we didn't get to her.'

'You are not to blame, not in any way.'

His dad's face was breaking, collapsing under the burden of the revelations of the last few days. 'But I am, Darren. I am to blame.'

Darren hadn't seen his dad cry for years, and he was aware that he was the one who had brought this to pass. He had started on a voyage of discovery to make it better but instead he had made it worse, so much worse than he could have imagined. He should have let it all alone. The truth wasn't going to set them free; it was a prison from which there was no escape. He tried to put his arms round his dad, but the older man pushed him away and stood.

'It's been ten years. And time hasn't altered anything. I still think she's going to open that door and walk in, smile that smile, throw her bag down.' He shook his head.

'I thought you had resigned yourself to her being gone,' Darren said.

His dad threw his hands in the air in a hopeless gesture. 'I have, but hope is irrational and never-ending.'

'I'm sorry, Dad, more than you can know.' Darren had to sit down. Something struck him forcefully. His parents must never know what he had done, of that he was absolutely certain. They had suffered too much already and he had made their traumas worse.

Dad began to laugh, snot and tears mingling in a sorry

mess. By lunchtime, Darren knew, he would have drowned his sorrows. 'Well, maybe there are some miracles in the world. You leave the ladder leaning up against the front of a house in south London, it hasn't been stolen and we haven't been burgled.'

58

Great Yarmouth

O lly ran to the corner of the street and pelted down towards the Spar, his school rucksack bouncing on his shoulders. He was trying out his new trainers, which Nan had finally bought him after a lot of nagging. He felt he could run for miles on these cushions of air. He also had persuaded Nan that he needed the same, newer version of the Nikes that Beggs had, so everything was good. He glimpsed the harbour in the abandoned lot between the end of the terraces and the Spar.

He sprinted past the shop and past the high wall. Where the wall ended and the little steps that led to the boats began, he nearly bumped into a woman walking away from the harbour. She had to step aside at the last minute to avoid being clattered into by him.

'Soz!' Olly shouted, wheeling away.

She carried on walking past the Spar, her face turned away, her blonde hair hanging low on her back.

It was the woman who liked staring at boats.

Olly slowed to a stop and looked down at the boats in the water. The day was still, the North Sea a mirror. Nan would be frying herself on the lounger in the yard when he got back from school. Olly watched the sun bounce off the water; the harbour was never busy, least of all on a weekday well after sunrise. At this hour it was all but deserted. His eyes tracked to the red boat, its tarpaulin a tight seal over the cabin and deck.

Olly looked back at the woman, but she had disappeared. She wasn't interested in all the boats, Olly knew; she was interested only in the red one. The line of crafts sat in the still water, but the red boat was bobbing up and down as if someone had just jumped off the deck.

Olly ran further along the road and looked into the car park for the owner's hatchback. Sure enough, it was parked there. He began to wonder where Gert Becker was as his boat was shut up, but then his eye caught sight of a stone and he kicked it with his new Nikes and was pleased to see it hit the wall and ricochet away. He headed off on the long road to school kicking every stone and discarded drink can he could see, the red boat and Gert Becker forgotten.

59

Darren finished the cold curry and went for a shower. He stood under the steaming water for a long time, scrubbing away the memory of that pitch black, never-ending tube. As he got clean he felt stronger – and angrier. There was somewhere he needed to go.

He went straight to Orin's office, barged past the secretary and her flapping arms and opened his door. Orin was up and around the desk immediately. His bulky form could move with speed and grace when required. 'It's OK, Margaret, I'll take this from here. Take a seat, Darren. I've been expecting you.'

'What kind of stunt were you pulling at the hospital? My mum was in there recovering from an operation—'

'Doesn't that make you mad? It would me. That *she*'s there, only metres away, being cared for by the state, and you don't even know?'

'That doesn't matter—'

'If I got her to feel even a sliver of fear, good. I'm not going to apologise. If I made those guards think, why am I protecting an enemy of the state? – good.'

'I care about my mum. Nothing else.'

Orin gave him a long look. Darren could see him taking a careful look at his hair. 'You sure about that, young gun?'

He began to feel uncomfortable under the big American's unwavering gaze, but knew he had to fight back. 'Who's your contact at Roehampton? Someone tipped you off that Olivia was there. You have no remorse, do you? No thought of how others might feel. Think of Molly's family!'

'I prayed for Molly's family, your family. You and I are in the same boat.' Orin had sat back down now, the forefinger of his right hand tapping quietly on the top of the desk. 'Your mum's been in hospital for at least two days. It's a strange thing when someone is confined to bed, there's lots of time to kill. A young, energetic man like you, you can't sit still, I'd bet.' Tap, tap, tap went his finger, beating out its threat.

'I—'

'Don't interrupt me. Someone got close to Duvall, far closer than they should have done, even when they moved her to the basement. They think it's a woman, but they're not sure, because this person escaped out of the hospital incinerator, if you can imagine such a thing.'

Darren swallowed. 'A woman?'

'Because they found long blond hairs at the top of the flue, fluttering in the breeze.' There was a pause. Orin's blue eyes never left Darren's face. 'Cut your hair and come and join my campaign.' Tap, tap, tap went the finger.

Orin knew. He had him right where he wanted him.

'Why haven't they arrested you for barging into St George's?'

'Because I have very, very good lawyers, and I have moral right and public opinion on my side. The question is, what was this person even doing in Duvall's room? She was unharmed.' Orin looked at Darren again. 'But that is a side issue. This isn't the reason why you came to see me.'

Orin was right. He needed to concentrate on the reason he had come. 'Something struck me about the papers you sent me.'

'How so?'

'They read like a police investigation. It's like you're searching for something.'

Orin snorted. 'You been paying attention, young gun? I'm searching for my daughter.' His finger started tapping again, a slow insistent beat on the table. 'I know more about missing people than most police officers in this country. I know how killers' minds work better than most profilers. I have access to information that officers spend their careers trying to get. I'm not in the service, but I can access the service.' He was sweating, a strange pallor on his cheeks. 'I accept my methods are unconventional.' He gave Darren a knowing look. 'But so are yours.'

'There's very little on Olivia's sister.'

'I gave you what I have on her. She went off the rails on a teenage fast track to destruction, the mother didn't have the guts to rein her in. One daughter killed herself, the other ended up killing other people. The sister's not relevant.'

'There you go again, it's as if you're eliminating lines of inquiry. Which means you're searching, which means you think someone else was involved in those girls' deaths.'

Orin was very still. 'I've waited ten years for a breakthrough in this case. I'm prepared to follow any lead, consider any theory. I've been told I lack perspective many times—'

'Perspective.' Darren stood up and put his hands on the desk. He didn't care if Orin could see the scrapes and bruises on them, he had to share the revelation he had experienced earlier that morning. 'A girl kneeling on the carpet, about to be bludgeoned to death by a woman, is an image to make a normal person shudder, isn't it?' He was thinking back to the moment when he had towered over his dad with the Tabasco bottle in his hand in the kitchen. 'But hear me out on this. Duvall is five foot four, but what if Molly wasn't kneeling? What if she was standing, and someone who was six foot tall, or taller maybe, hit her? With the same hand, at the same angle? Molly's body being revealed has brought with it a new wave of information, hasn't it? Information that can help us *solve* it.'

Orin got up suddenly as if the idea was electrifying. He stood staring out of the window across the river. 'One idea from left field doesn't unpick this riddle.'

'But it's possible, isn't it?' Orin didn't reply. 'This Eric guy, Olivia's boyfriend—'

Orin held up his hand. 'Just a minute.' He walked out of the room and came back in a few moments later, carrying a file. He sat down at his desk and opened the cover, licked his thumb and began to leaf through the pages. 'Let's get this straight. When Duvall took the girls Eric had been her ex for years, there's a girlfriend here in Hastings confirming it. The police found he had a solid alibi too, he was in a penitentiary –' his finger traced down a line of dates '– when Heather and Molly went missing.' Orin turned a few more pages, looking for relevant details. 'After he completed his sentence he went to live in Spain, this was corroborated by several people. But then information on him dries up – no one knew where he was. Seems he wasn't missed by anyone – even his mum didn't like him, said she didn't care what he was doing.' He shut the cover of the file and pushed it away. 'I tried to trace Eric Cox in the years after the trial, but I never found him.'

'What do you think that means?'

Orin pursed his lips. 'That this case can turn a sane man mad.' He paused. 'Or make a man do a stupid thing at a hospital. Cut your hair, come and join my campaign and maybe I can protect you from what might be heading your way, get you the freedom you need to pursue . . .' He paused, searching for the right word, 'pet theories.'

'Give me twenty-four hours.' Darren got up off his chair and walked out of the room.

Orin waited a couple of moments and picked up his phone. 'I need you to follow someone for me. Starting today.'

60

When Darren came home from Orin's office his mum's hospital bag was in the hall. He climbed the stairs to her bedroom and found her sitting on the bench seat in front of her mirror. She didn't turn round when he came in the room. 'Budge over,' he said.

She shifted gingerly across and they stared at each other in the mirror. 'I'm sorry I left you at the hospital,' he got out. 'I just had to go and . . . get some air.' It sounded so lame, such an awful lie. She didn't answer. 'Are you sure you should be home? Are you well enough?' he went on.

'I'm stronger than I look.'

'It must have been horrible being in there knowing she was near.'

'I want to move on. Forget about it.' She smiled briefly and pulled at her hair with the hand that she could still move freely. He was shocked to see a bunch of strands come away from her scalp.

'Oh Mum.'

'Just sit here with me.' She had Dad's electric razor on the dressing table in front of her and she picked it up now and turned it on. She ran a line through the right side of her hair and a leaf-fall of long strands cascaded to the carpet.

'Are you sure you want to do that?' But he knew it was the right thing really.

She winced, her body obviously still sore from her operation.

'Let me help you.'

He shaved her head for her. She seemed to shrink in size in front of him as he went. He saw a slow tear roll down her cheek and he felt a terrible fondness for her that words could not express. When he was finished she turned her head this way and that in front of the mirror.

'Feels cold,' she said and sighed. 'And exposing.' He didn't reply as they both absorbed her new look.

Darren walked over to the rail in the corner where her clothes hung. He was looking for a scarf.

'I like the orange and red one,' she said and he picked it up and brought it over. He stood behind her and folded it and tied it tight round her head and tucked it in. She looked surprised but also pleased. 'Now where did you learn to do that?'

Darren smiled and sat down beside her again. 'I guess I've got hidden talents.' He looked at the razor and looked back at his mum. He picked it up and ran it up the side of his ear, a cascade of sun-lightened blond and matted hair falling to the carpet. His mum gave a little gasp, and tried to reach up with her hand to stop him.

'No. It's time.'

He did another stripe, quicker. The razor vibrated against his skull, lowered its tone behind his ears. He kept on until it was all gone and he was finished.

He didn't know himself. His face was shockingly exposed, an outline of jaw and neck that was unfamiliar to him, cheekbones prominent. He was no longer a blond; a dark brown fuzz of fresh hair covered his scalp.

She smiled ruefully. 'You're a good-looking boy under all that.'

He took his mum's fingers, placed them on the back of his neck and turned so she could see the tattoo.

'It's Carly's initials,' he said softly.

He felt the light touch of his mum's fingers as they traced the inky lines. 'I know you loved her, Darren. I don't think I ever appreciated the pain you felt when she disappeared. I am still so lucky, you know? I have you, and I love you more than you can ever know.'

He turned back round and they gave each other a long hug. After a while she pulled away and looked at the floor, inches deep in discarded dreadlocks and her own hair. 'It'll be a struggle to get this lot out of the carpet.'

'I'll do it, Mum.'

'You can use a hoover, can you?'

Five hours a day, sometimes, he wanted to say, but he actually said, 'I can work it out.'

61

Great Yarmouth

Olly was gulping down his bowl of Frosties; breakfast TV was showing people fighting somewhere far away. The doorbell rang and Nan looked at him accusingly from the armchair. She rolled her eyes towards the door, indicating that she wasn't going to move to answer it. This was no surprise; she only ever got out of the armchair to get tea or go to the toilet. Olly put his bowl on the carpet and slid from the sofa. Beggs was at the door, a football under his arm, panting with excitement. Olly had to come to the harbour, Beggs had heard there was a right carry-on going on down there.

Olly yawned. Beggs wasn't selling it to him.

'There's talk of dead bodies and that.'

Nan was suddenly behind Olly at the door, urging him into his shoes and racing up the stairs to shed her dressing gown. She was moving faster than Olly had seen her do in years. No one loved a scandal like Nan.

By the time they got to the harbour, the crowd was three people deep, back behind blue and white crime scene tape. Nan started to complain that she couldn't see anything. 'It's not the bloody opera,' someone muttered, and Olly peered between necks and backs to see three policemen keeping the crowd well back.

Nan was not so easily put off, and wriggled and barged her way to the front, Olly and Beggs following in her wake.

A white tent had been erected over one of the boats; huge men in white boiler suits with white things over their shoes were moving about.

Beggs elbowed Olly in the ribs and pointed. A news van with something slowly turning on its roof had pulled up in the car park. 'That's Sky TV,' Beggs said in awe. The crowd was murmuring that a dead body had been found in the red boat. Olly had seen enough cop shows on the telly to know that the police wore white suits and TV news came only if murder was suspected.

Nan turned. 'Get to school, both of you.' She left her hard-won position to push them away down the road. Now that they really might be exposed to dead bodies and violence, she wanted to protect them from it. 'There's nothing to see here.' She watched them to make sure they were really on their way before hurrying back to the very thing she was keen to dismiss as nothing.

Olly and Beggs ran off down the road with the football, the unusual start to the day making them feel wild and transgressive. Beggs crossed the ball to Olly and he dribbled down the street and across an expanse of grass. He slowed to a stop, the ball coasting to a halt. The red boat was Gert Becker's. Was he dead? A strange feeling came over him, like he knew the answer to something but couldn't express it. He was thinking about the blonde woman he had seen – although, in the sharp light of this summer morning with so much activity and speculation, he wasn't sure any more that she had even been real.

'Oi, what you doing?' Beggs was waiting for him to pass the ball.

Olly shook off the feeling. After all, what had he even really seen, what had the blonde ghost even done? He ran up and kicked the ball and, as he had done so many times in his life, ran in Beggs's shadow to school.

62

'Bwoy, look at your hair!' Sonny slapped his thigh repeatedly, a grin exploding across his face. 'Or lack of it.' He frowned. 'From Rasta to skinhead – me prefer you the other way.' The smile was back as he turned to Corey. 'But the bwoy is fresh-faced under all that, what you say?'

'That is a sick style, cuz! He's showing his tats too.' Corey nodded appreciatively. 'What's that say?' he said, peering round the back of Darren's neck.

'It's just an abstract symbol.'

'Now what does Chloe say about this, eh? I hear you and her are an item! The whole hospital know, eh?' Sonny was grinning again. 'Hi Helen, how do you like Darren's new style?'

Darren turned. Helen was standing in the doorway, her face stony. 'Chloe? You're going out with Chloe?'

Darren cast around for a hole to crawl into, but knowing really that there wasn't one he turned and stared at the CCTV monitors so that he didn't have to meet Helen's eye. His eyes had settled on the one showing the kitchens and he could see Chloe in her white peaked hat moving baking trays around and Berenice wiping a counter. 'Um, I guess, well, we've only just started seeing each other—'

'They went surfing at the weekend,' Sonny put in, smiling.

'Surfing?' Helen said it with the surprise one might use for news of an outbreak of diphtheria in south London.

'Well, I've got to get on,' Darren said, and slid out of the door back to the safety of his cleaning trolley. He retreated up the corridor, planning to take refuge in the men's toilets. It had been a mistake to alienate Helen, she was his best bet for finding out more information, particularly about Olivia's befriender.

'Darren, can I have a word?'

He froze. Her voice was crisp and accusatory. He turned. The yellow cleaning sign in his hand showed a man falling backwards. He erected it on the carpet outside the women's toilets, knowing exactly how the poor stick figure felt. Helen was standing by the toilet door, holding it open like it was the mouth of hell itself.

Like a scolded child, he followed her in.

Helen decided to stand rather than lean, arms folded across her chest. Darren came in, his palm roaming over his scalp.

'So, um, yeah, like, I was going to tell you . . . that the way I'm feeling, it's kinda . . .'

She let him talk on, but she wasn't listening. Something had struck her when she'd seen him in security. Without his hair he was a different person. He was no longer Darren, the mumbling, shambling cleaner to be more pitied than admired. Under that thatch of dried-out locks had always lurked someone handsome, tall and young. And she felt a fear clutch at her heart; a sudden nostalgia for all the years that she had lost, for all the decades she had travelled and would never get back. She had crossed a barrier only visible to those who could look back; she had become all those words she used to scorn: mature, experienced – middle-aged, old.

Darren had his hands clasped together, trying to emphasise some point, his eyes roaming the washroom because they didn't want to alight on her face. She revelled for a moment in examining his teeth, his prominent cheekbones, the whites of his eyes. Such promise. Instead of feeling angry or used, she suddenly felt joy for the possibilities of all the years that were still to come. He had kick-started her on another road that she had never expected to travel, had helped her drag herself out of the shame and failure that was her divorce.

She held up her hand in a stop gesture. His monologue stumbled to a halt. She smiled. 'I wish you all the best of luck, Darren. Really I do.'

There was a pause. 'Huh?'

Helen shook her head and smiled. 'Darren Smith, you maniac.'

63

Great Yarmouth

By the end of the day, there was chaos at the harbour. The body on the red boat had been confirmed as its owner, Gert Becker, a millionaire from Birmingham. The crowd had swelled to a hundred strong, people from towns and villages far away. There were more news vans and an ice cream van. There was wild talk of a video confession by the victim, admitting rape and murder. The mood had changed while Olly had been at school and now people were pointing fingers, shaking their heads, speculating aloud. Only a few hours ago Gert Becker had been a victim; now he was a pervert.

Olly didn't hang around but headed for home. He knew now that this morning he had done the right thing in keeping quiet. The blonde woman was indeed just a ghost. He berated himself for even considering telling Nan about the woman, and how he had been sure she had been on Gert's boat, or about how he had watched the now dead pervert-good-riddance set out to sea many times in his red boat. It would have only pulled a whole ton of trouble on top of Nan's head, which in turn would have ended up on his.

64

Darren spent the boring, lonely hours on his shift thinking about John Sears and who or what he really was. When he was forced to leave Roehampton he could do worse than to keep an eye on what John did. When his shift finished he cycled to John's flat above the charity shop in Clapham and checked the pub car park. John's car was there. Darren waited on the corner, pretending he was on his phone. He looked anxiously around for the women he'd seen the last time, but the charity shop looked empty. At six on the dot the elderly lady he'd met the first time he'd gone in came out, locked up and walked away.

Commuters began to spill out of the nearby tube station entrance as the evening wore on. He became itchy and scratchy with boredom. He texted Chloe but she didn't answer.

As he was wondering how long he could tolerate just standing and waiting in a south London street, John's door opened and he came out, wearing work boots covered in dust and a white all-in-one. Darren shrank back into a nearby doorway and watched John walk towards the car park. A moment later his car emerged and pulled away sharply in the direction of central London. Darren got on his bike and followed.

John drove aggressively, but Darren had no trouble keeping up with him; he was faster on his bike in the rush hour traffic than John was on four wheels.

They travelled towards the river, the cranes of the Nine Elms construction site looming high in the night sky. John took the road that ran by Battersea Park and turned right into the huge development at Battersea Power Station. Darren figured he must be going to work. He stopped and considered. The lights in the unfinished buildings were all on, and while the large machinery had stopped for the night to let the nearby residents have some peace, Darren could still see cars in a makeshift car park and plenty of activity.

He coasted into the development and stopped by a huge awning with a monster-sized photograph of two blond children in the arms of grinning Caucasian parents, a sunny London river view visible through the windows of their flat. A large ticker tape ran across the picture, claiming that all of the luxury apartments had been sold off-plan.

Darren took a look at the car park and building site beyond, but couldn't see John's car.

The development was a maze of access roads, temporary fencing and plastic sheeting that obscured the huge towers thrusting skywards. Darren cycled down an unpaved road that lacked pavements or street lighting, and looked cautiously round a corner. He saw John's car turning left round another building and bobbled down the unpaved road, his bike wheels clattering.

John's car was parked by a large foyer that hadn't yet had its glass inserted. The interior was dark and unfinished. Darren locked his bike to a lamp-post missing its light and followed John into the building. He could hear men talking and laughing in a language he didn't understand, the sound of heavy bags of something being dragged across cement floors. He heard a lift arriving and turned to walk away. John was at the start of nothing more sinister than a work shift. Darren was wondering what time John finished when he passed a pillar and something heavy smacked him on the side of the head.

He slumped sideways to the ground, trying to get his hands up to protect himself. A foot connected with his stomach and he gasped in pain, doubling over tightly. He felt hands on his shoulder and braced for another blow, but instead he heard a voice close to his ear. 'Leave Roehampton, or next time it's worse.'

A kick connected with his back before a shout produced a volley of running feet. He tried to stand and glimpsed two figures being swallowed up by the dark.

A hand was pulling him by the biceps to get him upright, but the pain in his stomach was too great and he was on his knees and palms on the rough concrete.

'You all right, mate?' Darren flinched. John was standing in front of him. 'They take your wallet, mate? Which way did they go?' He was already half at a run out of the foyer into the road, scanning for the culprits or their car.

'No, no, they didn't, everything's fine,' Darren gasped.

John turned to look back at him. 'Don't look fine to me, mate. The security here's a bloody joke!'

Darren leaned back against the pillar and felt his head. He pulled his hand away and saw blood.

'You need to get that looked at.'

'I'm fine, really.' Darren made a move to leave but John put a hand out to stop him.

'Hang on.' He frowned, staring. 'I know you.' The hand pushed harder into Darren's chest, making him back up to the pillar again. 'I've seen you at the charity shop. On video. You were asking questions about me.' Now his face was hard and full of suspicion. 'Why are you following me?'

Darren tried to stand up taller than John, but he was still in pain and found it hard to straighten. His mind had taken a knock and he couldn't clear the fog of confusion. If John had saved him, who were the other guys?

John dragged Darren by his T-shirt, further away from the lifts towards a darker corner of the foyer. 'Why?' One of his fists was balled, ready to continue what Darren's attackers had started. 'You fuckers can't let an honest man alone, can you?'

The pain was beginning to pulse through Darren's frame now the shock had subsided. 'Honest? That's a joke. No one who's honest has two names and befriends a serial killer.'

The change was instant. John dropped his hand and stared at Darren. 'This is about her?'

'Why are you not who you say you are?'

The hand was back round his throat immediately. 'Hang on. I've seen you at the prison.' John paused, his mind working it through. 'You *work* there.' His hand jammed Darren against the pillar again. 'Who are you?'

'I want to find those girls.'

The hand didn't release its grip and his eyes narrowed. 'This is twisted shit.'

'No more twisted than you changing your name and going in to see her!'

'I've got a bloody good reason! But you, you're going to tell me right now why you're there and why you're following me.'

'Who were those women at the shop?' Darren thought he knew the answer, though, and he was right. John grinned nastily. 'My sisters. They're very protective of me. They don't like strangers sniffing around, police trampling on my privacy. So who are you?' The hand clamped tighter round Darren's neck.

It was hopeless. He had to tell him or he was going to get very hurt. 'I knew one of her victims.' The hand stayed where it was. 'Carly. Carly was my sister.'

The hand came away from his neck. John was very still. He looked Darren over, assessing his scuffed trainers and studenty clothes. 'This really is about her,' he said finally and pulled a cloth from his pocket and handed it to Darren. 'Put it over that cut, it'll stop the bleeding.' John shook his head. 'How many laws did you break to get a job there?'

Darren ignored the question, ploughing on with questions of his own. 'Why do you see her?'

'I didn't choose her, she was randomly assigned to me by the befriending organisation. I'm there to help her with the day-to-day stuff about being a lifer, things her legal team don't deal with. We sit in a bare room and she's supposed to talk. Most of the time I'm the one talking and she listens. She keeps me on the straight and narrow.'

'What do you mean?'

'Going in there is the best deterrent there is to a life of crime. I've no desire to follow in Lee's footsteps.'

'Who's Lee?'

'My brother. He's doing a seven-year stretch for dealing. Names have a habit of following you around, like bad smells.'

Darren understood that, probably more than John realised. His name had also been changed when he was adopted as a baby, to create a fresh start.

'I don't advertise that I see her. No one here would take kindly to knowing I visited someone like that.'

'What do you talk about?'

'That's private.'

'Tell me—'

'Listen. You think there are revelations here, but there aren't. She never talks about those girls.'

'Never?'

John shook his head and sighed. 'Maybe that's what makes her mad. She doesn't feel things like normal people would.'

'What does she talk about? Please, give me something.'

'You're clutching at straws.'

'Does she have any special requests, interests? Think.'

'If they find out who you are you're fucked! You'll end up in a place exactly like that!' John looked around, frustrated. 'She told me she reads the *Police Gazette*, she once came to see me carrying some kind of government journal—'

'What journal?'

'I can't remember. It looked dull, like it was about people who worked in the civil service. And no, she has never given me any clue about where any of those victims are.'

'How long have you been seeing her?'

'Coming up to three years.'

'Does she talk about her sister, Lauren?'

He shrugged. 'Rarely. I know she's dead, but I don't know anything else. This will be hard for you to hear, but Olivia's not tormented. She has no regrets and she doesn't try to justify what she did. That's rare, and believe me I know. Lee spouts justifications all the time: he's unlucky, misunderstood, he never hurt anyone, he's innocent, all this bullshit.'

'Did she ever talk about Molly?'

'The girl that's just been found? No.'

'She ever mention a Rollo, or anything about how tall he was, six foot two?'

John shook his head. 'I'm sorry. It's as if the past isn't very up front and centre for her. She's usually just calm and fairly pleasant.' He paused.

Darren seized on this tiny change in John. 'What? There's something.'

'There was this one time she wasn't calm. It was the most animated I've ever seen her. About a year after I started seeing her she came to our meeting and showed me a newspaper report. It was about a guy in Bristol who was exposed as a paedophile – all the messy stuff was on his computer.

Someone had tipped off the local police and the local paper and he killed himself.'

'What was his name?'

John shook his head. 'I can't remember. But what struck me was she was ecstatic and also angry. Really veering around in her emotions. It was very unlike her, as if she had stopped her pills and she was on an emotional rollercoaster. She kept saying the guy got what he deserved, that those abused girls got their justice in the end. You know some say she's mad and others say it's all a lie – that day, it was weird, she was clearly insane, but it was also the happiest I have ever seen her.' There was a pause. 'Look, mate, I don't know what you're doing, and I don't want to get involved. I'm just a plasterer trying to get by. I'm sorry about your sister but what I do is not against the law. Last thing I want is any trouble. Now, I need to get to work.' He began to walk away and then hesitated. 'You sure you're OK?'

Darren nodded. 'Thanks for getting them off me. I owe you.'

'Owe me by never saying hello to me at Roehampton. This conversation never happened.' A moment later he was swallowed up by the darkness.

Darren limped out of the building and round the corner, then swore. Someone had slashed both his bike tyres.

65

It was a long road home for Darren, pushing his damaged bike, feeling the bruises swell and the blood dry in a sticky mess on the back of his head. He didn't even have any hair to mop it up or hide under. It was the first time Darren had ever been beaten up, and he felt shaky and disorientated and desperate for home. He passed a cycle shop in Clapham and decided to lock his bike up for the night and take a minicab home; he could get the bike repaired in the morning.

By the time he got home his parents were in bed. He found a bag of peas in the freezer and held it against his head, trying to take down the swelling. His ribs were beginning to turn bright purple from the boot that had crunched into them and his eye was already turning blue and black. He took some paracetamol and tried to lie down and get some rest, but his mind was in turmoil.

Was John connected to the people who had beaten him up? It seemed unlikely; he had run out and frightened them off. Without him, Darren had no doubt he'd be in the hospital, and he'd had quite enough of hospitals for now. Why was he being warned off Roehampton? He must be close to something, but he didn't know what it was.

He typed John's brother's name, 'Lee de Luca', into Google and found someone of the right name sentenced to seven years for crack and cocaine dealing. He also found the evidence that put his doubts to bed once and for all – Lee looked like John.

He tried to think back through what John had said about his meetings with Olivia. He was right about her reading newspapers – he had seen the evidence in the dayroom and he had wiped newspaper print off the desk in her room – but other than that he hadn't found out anything more about her. Her sister didn't feature in what John had told him, which surprised Darren considering Olivia's reaction at St George's. That she wanted to keep up to date with the police and their activities was hardly a revelation to him.

Darren tried to find on the internet reference to the Bristol case that Olivia had mentioned to John. It became a depressing hunt through many newspaper and online reports about policemen, clergy, insurance salesmen and scoutmasters who hoarded indecent images of children on computers and shared them round the world. In among the criminal convictions and public shaming were quite a few suicides. He couldn't, though, find a case that exactly matched what John had said.

Feeling he'd come to the end of an evening that had taken him no further forward, he collapsed into bed, his whole body aching.

66

The police inspector picked up his first coffee of the morning and walked over to the detective tasked with the investigation of the security breach at St George's hospital. 'You need to see this, sir,' the detective said. He began scrolling on his computer through CCTV footage from the corridors at various points around the wing where Olivia had been held. The team had already discounted hours of surveillance and now they were looking at a grey and indistinct picture of a figure walking down a corridor, head bowed. 'The quality of these things is shot,' the detective muttered.

The hair colour was impossible to determine, but that was definitely a young man, with longish hair.

'You can see the Adidas stripes on his trainers,' the detective added. The man showed up on another camera near a door that led to Olivia's corridor. 'Look – the camera doesn't show the actual door, but he doesn't appear on the camera on the next bend, where he would have come had he not gone through that door.'

The inspector was sure. 'It's the same guy,' he said.

'I think so too. But there's something else. I don't think the guy was with the protestors. Look.' He closed the file, opened another and fast-forwarded through. 'This is the lobby, four hours before anyone even knew Duvall was in the hospital.' The inspector clearly saw the same man, a Sainsbury's bag banging against his knees, lope past the camera. He made no attempt to hide his face. 'And this is even better.' He inserted another disk, this time of another corridor. The same man, still holding the bag, going through a door.

'What ward is that?'

'Northampton. He's visiting someone.'

'Great work,' the inspector said.

'But here's the thing,' the detective said. 'I got a list of people who were staying in that ward that day. Ten women. I looked them up, and *this* is what I found.' The detective opened a browser and typed a name into Google Images. 'She look familiar to you?'

'Kind of . . .' The inspector tailed off, trying to place the woman.

'She's Melanie Evans, the mother of Carly Evans, who was abducted by—'

'—Olivia Duvall.' The inspector finished the sentence.

'That man, I'm pretty sure, is Melanie's son.'

67

Darren struggled awake, clawing with his hands, crawling from a tight endless hole. He woke gasping for air in his bed, the lingering nightmare about still being in the hospital incinerator making his heart dance with fear. He struggled to sit upright, his ribs groaning with the pain of the bruised flesh from his beating last night. He felt the back of his head; a painful swelling marked the place where someone had warned him off. He needed to lie in bed, curtains closed, complete the latest GTA video game and smoke all his dope. Forget. Repair.

Instead, he struggled to his feet and tried to stretch. Someone had warned him off Roehampton, but that was exactly where he was going.

He also needed to talk to Orin. He managed a shower, then came downstairs and put some bread in the toaster, remembering as he did that his bike was in Clapham and was unrideable. He picked up his bag and hunted around for some cash, then got a minicab to Clapham.

He sat over a coffee in an American chain as he waited for his tyres to be replaced. Orin phoned him.

'Young gun, you made up your mind yet?'

'Sorry Orin, I've had a really hectic night, a lot of stuff has been—'

'I know who Rollo is.'

Darren pushed his coffee aside. 'Tell me.'

'Rollo McFadden. He was Molly's mum's boyfriend. I didn't

recognise the name when you asked me because he appears in very few of the reports on her. She had a string of men in her life – he was just another name in a long and sad list.'

'What do you know about him?'

There was a long pause. 'You're a terrier with a bone, young gun, I respect that. But why is he significant to you? You haven't explained and you sound like you've just been given a knock that's sent the sense straight out of your mouth.'

Darren put his hand protectively over the big bruise on the back of his head. 'Well, Streatham is a dangerous place.'

'I wouldn't know, I never go to south London.'

'Where do you live, Orin?'

'Knightsbridge.'

He imagined an elegant Georgian terrace, the thrum of black cabs. Death brought people from all walks of life together. 'I guess your nights aren't disturbed by fourteen-year-old joyriders on mopeds.'

'No.' Orin paused. 'My nights are ruined by Arab princes racing Ferraris. It's a goddamn nightmare. Good job I don't sleep.'

Darren smiled ruefully. Despite himself he was beginning to warm to Orin.

'Do you have a photo of Rollo? Does he look like he's tall?'

Orin gave a low laugh. 'He's built like a Georgia outhouse. He's six foot two exactly.'

Darren frowned. 'How do you know that?'

'Because I've got the summary sheet of his murder right in front of me.'

'His murder?'

'And I'm not telling you another goddamn thing until you share your theory, tell me how you got Rollo's name and go public with me.'

Orin hung up and walked out of his office towards his

research room. As he opened the door he turned to his secretary. 'Type up a press release saying we have a new high-profile member of The Missing campaign. The brother of Carly Evans. I've waited long enough for Darren Evans to pull his finger out of his ass. I'll extract it for him today.'

68

D arren locked his bike up and went into Roehampton. He left his bag in a locker and changed into his uniform, and was standing in the corridor when Kamal emerged from his office. Kamal took a long look at the cut on the back of his head. 'Are you going to fill in that leaving form now?'

Realisation began to dawn. It was his boss who had sent the men to follow him to Nine Elms. Kamal really wanted him gone and had gone to some length to achieve it. Darren's scab itched, his body ached and he was so tired – but not tired enough that he couldn't feel angry at what had happened.

Kamal began to dole out the cleaning routes. With the new revelation from Orin about who Rollo was, Darren was more desperate than ever to get a moment with Olivia. He tried to double-bluff Kamal. 'Can I clean the kitchens today? After what happened I find the cells bring back bad memories.'

Kamal grinned nastily. 'Think you're smart, college boy? Think you can double-bluff me? You're definitely doing the kitchens.'

Darren's heart sank. He was looking at another eight-hour shift without getting a glimpse of Olivia or any chance to talk to her. He felt the pressure of time he didn't have, of a door of opportunity closing. He turned away and waited for the buzzer to sound and the door to slide open, his only solace being that if he was unmasked Kamal's little empire would also fall.

He trudged the corridors, figure-eighting and wiping, and came to the kitchen, passing a straggle of inmates and two nurses who were moving in the other direction. Olivia was not among them.

Inside the kitchen the clattering of pans and the babble of voices was a welcome relief from the oppressive silence of the corridors.

He couldn't see Chloe. She was working that day, he knew, but he didn't even catch a glimpse of her. Instead he found Berenice roaming the room, rearranging chairs. She caught sight of him and came over and gave him a hug.

'Darren!'

'You're in a good mood today,' he said, the breath squeezed out of him.

'You betcha!' She picked up a tabloid from a table and gave its pages a shake. 'Look at this man! He's a big noise, an upstanding highly regarded member of the community. He's a family man, but he's been exposed as a multiple murderer. He's confessed on camera to being one of Britain's worst ever serial killers. Worse even than Duvall.'

Darren looked at the paper she was holding. A middle-aged man in a suit and tie stared out of a photo. Gert Becker had been sniping at Darren's subconscious all morning – snippets on the radio at breakfast at home, the front pages of the newspapers people held up in the coffee shop in Clapham, the headlines on a pile of freebies outside the tube station. It was an extraordinary case. The millionaire businessman from Birmingham had confessed on camera to kidnapping, raping and murdering fourteen women and girls over a period of nineteen years. He had targeted runaways, prostitutes and foreigners – had bought girls from criminal gangs operating out of five European countries. He had made his confession from his fishing boat in Great Yarmouth, over whose very sides he had thrown the corpses into the North Sea.

He knew the names of only seven of his victims; just five were registered as missing at all.

Gert Becker hadn't been alone when he made his confession. Someone had taken the video and posted copies of it to the UK's major news outlets. Becker was found the previous day, hanging by a noose from the side of his boat in what first indications had suggested was suicide.

Berenice was flushed, anger and disdain chasing themselves round her fleshy face. 'It makes you think, doesn't it, how cheap the lives of women are. So cheap they can be thrown away like a used tissue. The police didn't even know a crime had been committed. These women we serve in here are saints by comparison! This man was cold, calculating, unspeakable.'

'You obviously feel very strongly about it,' Darren said.

'Yes I do. Oh Darren, today is a good day, a magnificent day. When justice is finally done, the world is a better place.' She stopped and stared at him as if for the first time. 'My God, what happened to your head?'

He couldn't explain it, but he felt the panic of tears beginning to form and he didn't want her to see them. She was so happy and the day was so bright and summery and he was so tired and ground down. But Berenice did notice, and took a step towards him and put her fleshy hand on his arm. 'I was beaten up last night—'

'I'm so sorry.' She shook her head. 'It makes you doubt everything, it makes you hate yourself.' She squeezed his arm. 'I know how it feels because it's happened to me. I'm going to make you a cake, make you feel better.'

A tear dribbled down his cheek. Here in this kitchen was the kindness of strangers, something the girls who encountered Gert Becker had never found, something that Carly had needed so desperately.

Berenice had the good grace to stand in front of him to block his tears from the team in the kitchen behind her. 'You're going to be fine, it'll just take a while. I've got to bake like mad for market day tomorrow – it's full on production at the lock-up – so I'll bring one in on Monday. Comfort food, there's nothing like it.'

She pushed a pile of trays further down the counter and turned back to him, wiping her hands down her apron. Her voice was quiet when she spoke. 'When I was attacked I was like you, I was very young. But I knew that one day I would feel better.'

Darren nodded, scrubbing the floor furiously with his mop, half imagining Kamal's face under the water-soaked strands of cloth. She was talking a lot of sense.

'I knew I would be over it when I got my revenge.'

Darren looked up at her. 'And did you get your revenge?'

She gave Darren a strange look that he didn't understand. 'Completely.'

69

Helen was coming out of Roehampton with a leaving card for Dr Chowdray. He was moving to Oxford and she needed to get the staff to sign it before they all left for the day.

She came out of the staff entrance by the kitchens and found a group of women on a smoking break. One of them was Chloe. 'Hiya Dr McCabe,' she said.

'Oh hello, Chloe, isn't it? Please call me Helen.'

'That was a nice drink at the pub the other night.'

'Yes, it was nice to sit outside in this wonderful weather.'

'Darren's been amazing, hasn't he?'

For a horrid moment Helen wondered if Chloe knew all about Darren and her, but then she realised that she was just being friendly. 'Yes indeed.'

'He's been through a lot though, hasn't he? Seeing that attack, and his mum's got cancer, did you know that?'

'Oh, I didn't. I'm sorry.' So Darren had a sick mother – that was a turn-up. He hadn't felt able to share that with her. She felt for him – distractions were what he had been seeking, she understood that.

'Even his dog Chester died recently – it can all pile up, can't it?'

Helen nodded at that. 'That's too true, Chloe, isn't it? Here girls, Dr Chowdray's leaving us for the green and pleasant lands of Oxford.'

They oohed and aahed and she held out the card.

They reached for the pen and filled the blank space with well-intentioned scribbles. 'Thanks.' She skirted the car park to enter the building via another door, thinking she needed to remember to talk to building services about the fag butts littering the entrance.

So Darren's dog had died. Helen had never liked dogs, though she did sometimes wonder whether it was time to get an aquarium. Chester the fish. She smiled. It was a good name.

Helen stopped. When her brain made connections the world held its breath, as if waiting for a stone to land in a well. Chester. One of Olivia's victims had had a puppy called Chester. Her mother had come to the prison recently – because she had cancer.

The stone hit water at the bottom of the well. Carly Evans had a brother.

Helen ran for the door and through security. She took the stairs to her office two at a time, burst in, typed her computer password and scrolled through Olivia's file. She had to be sure, but with every second that passed she knew with greater certainty.

The page with the details of the victims was before her on screen. Carly Evans. Her mother was Melanie, father Andy. They lived in Streatham. Carly had a brother called Darren.

It was him. *He* had been in Olivia's room that night at St George's.

As Helen ran out of her office and along to security she thought of many things, none of them good: grooming, revenge, obsession, copycats and the fact that she had been used. Darren hadn't dated her because he liked older women or was intrigued by his boss or because he fancied a fuck: he did it because he had wanted information. Their affair would not stay secret after this and the one thing that Helen prized above all others, the thing she never wanted to lose, was at stake: her professional reputation.

'Lockdown! Put this place into lockdown!' she screamed at Sonny.

Sonny took one look at Helen's face and felt the sharp stab of action, so long anticipated, never before deployed. Her face was livid, her hair flying. 'Now!' she screamed.

Sonny turned to the big red button on the wall, its protective sheet of perspex reflecting the light. He was confused: he had seen nothing untoward on the security cameras, had had no phone call; but he was being given his chance and he was taking it, because he had waited for nineteen years. He got up, balled his fist and smashed it on to that big red button.

When he turned back round Helen was already gone but the noise – short, pulsing firecrackers of sound – was beautiful to him.

70

Darren was pushing open the last exit door at the end of his shift when the siren went off. Nathan, standing by the security barrier, hurriedly reached for the radio on his belt.

The siren was making Darren's mind jump in crazy directions. He let the door fall shut behind him and glanced back over his shoulder. He saw the way Nathan was looking at him as he listened to whatever was being said by the person at the other end of the radio.

Darren ran.

He heard Nathan shouting behind him. He was out in the car park. The siren was louder out here; people stopped and turned. He had just seconds to spare. The bike racks were at the far end of the car park. He dodged parked cars and raced towards them, pulling the keys from his pocket.

Nathan and another man were in pursuit, blocking his path to the exit gate.

'Darren,' Nathan called, slowing down and walking towards him, 'stop and we can work this out. It'll be a misunderstanding, mate.'

Nathan didn't know yet what was at stake, but Darren needed to be gone from here, right now. Behind him was a bank where shrubs grew and beyond that a low chain-link fence by the road.

He could hear the faint shrill of a police siren.

'That's it, mate,' Nathan said slowly, his hands out wide

like he was herding sheep. 'Just come back inside and we can talk this through.'

Darren picked up his bike and ran up the bank, hurling it over the fence into the road.

Nathan ran at him as he vaulted over, a car screeching to a halt. He began to climb the fence, shouting at Darren to stop.

Darren got on the bike and pedalled away.

71

Orin was standing checking a press release over his secretary's shoulder. It was about to be emailed to all news outlets and put up on The Missing's website. A photo of Darren with his new shorter haircut had been screen-grabbed from the security camera Orin had running in the office reception and blown up. He looked thoughtful, committed, respectable. It was perfect. The fact that Darren hadn't actually agreed it with Orin didn't concern him; he hadn't got where he was by toeing the line. 'Send it,' he told her.

Two minutes later Orin got a call from the man he'd sent to tail Darren. 'That guy on the pushbike's just done something really stupid, from what I can tell.'

Orin listened to the story, hung up and stood very still. He walked back into his office and closed the door. He unlocked the bottom drawer in his desk, pulled out his washbag and carried it into the toilet.

Darren got off his bike in a housing estate in south-west London and stood in the road. He didn't know where to go. He didn't know what to do. He had a crushing sense that his life, in the form he had lived it up until now, was over. And the worst thing was he couldn't get out of his head the idea of Olivia lying on her cell bed, enjoying his failure, revelling in her victory.

What had he achieved in the month he had been cleaning at the hospital, trying to get to her? Precisely nothing. He had got Linda killed, nearly got arrested and stuck in an incinerator, had alienated his family by getting into bed with Orin Bukowski, had lied to those he loved.

He had got Molly back. That was something; but it had come at a heavy price. Her bones had raised as many questions as they had answered. Closure, Darren realised, was not something that you were given, it was something you found within yourself.

Murder laughed at him.

He lashed out and punched a lamp-post, then snatched his hand back with the pain, his knuckles cut and bruised. Tears stung his hot eyes.

He was out of time and he clung desperately, like a man at sea, to the only thing he had that could keep him afloat: Rollo McFadden. This was the only clue he could still pursue. Why had Olivia given him this information? He had to go to Orin's to take a look at what he had.

He needed to move fast, before Orin got hold of the news of what had happened at Roehampton.

He tried phoning Orin but there was no answer, from either his mobile or his office. He tried again: nothing.

Darren got back on his bike and began the long ride to Orin's office on the South Bank.

72

Melanie was feeling sick again, a great wave of nausea overwhelming her like sea water on a harbour wall. One of the drugs in the cocktail she was taking was making her skin itch so that she couldn't sit still, so the doorbell ringing was a relief – she could distract herself by going to open the door.

When she saw the two policemen standing there in uniform, she didn't react. She was calm. Uniformed police had visited her door often at the beginning of that hellish ten-year period. It was with considerable surprise, though, that she listened to them say that they were here about Darren.

Andy was at her shoulder now as she invited them in to the house. The itching of her arm was intense now, burrowing deep into her tissues.

'We're looking for Darren urgently.'

'Why?'

'We really need to speak to him. Do you know where he is?'

'He's at work.'

'Did you know that he was working at Roehampton High-Security Hospital?'

Melanie was too surprised to reply.

'He works at King's College Hospital, in the records department,' Andy said.

The policemen looked at each other. 'It seems he faked an identity and was working as a cleaner to gain access to—'

Melanie took a quick step forward to counter what she knew was coming. 'That is rubbish.'

The policemen looked at each other again.

Melanie didn't answer. She walked out of the room and took the stairs two at a time to Darren's bedroom. When Andy and the police officers came into the room behind her, she was already rifling through disorganised piles of paper and drawing pads, cigarette papers and clothing.

'As you can appreciate, this is a serious security breach and Darren has committed fraud,' a police officer said. There are concerns that he may have passed Olivia Duvall inappropriate material, or been subjected to influence that may be dangerous.'

'Dangerous to who?' snapped Melanie.

'The public, Mrs Evans. As a relative of a victim he is in an acutely dangerous position having access to Olivia Duvall. Inmates such as her are manipulative and potentially a danger to those they interact with.'

Melanie's itching was overtaken by her anger.

'Darling, what are you looking for?' Andy asked desperately.

Clothes were raining down from shelves, dusty video game cases clattering to the floor. 'He told me he was seeing someone he worked with—'

She stopped, her hand on a cheap blue polyester top. She unfolded it and froze. There, above where Darren's heart would be, was Roehampton High-Security Hospital's logo.

Melanie turned to Andy and felt herself tipping sideways. Her desire to find Carly had made her go through the madness of meeting the Witch, and inspired by her, Darren had chosen his own, more extreme and dangerous version of the same thing. She was convinced she herself had sown the seeds of his destruction.

And as so often in recent times, as she fell to the floor she saw Andy reaching out in a desperate attempt to save her.

73

The ride to Orin's building took Darren forty minutes. He tried to go up to his office, but when he got there the door was locked and no one was around. He cursed silently. He had hit a dead end. He came back out into the street and walked round the corner to a walkway by the river. He tried calling Orin again but there was still no answer. He hung up and saw that he had two missed calls, the first from his mum.

When he played back her message it nearly broke his heart.

'Darren? Where are you? You need to come home. The police are here. They say you've been seeing the Witch.' Her voice caught in her throat. 'You need to ring me and tell me it's not true.'

The next person on the voicemail was Chloe. 'You lying toad! I don't even know what your name is. I hate you! I trusted you, I shared things with you and you lied! Over and over again.' She didn't say goodbye when she cut the call.

He took his phone and hurled it as high and as far as he could into the river, then stood staring at the grey swirling surface. He stood there for a long time, marooned. He knew he had to go home and face the music, but he couldn't do it. He was a coward and he couldn't do it.

He looked about him. He was near Borough Market, where Berenice was baking cakes to sell in the morning. She would give him a sympathetic ear; she wouldn't condemn him for trying to get to the truth. Hadn't she only this morning revelled in the revenge she herself had enacted on the man who had attacked her? Her reaction to the paedophile in the paper this morning convinced him that Berenice's was where he needed to go.

The market was closing when Darren got there, road sweepers cleaning away blown-about newspapers and take-away cartons, council refuse trucks emptying huge rubbish bins that made the unpleasant summer smells of the city puff across the expanses of tarmac. Borough Market had once been the capital's premier fruit and veg market, sheltering under the railway lines that tangled their way from Blackfriars and London Bridge stations to south-east England, boxed in by Victorian buildings in no regular pattern. During the day asparagus from Surrey and apples from Kent crowded next to expensive fudge stalls for tourists and tables groaning with French cheese, and at night bars and restaurants did brisk trade selling food from every corner of the globe.

Darren coasted around on his bike, pausing to ask a man packing up a van if he knew Berenice or where the cake-maker's railway arch was. The guy shrugged and shook his head. Darren came round past a tapas restaurant where, on this hot night, diners were spilling out on to the pavement, and took a side alley. He asked an old man leaning against a wall enjoying a cigarette if he knew Berenice. He got a shake of the head in response.

Darren began walking around grimier and quieter alleys, reading signs and painted hoardings, checking the storage sheds under the railway arches, looking for Berenice's name or that of her business. He didn't find it. There was no logic to how the market was laid out and he lost his sense of direction a few times as he travelled down cobbled streets and across bumpy concrete expanses.

He began to panic. He couldn't find her and that meant he had to think about going home. He coasted into a narrow side road by a row of railway arches that had been adopted as workshops and storage units and stopped. He could see a white Ford Transit van parked by a high brick wall on the other side of the road. He cycled up to the window of the van and looked in. Bingo. A couple of farmers' market magazines lay on the passenger seat, along with a Tupperware container. He knew it was Berenice's van: he'd seen it on the security monitors at Roehampton.

He stood back and shouted her name. He tried again and a man appeared from behind a blue door set in an arch and directed him further down the street towards a railway arch filled in with bricks with a red metal door set into it. There was no name. Darren knocked. Nothing happened. He knocked again. He stood back and looked around.

A moment later Berenice came round a corner, a bag of shopping in her hand.

She stopped in confusion when she saw him, looking around nervously. 'What are you doing here?'

'I wanted to come and see you.'

She didn't move. 'I know who you are, Darren. Everyone at the hospital knows.'

'I just want to talk. Please.'

'Aren't the police looking for you?'

'Probably.'

She gave him a look that suggested pity. 'They'll be sympathetic, but not if you run and make trouble.'

'Trouble's already come.'

There was silence. He looked around. 'Is this your arch?'

She nodded, but seemed reluctant to move.

'I'm starving. You got any food in that bag?'

She relented and walked towards the red door. She unlocked it and put the keys back in her pocket.

'You don't have your name on the door.'

'I don't want to draw attention to myself. There are often

break-ins.' She stepped inside, turned on the light. He was in a commercial kitchen, with brick walls and no windows, a cooker and fridge and sink along the right-hand wall and low lights hanging from the high curved ceiling. The middle of the room was dominated by an island topped with stainless steel. Beyond, the back wall of the lock-up was lined with shelves and two wooden trestle tables were propped up against it.

Berenice closed the door and put the shopping bag on the island.

Darren took his backpack off and did the same. 'It's nice in here. How did you end up with this?'

She looked around. 'I won it in a card game. Don't look so surprised. I've come from nothing and fought for what little I've got now. This was one of my few pieces of luck.' She turned away from him towards the shelves, pulled a knife block back with her and put it on the island. She pulled a loaf of bread from the bag and began to slice it. A train rumbled loudly overhead.

He began to walk around the space, examining it. The shelves along the back wall were cluttered: at waist and shoulder height there were Tupperware boxes in myriad shapes and sizes, a blender, laminated certificates for a cookery course completed and a hygiene certificate from the council, storage jars with flour and dried fruit and other ingredients Darren couldn't identify. He ran his hand along the top of one of the trestle tables and noticed that in the corner leaned a skateboard.

Berenice saw Darren staring at it. 'If I tried to ride that I'd probably end up in A and E. I use it to move my trestle tables to my pitch. They weigh a ton. This way, the wheels do all the work.'

They looked at each other as silence stole up around them. When Berenice spoke again her voice was quiet. 'You need to go home, Darren. Your mum needs you. You need to sort this out.'

'I did it to try and find my sister. My mum's ill with cancer.'

'I know,' Berenice replied. 'Did Olivia ever tell you anything, anything at all?'

He shrugged, realising she was the first person he had talked to about his demented plan. She seemed ill at ease and Darren wondered if she was scared of him. The thought horrified him. 'No, not really. I think she has issues with her sister's death, and with Molly's mum's boyfriend.' He tailed off. It sounded pathetic, what he was saying; what he had discovered was so shallow and slight as to be meaningless.

He saw her relax and a thought came to him. 'Why do you work at Roehampton? It's not a very nice place and the pay's bad. This space you have here is so much more – dynamic somehow.'

She became defensive. 'It's not that bad. I get Thursdays and Fridays off to come here. Not everyone has endless choices. I'll make you a sandwich and then you need to go.'

He felt ashamed for seeming to criticise her. After what *he* had done! He backed into the corner as if retreating from his own ill-considered comment. He cast around for something to hold on to, something to do to delay all the problems he had to face for just a little while longer. He put his foot on the skateboard. It was old and well used, with chips on its edges and grime in the textured surface.

He had been a good boarder when he was younger. Riding pavements and riding waves, free and uncomplicated. Oh how he wished he could push himself off and coast away from his troubles. But it was a fantasy and he was so very tired. He put his toe on the end of the board so that the other end poked skywards and caught it in his hand. He felt the rough grain of the riding surface under his palm and the comforting weight of it. It was a childish toy. The things he had done belonged to a grown-up world and he had to face the consequences. He had to face them as a man.

He turned and put the skateboard back next to the trestle table, its wheels facing him. Between the wheels was a graffiti tag. Most skateboards had them, a riot of colour and action. This one was different, a white squiggle on a black background. The curve of a C under the embrace of an E. He froze. He knew that tag, as individual as a signature. It had been drawn on the end of a surfboard that now lay in a Streatham attic, and had been engraved in an act of love on the back of his neck. Now somehow – somehow – it had ended up on the bottom of this skateboard.

Darren spun round but he was too slow to avoid the punch to the side of his head. He fell to the floor and rolled under the kitchen island, shock and confusion coursing through him. Berenice came round the island and jabbed down at him with a knife, scraping it along the floor as he scrabbled himself upright away from her. He danced back, reaching behind him for anything on the shelves he could throw at her.

She was panting with exertion, her eyes wild, her face set with determination. Darren thought he must have hit his head on the floor, as a thousand images burst across his retina simultaneously: Chloe's words in his car at the beach in Devon, *White vans are great for transporting bodies in;* Orin standing by his window in his office, *You know how hard it is to bury a dead body by yourself?* A heart carved into a scoop of mashed potato on a tray that came back to the kitchens every day, a simple message system. He had mistakenly thought the heart had been for him, but it had been for her. There *had* been someone else acting with Olivia, and Darren was looking right at her.

She held the knife like a dagger, tracking him round the island.

He hurled the blender at Berenice's head, catching her on the shoulder. It clattered away across the room. 'You killed Molly,' he gasped. 'You two did it together. You did all of it together, it's just that only one of you is locked up.'

Berenice scowled. 'You know nothing, little boy. You couldn't stay away, you couldn't leave it alone. You don't know what you're dealing with and now you leave me no choice. Stupid boy!'

'Where is Carly?' he screamed and she raced round the island for him, the knife slashing down. Darren danced backwards but the knife caught him in the front of the thigh, a searing pain exploding up his leg. He kicked out at her desperately and she backed away round the island again, waiting for her chance to attack.

He was panting heavily, feeling his trousers, wet where the blood must be soaking through them, but he couldn't take his eyes off her for a second. His rucksack was on the island. He risked a glance over at it and blessed his absent-mindedness: he'd never closed the zip.

He needed to keep her talking. 'How did the police never find you? How could you be so well hidden?' It could only have a chance of success if the whole thing was carefully planned, a long time in advance. 'Why did you do it?'

'You're so naïve.' She began to move slowly round the island so he had to reluctantly move away from his bag. 'A man.' She spat the words out. 'Who's responsible for all the evil in the world? All the violence and the suffering? All because of what hangs between your legs.'

He got angry then, thinking of Molly rotting in a hole in the ground. 'You're as deluded as Olivia. Where's my sister?'

'It's so simple to you; someone is lost so they must be found. Sometimes people can't be found, and sometimes they don't want to be found.'

Darren lunged for the rucksack, using the bag to uppercut

Berenice in the face. He slammed backwards into the shelving, rooting desperately in the bag for what he needed.

She jumped forward and the knife slashed down near his face. He feinted and grabbed at the shelf to use as leverage and, in a panic, saw that the shelf was coming away from the wall, items scattering to the floor. Panic became shock as the entire unit swung outwards from the wall, revealing behind it a door. The back wall of the lock-up, Darren realised, was false; the cake kitchen took up only a small part of the space. A trapdoor flew open in Darren's mind; something horrible lurked behind it.

Berenice faltered and at that moment Darren dropped the bag and lunged at her with the paint-stripper gun. A jet of blue flame hit her face. She howled and recoiled, tripping over the skateboard. Darren was on top of her in a moment, the gun burning her eyes, her knife flailing madly. She caught him in the side, a pain so agonising he couldn't breathe. He pressed the gun in closer and she had to drop the knife and scrabble to push the burning jet away from her blistering skin. Her shrieks reverberated round the damp arch.

'Where is my sister?' he yelled, a smell of burning flesh in his nostrils. She was bucking hard underneath him, her face straining to escape the fierce heat. He pinned her arms with his knees and dropped the gun, grabbing her neck and slamming her head down on the concrete. She stopped moving immediately.

He pulled the keys out of her pocket, stood up and staggered against the island, pain and faintness overwhelming him.

He stood in front of the concealed door. There was no handle and it opened inwards. He tried two of the keys before he found the one that fitted the lock. Bleeding heavily and feeling fainter by the second, he opened the door.

74

A thick black curtain hung across the doorway. Darren pulled it hesitantly aside.

Behind the curtain a light was on, and he saw a large living room, the walls made of brick and covered with paintings. It was like a loft, only without any windows. It was comfortably furnished, with sofas, a table and chairs, a TV on a stand and a computer. There were rugs on the floor and a boxing ring set up in the middle of the room. Next to the boxing ring was a running machine and a pull-up bar.

Movement caught his eye from behind one of the sofas. A woman's head was peering over it, staring at him. Darren felt the faintness rush back at him and he thought he was going to collapse. There were bunk beds in the far corner and another woman was under one of the beds, her dark eyes blinking at him.

'Darren?'

That voice. He turned to his right and his heart exploded. Carly was standing there, in the kitchen of the concealed room. She was perfectly still, her eyes discs of shock in her face.

'Darren?' She said it again, as if not believing he could be real.

He couldn't breathe or move. He had so much to say that a lifetime wouldn't be enough. A woozy panic rushed through him; he felt that, now he had finally found her, he would die before he fully absorbed the fact. Trying to shake it off, he took a step towards her, but before he could say anything she screamed a warning. He turned. A hard smack hit him across the head. As he fell to the floor he saw Berenice standing over him, one of her eyes a running mess of scorched and disfigured tissue.

The room erupted into action. Carly sprang towards Berenice and jumped on her, pulling her to the ground and punching her. Darren couldn't move; his limbs were jelly. Blood from his head poured into his eye. Now Berenice was down and not moving and Carly was kneeling over him.

He felt someone pulling his ankle. 'He's my brother, leave him alone!' Carly cried.

A woman with long blonde hair was trying to drag him across the floor. 'It's not safe and you know it, Carly.'

Two other women were standing by the blonde-haired one, and he realised one of them looked like Rajinder, although her hair was in a different style. The other woman had brown hair.

The brown-haired woman was whimpering. 'Is she dead?' She was looking down at Berenice.

'Run!' Darren shouted.

'Darren, get up, now.' Carly had her hands under his armpits, pulling him upright. The woman with blonde hair was still hanging on to his ankle.

He was woozy and wanted desperately to sleep, but managed to say, 'Run, Carly, run!'

'Stay here, Carly. I mean it!' Darren realised that the woman with blonde hair must be Isla. She looked so different from how he remembered her as a child, but her voice, so like Orin's, was familiar.

'It's over, it's finally over,' Darren tried to shout, but the sound died in his throat. Everyone was moving so slowly. He didn't understand it; they were prisoners in this hellhole, suspended for a decade in a horror he couldn't begin to contemplate, and no one was moving.

He heard a noise behind him and saw Rajinder hammering at something on the table. A piece of computer disk flew up in the air.

'He is innocent!' Carly was pulling on his arms. He was being stretched between the two women.

'We are so close!' Isla shouted.

'It's over,' Carly said.

'Run, Carly, run!' Darren finally managed to shout.

Carly was galvanised into action. She pushed Isla away from him, grabbed him under the armpits again and got him to his feet. She was surprisingly strong. Leaning on each other, they came out of that room and they led each other back into the world.

The brown-haired woman came close behind them, gulping in air and crying. Isla had followed too, he realised. She was standing inches from him, staring intently.

'It's over, Isla, you're safe,' he struggled to say.

Isla said something he couldn't hear and backed away to a wall. 'No we're not.'

'Your dad—' A wave of pain erupted in him.

She shook her head. She said 'no' again, louder, then turned and ran away, disappearing round the corner.

'Wait!' Darren tried to follow her but he had no energy left and he stumbled and fell. Something was badly wrong inside him – every sinew in his body was straining but he was floating away, unable to stay grounded.

Carly was kneeling by him on the floor, cradling his head in her lap, pawing him to stop him falling into unconsciousness, saying his name over and over, trying it out, seeing how it fit.

He felt much weaker and only had the strength to whisper. 'I looked so long, so long I looked for you.'

Carly gazed up at the sky and she howled from the depths of her soul, a pain profound and raw and triumphant. Darren felt an acute agony in his heart, such an intense moment of joy he thought it might overwhelm his body and kill him. Tomorrow she would see the sun, and all the tomorrows after that. She had emerged, kicking and screaming back into the world, a rebirth, a miracle. As he floated away he knew one thing: love was strong, stronger than life.

75

When the police arrived at Melanie's door for the second time that night, they told her that Darren was in a critical condition in hospital with multiple stab wounds and was under police guard. The young officer looked grey with fright and twitching to get going. She sat far from Andy in the car, staring dully out of the window at the London night. She had suffered the worst that life could throw at a mother, people said, it would never be as bad as that again, they said. But they were wrong, as she had always known they were.

Melanie had read on the internet that cancer drugs could make you hallucinate and that emotional stress could enhance the hallucinogenic effect. Which was why while she stood looking at one half-dead child wrapped in bandages and on a drip in a hospital bed with a face battered black and blue, a vision who looked like her own younger self was coming across the room towards her, floating and shimmering in a chaos of police and people in white coats. The vision looked like Carly, but the room was so noisy and crowded and Andy was gasping in her ear and she heard a sound that only her most fantastical dreams had allowed her to dare imagine.

This vision shouted 'Mum!'

A moment later Carly was in her arms; she could feel the warmth of her, smell the shampoo in her hair, hear her daughter crying into her neck.

Melanie sank down on to the bed, her legs unable to support her. She grabbed Carly's face between her palms, drinking in how her teenage features had changed into an adult's: her cheekbones were more prominent, her eyebrows thinner, her face sadder and more set. But she was vital and alive and right here.

As Melanie clung to her daughter she was transported to a time years ago when she had sailed out into the English Channel to watch a solar eclipse. As the boat bobbed in the water, the seagulls had suddenly fallen silent and the wind had dropped. She had felt a spike of fear as a huge threatening shadow had raced over her across the miles of open water. She had been stunned at the speed that the earth was travelling, had been in awe at the scale of the universe. It felt to her now as if that monstrous darkness, the pain and loss of the past ten years, was receding at lightning speed away from her and her child. She had been forgiven. She thanked every god and spirit she could think of for her daughter's deliverance.

'I'm so sorry,' Carly sobbed.

'I knew you would come back, I *knew*.'

The harsh alarm on Darren's monitor exploded into life as his heart gave out.

76

Olivia was woken by the cell door opening. A group of guards filed in. Suspicion swam round in her mind as she sat up. No one ever came this early or in these numbers. The routine was out.

She'd heard the alarm yesterday – it could be heard in every cell in the accommodation block – but when she had pumped the guard for information through the hatch in the door, she got nothing more than a terse denial of everything. She could feel the tension though, the quickening steps, the long periods of silence as people did things elsewhere. She had never heard that alarm before; it must be used only for escapes or large-scale events. She wondered what had happened. It had been turned off less than ten minutes later, but the biting tension remained.

They must have discovered who Darren was. This wasn't a surprise; it was always going to happen eventually. But somehow the mood this morning didn't fit that theory: one of the guards was grinning. She stood up, anticipation crackling in the soles of her feet, but she was ordered to sit back down. Helen appeared in the doorway.

Berenice, she thought in despair. Her first thoughts were always that something might have happened, that a revelation had been made that would break their tenuous connection – the slim strands of snatched words in the lunch queue, the glorious moment twenty-nine days ago when she had been close enough to touch her arm. It was four and a half months since she had been near enough to smell her.

Helen looked dishevelled, like she hadn't slept. Her make-up was heavier than normal. Olivia saw restrainers in the arms of one of the guards. She stood sharply, and this time they didn't bother telling her to sit back down.

'The women have been found,' Helen said. She turned to leave the cell. She didn't even bother to look at Olivia. 'Darren discovered them.'

'All of them?' Olivia's voice was coming from far away, from someone who was not her at all.

'Berenice McArthur is dead. Carly Evans killed her.' Helen put a hand on the door.

'Wait!' But Helen didn't wait. She disappeared round the door. 'Wait! Did they say anything? What did they say about me?'

She tried to run after Helen, the questions piling up into a great mountain of anguish and failure, but the guards didn't let her. Helen didn't come back. It was over. She screamed as loudly as she could, and lashed out with her nails at the nearest guard. She was wailing, unable to contain the grief and the endless questions. The guards were more than ready. They circled her in a practised manoeuvre, restraining arms and legs, avoiding her gnashing teeth. She kicked and thrashed, the few words Helen had said more brutal and final than any she could have imagined.

Darren and Carly had destroyed everything that made Olivia's life worth living. She had been in control, and somehow, the clueless cleaner had undone ten years of work. So much work!

Her hands were clamped together now. She saw one of the nurses preparing an injection and she howled expletives down on them all.

There was something even worse than what Helen had

told her. The men in her cell were grinning, as if she didn't matter any more. As if the power she had held was drained entirely away; she was already a nobody. Theirs were the grins of the victors.

77

Five Days Later

Darren was pulled back to consciousness with a hard slap on his left arm. He was disorientated, the light too bright for his eyes, his limbs like lead. An African nurse was shaking her head, remonstrating with Orin, who stood next to her. 'He needs to rest to get better! You get five minutes, then you're out.' She pressed the button on the bed and Darren began to rise to a semi-seated position. She turned and left the room and Darren saw that Carly was also there, leaning on a windowsill.

Darren was too weak to move. His hand was connected to a drip by the bed; he had difficulty keeping his head upright. That was OK though: he didn't want to do anything except gaze at his sister. She smiled at him uncertainly and he thought he could sit here for the rest of his life and stare at her like an idiot. She looked the same, yet so different. Her face was thinner than he remembered, her hair longer and darker. She was striking now that her face's childish plumpness was gone, but there was sadness in her eyes, an air of being old before her time. He was staring at a beautiful stranger.

'Partially collapsed lung, stab wounds to the vastus med-ialis and the right deltoid and a depressed fracture of the skull.' Orin had picked up Darren's notes and charts from the hook at the bottom of the bed and read from them, his voice a monotone. 'Your heart stopped twice, you came out of intensive care this morning. You've been out of action for five days, but you're back now.' He hung the notes back on the bed and stood, arms crossed, feet splayed, looking down at Darren. 'Where's my daughter?'

Darren looked at Carly and frowned. His mouth was dry, he couldn't speak, confusion rendered him mute.

'Your sister wouldn't talk to me unless you were present. This is the first time I've seen her. What happened at the railway arch?'

Carly saw Darren was struggling and came over to the bed, handing him a glass of water from the trolley. 'You can do it Darren, tell him what you remember.' Her voice was low and calm, she put her hand on his forehead.

'I went to see Berenice, I saw your tag on her skateboard, we fought . . .' He trailed off. Orin didn't take his eyes off him. 'I got the key and I opened the door and—'

Orin interrupted him. 'The police are combing that arch for every bit of information they can get.' He turned to look at Carly in an accusatory way. 'They don't understand what they're finding.'

Carly said nothing, just looked out of the window. Tension bristled in the air. 'Tell him what happened,' she finally said to Darren.

'I opened the door, I saw Carly, all of them, in there, just standing there. Berenice came at me again and Carly shouted a warning to me. She saved my life.'

'What about Isla?'

Darren paused. He couldn't remember. The world had turned strange at that point. Flashes of what he'd seen came back to him. There was something he was trying to remember, something from the corner of his vision. 'Isla was dragging me by the leg . . .' He tailed off again. That wasn't what was troubling him. 'We came outside, a woman, I guess it was Heather, was crying.' Darren watched Carly, staring out at nothing through the window. What had happened during all those years? She looked normal, sounded normal, was well fed and healthy, but there was something he couldn't place. 'Carly was shouting.'

Orin turned to her. 'What were you shouting?'

She still didn't move. 'I was shouting it's over. It's all over.' Her eyes filled with tears.

Darren took up the story. 'Isla came out of the lock-up. I said "You're safe" and she said "No". And she backed away to the corner and I tried to get up and follow but I couldn't. I was calling out her name, but she was gone.'

There was silence. 'So she went voluntarily,' Orin finally said.

'Yes. Have the police not found her?'

'They're looking of course, but I've hired my own private detectives to find her using more aggressive means. There isn't a flophouse or railway arch that won't be tossed by my men.'

An image flashed in front of Darren of an army of the homeless and the hopeless being upended by Orin's people. He was still struggling to recall what he had seen in the arch.

'Where are Rajinder and Heather?' he asked.

'Rajinder's with a cousin and is refusing to speak to the police or her family. Heather's gone to a convent. She has no family. During her incarceration she became deeply religious.' Orin turned to Carly. 'Which leaves you. Isla didn't just put on a coat and stroll off. Where is she?'

In that instant Darren remembered what he had noticed as Isla dragged him across the floor. Behind her, on the wall, was a row of coats and on the last hook hung an umbrella.

They had been allowed to go outside.

Carly got off the windowsill and walked towards Orin. 'I don't know where Isla is. But it's important you know what was really happening in there. She disappeared not because she can't come home but because she doesn't want to.'

'This is ridiculous,' Orin spat. 'She has been shut up by a madwoman in a cage for ten years, now she's alone and afraid and half mad and seeing the world for the first time and—'

'You don't get it.'

'No I don't, young lady. My daughter is alive after years when we thought she was dead. She could come to harm. She needs to be found.'

Carly shook her head. 'She hasn't been chained up for ten years. We weren't rotting away in there. We were busy. We were at work.'

Orin looked too stunned to speak.

'Does the name Gert Becker mean anything to you?' Carly continued.

'The guy on the video on the boat?' Orin asked.

'Isla took his confession.'

Darren closed his eyes, trying to shut out the ramifications of all this.

'She was outside?' Orin's voice was quieter than Darren had ever heard it.

'Berenice was one of Gert Becker's victims. She had the misfortune to run into him when she was fourteen. He tied her up and kept her for three days before she managed to escape.'

'Why did she never report him?' Orin demanded.

Carly laughed, but there was no humour in it. 'A runaway from a children's home who'd been kicked out of three schools and who hated the police? A girl like that accusing a high-profile, wealthy businessman, a pillar of the community?' Her voice was thick with sarcasm. 'He knew exactly what he was doing. Gert chose his victims very carefully. He revelled in being untouchable. Years later Berenice, emotionally unstable and physically scarred, drifted down to Brighton and met

Olivia on the seafront.' She faltered. 'Olivia saved her. Put her back together. They had a connection, because what happened to Berenice had also happened to Olivia's sister Lauren. She was used and abused by a man who seemed untouchable – one of her dad's friends. He worked in London. Olivia's parents had lots of parties at their fancy country place – powerful people from the City and the government would come and stay. But Lauren wasn't as strong as Berenice and she couldn't cope. She killed herself when she was sixteen.'

Darren felt his heart fill with despair. His sister, so young and impressionable, had been fed a modern version of a Grimm's fairy story, only real and brutal and sick.

'Hell, this is horseshit! If these women had done the right thing other women and girls would be alive today – Becker would be rotting in a penitentiary!'

Carly got off the windowsill. 'You *know* that's not true. Men like him get away with it – all the time. That's why accusing him wasn't enough. Olivia and Berenice wanted a full confession, all the details, all the names and dates—'

'Stop, please stop,' Darren pleaded. Carly was too young to think the world was made this dark. 'Not all men are like that. They're not all monsters—'

'Where I grew up they are.'

Orin's strength seemed to fail him and he sat down heavily on the bed next to Darren. Darren didn't know what to say that could make the other man feel better – a moment of joy Orin must have wished for countless times and never dared to believe could come true had been snatched away from him.

He looked at Carly and his heart bled anew. He thought about all the education she had missed, the relationships she had never had a chance to form, the good in the world that had been denied her. 'Olivia and Berenice trained us, in computer techniques, in impersonation, in interrogation, in how to tail someone. When Olivia was arrested, we carried on the job without her. Your daughter's not running, Mr Bukowski, she's hunting. She's hunting the man who cut Lauren's life so short.'

'Who is he?'

'We don't know.' She paused, staring at nothing through the window. 'It's complicated. It's like we're hunting a many-headed beast. Once we find evidence against one man, it leads to someone else. There's a network of people who are connected.'

Orin made a noise Darren couldn't quite make out. He was pacing round the room, unable to stand still. He came over to Carly and stared out of the window alongside her.

'There's something an American notices when they come here. It's small. So many secrets in somewhere so small.' There was silence. He turned round. 'I am going to use all my money, all my connections and all my energy to search every inch of this goddamn tiny, grey country to find her, and then I am going to finish this.'

'Carly is not to get involved, she needs to concentrate on readjusting to normal life, on repairing herself—'

'That's sweet, Darren,' Carly interrupted, 'but there's another problem. I don't like your daughter, Mr Bukowski.'

'But you know her, better than anyone. Hell, I don't much like your brother, but I need him. And he owes me. I'm finding Isla. I have the money to mount a search, I have the police connections, and Darren –' he turned to the bed '– has got close to the architect of the whole sorry saga as she rots away in her cell. So are you two young guns in or out?'

78

O livia hadn't left her cell for days. She wasn't sure she knew how many; time was blurring and folding in on itself. They had tried to take the restraints off a few days ago but she had punched the wall so hard as soon as her hand was free that they had got her back into them and moved her to a padded cell. The pain of the open knuckle was a welcome distraction from the terrible visions that had set up home in her head.

They had tried to feed her soup and she had spat it back out in their faces; water she did the same with, until they began drugging her again and she simply drifted in and out of consciousness. That was fine by her; she wanted to stay suspended in this state as she starved herself to death. She knew she had the willpower.

She had been wrong about everything she had worked for and believed in, and so it was better that it be over. She would spend every waking moment working out how she could kill herself. She relaxed a little then. She was efficient and cunning – she would be dead before the month was out. She needed to pull herself together and get out of these ties and then she could work on annihilating herself.

The door opened and two female guards came in. They manoeuvered her into a wheelchair and took her down long corridors. She didn't bother to ask where they were going because she didn't care.

They parked her in a room with a desk and a small window

through which she could see the sky. It was blue and the memory of Berenice with her in Brighton filled her up and made tears spring into her dried-up ducts. She could weep for a thousand years.

The door opened and Helen walked in, a file under her arm. 'Good morning, Olivia.'

Olivia tried to work some spit together in her mouth to lob at her.

Helen sat down and put the file on the desk, interlaced her fingers and leaned forward.

The tears had helped; there was a big glob of snot forming at the back of Olivia's throat. She could splatter Helen's silk shirt from here.

'Isla Bukowski has gone missing.'

Olivia swallowed the spit in her mouth and stared at her.

'When the women were discovered in the lock-up, she fled the scene and cannot be located. She is, apparently, looking for someone who she believes drove your sister to kill herself.'

Olivia felt a great peace wash over her, more profound than anything she could have ever imagined.

Isla was fighting the fight, keeping the dream of justice for Lauren and countless others alive. Even after the greatest test she had faced, being confronted with the possibility of return to normal life, to the instant gratification of love and family, she had stuck to the path she had been set on all those years ago. A decade of suffering in here had not been in vain after all.

'You know, Dr McCabe, I've missed our chats.' Her voice was croaky and hoarse, her vocal cords damaged from prolonged screaming.

'If you were to cooperate and give us some idea of who this person is, your therapy with me could be continued.'

'I would feel more able to give you information if we could talk like normal human beings, without all this unnecessary baggage.' Olivia nodded down at the thick straps that wound round her wrists.

Helen remained calm. 'It's very important for you to feel you have some power, however illusory, isn't it?'

Olivia grinned. Her lips were so dry that she could feel the skin cracking and taste blood rushing to fill the tiny fissures. But more than that, she felt life and possibilities rushing back into every shattered cell of her body. 'Dr McCabe, let me tell you something about power. Power is held by the person who is thought to wield it. And in this room, today, who do you think that is?'

Helen gave a small smile, as if something Olivia had said amused her. 'It doesn't matter who I think it is, Olivia.'

Olivia found herself thinking her psychiatrist's brown eyes more appealing than any she could remember. Her hair was so thick and glossy. She imagined for a long blissful moment how wonderful it would be to stroke it. If she helped in a small way her mental dance with Helen in their therapy sessions would continue, hopefully for years. She thought with joy about all the entertainment, amusement and distraction it would provide.

'Welcome back, Dr McCabe.'

She had come home. And it was beautiful.

79

D arren was preparing to leave hospital. His overnight bag was on the bed; someone, probably Mum, had packed it and brought it in when he was unconscious and in intensive care. There was his washbag, a selection of clothes and, in a fit of enthusiasm, his mum had packed some art supplies. There were some files shoved in on top of it all with The Missing charity logo on them. Orin must have delivered them to the hospital some time over the past week.

He had only a few minutes – Mum and Dad had gone to get the car and Carly was outside in the corridor getting water. Darren sat down on the bed and pulled the files out. The first one was a short profile of Olivia's sister and a photo of her that was grainy and very blown up and probably from school. The second contained information about the murder of Rollo McFadden.

Orin had paperclipped a note to the front in his spiky scrawl: 'This is all the extra I could get. Remember the work of the charity is still as important today as it was yesterday. Come and join me.'

He put the file aside. Orin had dug out this information in an attempt to woo him back when they were still grasping at the shortest of straws, when the possibility of finding all four of the remaining missing alive and well would have seemed beyond fanciful. Molly was the only girl who didn't make it. *Rollo is six foot two.* Olivia's words came back to him and he felt dread flicker down his spine.

He picked up the file and opened it. There was a detailed report on Rollo's murder. He had been a nightclub bouncer in Brighton and had had running feuds with several local drug-dealing gangs; he had two convictions for ABH. Rollo had been beaten about the head several times by unknown assailants in the front room of his house in Hove. The photo-copied photos were evidence enough that his end had been bloody, brutal and vicious. Darren couldn't stomach it; he had endured enough violence to last a lifetime. He was about to close the file when he noticed that the date of the murder was the day before Carly and Isla went missing. He tried to flick back to the front of the file but he fumbled the papers, and several photocopied photos from the back of the file fell to the floor. He swore. With his injuries, he couldn't bend over to pick them up. He stared down at the photocopies of evidence collected from the crime scene and saw something that made his newly constructed joy drain away.

A few moments later Carly came back into the room. She saw the change that had come over him and faltered when she saw what was on the floor. She shut the door.

Darren was staring at a photo of a dirty carpet stained with Rollo's blood. Lying by an upended ashtray, among a scatter of cigarette butts, a lighter, a crushed child's textbook and a woman's shoe, was a woven bracelet. The blue and green threads were knotted together in a Carrick bend.

'What were you doing in Rollo's house?'

She sat down on the bed. She didn't take her eyes off him. 'There's so much that you don't know or understand, Darren—'

'Just tell me the truth!'

'Molly didn't run away and then end up being abducted by Olivia, she retreated there of her own free will. She lived at Olivia's for more than a year with Rajinder and Heather. She ran away from Rollo.'

'What were you doing at his murder?'

'Rollo did terrible things to Molly, appalling things to that child. She told Olivia everything and Olivia offered her sanctuary at her house.'

'I want to know about *you*!'

Carly broke eye contact and looked at the floor. 'Isla met Olivia at a Reclaim the Night type protest. We all believed that as women we should be able to walk around without feeling scared, should be able to go about our lives in peace. Not long after that she invited us to her house because there were other girls there. Rajinder and Heather were older; Molly was this little fireball of a personality. It was a great place to go, like a fantastic youth club just for girls. Isla in particular loved it. Berenice was like a big mother hen and Olivia was the founder of it all. We had such good times there, but it was always our secret. We never told anyone else about it, we made sure we weren't seen coming and going. Right from the beginning we understood that that was important.' She paused. 'It's like we had been chosen, we were special, and we were proud of that.'

Carly was off the bed now, walking round the room, animated as she spoke. 'But there was a shadow that hung over our group. Berenice, Rajinder, Heather and Molly had terrible experiences in common: they had been abused and the culprits had got away with it. Olivia's sister had killed herself after a similar experience. Olivia wanted retribution and we wanted to help her.'

'My God, Mum and Dad had no idea what was happening—'

Carly interrupted him, desperate now to get her story out. 'Molly was the worst affected, I think, by what had happened to her: Rollo raped her over and over again for months. The longer Molly was at Olivia's, the angrier she became. We thought we understood that anger; we were fired up about the injustice in the world. Isla in particular was desperate to really *do* something to put things right. She was the one who looked up to Olivia the most. She said there was no point sitting around and talking about it – that's what victims did, and Molly was a victim no more. So she hatched a plan without Berenice or Olivia knowing. We were going to get Rollo to admit to what he had done to Molly.' Carly came and sat back down on the bed. 'Isla can be very persuasive.'

'My God, what did you do?' Darren asked, but he didn't want to know the answer. After so many years of being desperate to understand, now he would happily die in ignorance.

Carly's voice had become very quiet. 'We were so young and naïve. Molly lured Rollo to Olivia's house. When he walked in, we jumped him. Isla hit him over the head and Rajinder, Heather, Molly and I tied him up. It was a mock court: the victim and the accused. And Molly set to work, accusing him of all the things he'd done to her. In front of us as her witnesses.' She paused. 'Rollo had a look in his eyes like I'd never seen. Such outrage and fury.'

'What were you going to do then? Were you just going to let him go?'

'We had a plan all worked out. He was going to sign a confession. But then Olivia came home. And that's when it all went wrong. She was furious that we had jumped the gun, gone ahead without telling her. There was a big argument, Olivia shouting that we weren't properly prepared to take his confession and at that moment when we were distracted, Rollo got free. He was a big guy and he was as mad as hell. He grabbed a metal doorstop and he smashed Molly in the temple with it. He killed her instantly.'

Carly rubbed her hands down her jeans and got off the bed. 'It was chaos after that. He bolted for the door. Isla and I ran after him. He was injured from where Isla had hit him earlier, stumbling and weaving down the road. We followed him.'

'You were children!'

'Yes we were. But we felt we were righting a wrong. The world was black and white to us then, a world of absolutes. We watched him go inside his house and . . .' She faltered. 'I was so angry. More furious than I had been about anything, or could ever imagine being. Molly had told us how Rollo used to lock her in at night, and she would escape by coming and going via the window with a broken catch in the toilet. Isla and I went down the side of the house. It was strewn with rubbish, Isla picked up a discarded metal bar and we climbed in through the toilet window. The house was dark, but we could hear him crashing about in the living room.' She paused, distracted.

'We never doubted what we were doing. We stood in that rank hallway and we nodded at each other. Isla raised that metal bar and we ran through into the living room to meet him head-on. Isla swung that metal bar so hard. I remember the noise it made when it connected with his skull.' Carly's voice was a monotone, as if she had relived this moment thousands of times from every angle. 'He was on the floor, his cheekbone was caved in. He was growling, this animal sound. He grabbed at me, hurling me to the ground. That's when he must have yanked my bracelet off. He pulled at Isla's legs and got her to the floor. He had his hands round her neck. He'd turned her over so he was lying on top of her. I wriggled free and picked up a barbell from the corner. I turned and smashed it down on the back of his head. I did it again and again until he stopped moving.'

Darren was speechless for a second. 'You could have gone to the police.'

'We had forced our way into his house. I had moved across the room to pick up that weapon. I was fourteen, criminally responsible. I would have ended up living away from you, in the institutions Berenice and Heather feared so much and had run away from. If we disappeared, right then, like Molly had done, like Heather and Rajinder had done, there couldn't be any comeback over Rollo. Isla urged me to do it, she was happy with choosing that path, but I was so much more conflicted. But I felt I had no choice. Isla had come up with the plan to capture Rollo, but I had freely gone on to kill him.

'That night we took Molly out to the Downs, all of us together, and we buried her. It was a place she had walked with Olivia once, and she had liked it. After that, Olivia and Berenice took Isla and me in.' She looked down at the floor. 'We moved to the railway arch with Berenice and made it into a home. Berenice was unhooked from normal life – she had no job or identity or family – she was untraceable. Many people are. Olivia stayed in Brighton.'

'Why did she confess to murder?'

Carly shook her head. 'Her cause was more important to her than her own freedom. She didn't want our group to disband, she wanted us to hunt down who had abused her sister and caused her death. And her confession probably kept Isla and me out of jail.'

'She really is mad,' Darren said.

'Perhaps,' Carly said. She took a deep breath. 'Her saying she'd killed us made our decision to run away final. By then we were like a military unit – united by what we had seen and done and totally committed to each other. We mourned Molly and Olivia like fallen comrades and then we went to work. We didn't follow the court case, watch the TV or read the newspapers, we all agreed it would be too painful. If I had seen even one image of you or Mum and Dad I wouldn't have been able . . .' She tailed off and struggled to compose herself. 'And on some level I felt that I needed to be punished for what I had done.'

A little track of tears had opened up and was travelling down her cheek. 'I missed you more than I thought possible. But I had made my choice, because I had no choice really. My revenge for Molly caused you all such pain.' The tears were flowing faster. 'But when I saw you at the lock-up, Darren, injured and looking for me –' she was crying now '– I chose you. I chose family over my childhood ideals.' She took his face in her hands so he was forced to look directly into her eyes. 'Remember what I said to you on the beach that day you got lost, Darren? "This is me, and this is you. We're family, we can't ever be parted."'

Darren had a thousand questions to ask, a million ways he wanted to rant and rail at his sister for the pain and heartache she had caused, and for the years of her precious life she had wasted, but he was interrupted. The door opened and Melanie came in. She saw Carly's tears and gathered her up in her arms. 'Oh baby, don't cry. It's been a long road. But we can all finally go home, together.' She closed her eyes and put her face in Carly's hair, revelling yet again in the glorious idea that she was back. She had no idea what Carly was really crying for.

Darren put his foot over the photo and crushed it under his shoe.

80

Five Days Later

Darren was back in the lobby at Roehampton. The place had a smell he had come to recognise but that didn't stop it making him feel ill. How different things had been the last time he was here!

Helen came to give him a pass and led him through the visitors' entrance. She smiled as she greeted him and looked him up and down. 'Do you need a wheelchair?'

He shook his head. 'I just need to go slowly.'

They made their way towards the first security door. He heard the buzzer and shuddered.

Helen paused. 'You don't have to do this, Darren.'

'I know.'

They walked down the long, dirty white corridors of the hospital until they came to a shut door.

'It's the same drill as last time. She will be chained up, you can't touch her or give her anything. We'll be watching from behind the glass.' She walked away and Darren opened the door.

Olivia was sitting at a table, her hands cuffed in front of her, a chain running down to shackles at her feet. The contrast to how she looked when he had last seen her – laid up in a hospital bed in a basement, weak from her operation – could not have been sharper. She glowed with health, her skin shone, her hair was smooth, the colour was up in her lips and cheeks. He sat down opposite her.

'You look tired, Biological.' Her eyes were sparking with flecks of gold, as if a thousand thoughts were colliding in her mind.

'That's not surprising. There's been a lot to process recently.'

'Reunions are such a messy business. The reality often doesn't live up to the fantasy. Are you finding that?'

Darren forced himself to stay calm despite her triumphant mocking. It was important that he didn't get distracted, that he didn't let Olivia rifle around inside his head; he was too fragile. He reminded himself he had come back here for one reason. 'Where's Isla gone?'

Olivia sat back, at ease in her chair, seemingly at ease with life. 'You know how many people have applied to come and have an audience with me? Have begged for five minutes of my time? I let only one in, Biological. You. You were very lucky to find those girls, but I forgive you, because you are very like me. Even in your cleaners' clothes I saw the pain in you, the burden you bore of the unanswered questions about your sister.'

'I'm nothing like you—'

'You risked everything for answers – you nearly went to jail, almost lost your life. You tore down the world for your sister, and so did I. I don't regret it.' He couldn't look away from her. She was insane, yet she was compelling. 'Berenice and the girls have exposed fifteen men, you know. Seventy-five girls got some kind of justice from our methods: public confessions of murder, of rape and sexual assault. Even if the perpetrators didn't end up behind bars they were named and shamed, their lives ruined. Gert Becker was simply the most extreme.

'You know how I picked my girls? What brought them in particular to my attention among the river of sorrowful young people I swam through in my job as a social worker? They were fighters. They didn't stand by. It's a woman's way, isn't it, to put up and shut up, to tolerate and to keep secrets. The girls I picked were exceptional. They had fought their way out: of violence, of their callous care homes, and for Carly and Isla, out of their *comfortable* lives and loving families. They gave up everything, risked everything they had, to be able to *change* it.'

He needed to stick to the task, not get distracted down the byways and chambers of Olivia's mind. 'I'm here about Isla, that's all.'

She smiled indulgently. 'Darren, our greatest delusions we save for ourselves. I know why you look tired. Your joy at Carly coming home is tempered by what she did, by what I know.' The smile disappeared as quickly as if a magician had whisked it away. 'What I sacrificed for her.'

Darren swallowed. The threat was plain. To save Carly and Isla Olivia had confessed to murders she hadn't committed. Olivia having such a power over Carly and over him was almost too much to bear. 'You wanted to punish me, you wanted to destroy my life because I dared to come near you,' he said. 'So you set me on the path to Rollo because you knew what devastating information I would find. But I found the women instead, something you never thought I was capable of.'

'Calm down, Biological. It looks like it's a win-win from where I'm sitting. Carly's secret's safe with me. Carly did more good from that railway arch than she ever would have done in the young offenders institution where she would have been sent for killing that bastard.' She paused. 'As for Isla, she's not coming back. She was always different from the others. She craved an exceptional life, even at fourteen she wanted to upend the world. Orin will have to suck it up.'

'Who's she hunting? Who was it who ruined your sister's life?'

Her face dropped into its mask-like state, the light in her eyes gone. 'I don't know. We narrowed it down to a core of thirty of my dad's contacts. Lauren talked to me about it only once before she put herself out of her misery. She was too scared to even utter his name.' Her voice was low and unhurried, like acid dripping on metal and slowly discolouring it. 'It's been ten years. It takes a long time to eliminate suspects, to tail them at night and to befriend them online and to break passwords and to delve into the most hidden parts of a man's life. But we will get there. When Isla gets close, it's going to get dangerous. She'll need help. When it's required, Carly will fight the fight, and no amount of doltish adoration from her brother or fluttering hands from her mother will stop her. You know now what she's capable of. She's pretty impressive, your sister.'

Darren glanced at the long black window at the side of the room, where normal people, good people, were waiting to lead him away from this. He felt so tired, so beaten down by the scale of her ambition. 'It's over, Olivia. It's done.'

She smiled and threw her hair back, and he saw she had a terrible, uncompromising beauty. 'Did the police tell you what was found at the scene of Gert Becker's death?' Darren felt dread coat his stomach. 'The avenging angel left a note, a calling card, if you like. "The Silent Ones". It won't be the last time you see that name. It's not over, Darren, the fight against the men who hate women is only just beginning.'

'You can't take the law into your own hands—'

'A woman's hands are all she's got. Sexual violence is such a distinctive, peculiar crime; the victim goes on trial with the perpetrator, more often than not the man walks free. Not in my world. I've made my mistakes—'

'What mistakes?'

She was in a mood for revelations. 'Eric Cox was one, but my methods improved.'

'Your old boyfriend? What do you mean?'

'You know why Eric went to jail? For fencing stolen cars. He saw the inside of a cell because he took a car. He raped underage girls but he went to jail for theft.' There was a long pause, during which a smile began to creep out from the sides of her mouth. 'I got him to confess to his real crimes. It took time, but I got there. What I didn't get was a recording.'

Something in her tone made the hairs on Darren's neck rise. His voice was so quiet when he spoke that he wondered that she could hear him at all. 'The blood that the police found in the back garden of your house, it couldn't be from the girls. So whose was it?'

Her smile widened and it chilled Darren to the bone.

'Was that Eric?' he asked.

'Among others.'

Darren stood up sharply. He opened the door, desperate to get away. 'I hate you.'

As the door began to swing shut behind him he caught a last glimpse of her. Her eyes were flaming with flecks of fire as she mouthed, 'I love you.'

81

The man heard the knock on his office door and shouted 'Come in.' One of the countless middle-aged lackeys who populated his department stepped in and the man tried hard to look like he was pleased to see him.

The lackey sat down and pointed at a photo in a frame on his desk in a bid to be conversational. The man wondered what favour was about to be grovelled for.

'You've gotten far too prosperous in your old age,' the lackey said. 'You look thinner in this picture here.' It was his family bathed in sun, leaning on a gate in the Cotswolds. He was glad he had dusted it off and put it on show; people had a strong desire to believe in the myths they saw in photos. It also served another purpose. Now that the revelations about Gert Becker had exploded into international news, he needed to polish his family-man credentials. 'How old is your daughter now?' the lackey continued.

'Nearly all grown up, off to Oxford in October, if she gets the grades.' He sighed, as if seeking sympathy. 'It seems harder than it was in our day.'

The lackey smiled with recognition. 'Anyway, the reason I'm here—'

'And I thought you'd come by because you liked me.'

A sycophant's grin spread across the lackey's face. 'We all have to bow at the feet of the powers that be, Harris.'

Harris pulled on the cuffs of his blue shirt.

'So, it's about this Isla Bukowski thing and the Gert Becker video confession.'

The smile died on Harris's face.

'The minister wants to make a statement in the house.'

He was surprised and didn't hide it. 'Whatever for?'

'It's pandering to public opinion in the most craven way, if you ask me. The press can talk about little else. You know questions are being asked about why the police never found those women before, about the Bukowski girl playing the avenging angel and going AWOL. The minister's looking for somewhere to park the blame and walk away.'

'Well she's not parking it with us,' Harris said indignantly.

'Of course, but we need to be seen to be doing something. An inquiry, most likely.'

'Well, that's not a problem. We can find someone to be knee-deep in old paper for a couple of years.'

'Indeed.' The lackey paused. 'But there's another area that needs attention. These women were being trained, supposedly. Trained to seek out men with,' he waved a hand vaguely as if the right word was about to float by on an air current, 'predilections to unsavoury behaviour.' He fiddled with his tie and then smoothed it.

The idiot's so constipated, Harris thought, he can't even mention the word sex. Or rape. Or murder.

'Terrorism fears are at fever pitch at present. A secret group being trained covertly comes under the remit of this department to some extent. We need to keep an eye on these women, undertake surveillance, make sure there's no blow-back on the department. The lowest level, I'd suggest, just to keep tabs.'

Harris stood up fast. He yanked on his blue cuffs again, hard this time, and banged his hand so loudly on the table that the family photo clattered to the floor.

'Fuck! Can't you see the bigger picture? If something happens to an innocent male member of the public because of these women, it's bedlam, vigilante justice at its worst. Every man in the country will be quaking in their beds fearing they're going to be pulled from them and stuck in front of a video camera with a knife to their bollocks!'

The lackey reeled back in his seat. Harris leaned forward, menacingly. 'Low-level surveillance, are you mad? We have the budget – find your balls and get a team! Jesus, I'll take control of it and end this once and for all.' He pointed his finger at him. 'You know what, this is personal. Personal, because I've got a pair, like thirty million other Britons.'

The lackey grinned, pleased he could tip the whole troublesome matter out of his in-box and into someone else's. Harris didn't let up. 'And what in hell is happening with the one who hasn't been found? This Bukowski girl?'

'Word downstairs is that the police have no idea where she is or who she's with.'

Harris swore. 'The DCI presiding over this mess is going to be over my knee getting spanked by the end of the day. He will report to me by Friday too.'

'By all means, Harris, take control. It does seem as if someone needs to and having a senior person on board who is passionate about the issue is all to the good. I'll inform the Home Secretary. Keep me abreast of developments.' He stood up and turned to the door. 'Remember, come to our party in Kent next Saturday. Bring Julia, Sally would love to see her. And pray for sun.'

The door closed and Harris yanked his shirt cuffs down again. He looked out of his window at the spire of Big Ben poking over the squat sixties tower blocks. Gert Becker had been exposed. Harris wasn't hugely worried – ever since he had first begun, years ago, to target the vulnerable daughters of friends and associates he had taken precautions – but the Bukowski stunt was audacious. Olivia Duvall obviously couldn't connect him and Lauren, even after searching for ten years. His position seemed secure, but he didn't know what information Becker had given up under his torture. He needed to be front foot and ready, that was all. No one was going to unseat him from this spot of power and influence. He'd risen until only the pigeons pecked higher.

He felt the familiar itch begin its faint thrum in his heart, the drumbeat of excitement, transgression and desire. A 24-year-old, friendless waif, unused to the world, without a family or a home, partially locked up for a decade and scarred by extreme images she had seen as a child. She was pitting her pathetic sense of justice and retribution against the security apparatus of one of the world's richest countries. One thing was for certain: he would enjoy Isla Bukowski when he finally got hold of her.

82

September 2014

The tide was low, the great expanse of yellow beach unpeeled and staring up at the sun. It was going to be an Indian-summer scorcher of a day, the news had said. It was still early and the teenager in cut-offs and a T-shirt with a money belt slung low on her hips like a Wild West gunslinger had plenty of change for the car park fee. Darren pulled in and rolled down to the spots nearest the beach. He sat staring at the view for a moment as everyone else opened the car doors and began to unload the mountains of gear that they had with them.

Dad was fussing over the portable chairs and an umbrella. Mum was putting the lead on Carly's puppy – she had named him Skye. Chloe was picking up plastic bags full of food that looked like they would split under their own weight. She had a towel, a cricket set and a bodyboard too. Darren got out of the car and began to untie the surfboards from the roof. Carly stood on the other side of the car and threw the straps back to Darren. He caught his sister's eye and grinned.

'It's corduroy,' Darren said.

She nodded, staring west, and for the thousandth time since she had burst back into their lives Darren wondered what she was thinking, marvelled at how she had coped and remained stunned at her ability to rise, relatively unscathed, from the darkest depths of human despair. He pulled the surfboards from the roof and placed them on the ground, looking at his reunited family.

Mum was running in tight little circles chasing Skye, Dad was pointing out to no one in particular something about rock formations. Chloe was good-naturedly coping with the madness of the last few months and throwing Darren a lifeline of love and pleasure. He didn't deserve her, he felt, which made her love for him all the more precious.

They had waited so long for Carly to come back to them and that road had not been easy. For Carly, too, there had been so many challenges to meet: long months of intense counselling and adjustment to family and adult life when most of her childhood had been stolen, all carried out under a white-hot media glare, the swirl of theories and speculation about Olivia, Berenice, Isla and the other girls.

At times it had seemed that they would drown in it, the ramifications like a tidal wave from an underground earthquake. Darren had begged Orin to give them time, time to heal and adjust before they began work to find the last one missing; the police were still sifting through a mountain of evidence from the lock-up and Gert Becker's confession. But these were details that felt far off; the adjustments closer to home were more heartfelt. Guilt ate away at Dad still, guilt that he had not had faith like Melanie, he had not believed. For Mum herself, her battle with cancer remained something she was determined to win, but her treatment was ongoing and the outcome still uncertain.

Darren changed into his wetsuit, picked up Carly's board and his own and began to walk down the steps to the beach. Later in the day they would queue for tea and ice cream at the shop, sunkissed and wave-cleansed, the city and its concerns blasted from their skin and their minds.

He felt the cool sand between his toes, his shadow still long as he walked to the sea. They crossed the sand in a straggle: a family – compromised, complicated, but all heading in the same direction. He looked at the huge Devon cliffs soaring skywards, monumental and everlasting. There were decades of life still to live, years and years of it to enjoy and to take on. He turned to his sister and felt bliss in his heart. She could, and she would, recover. Her life would be long; finally she could dive in and live it.

Carly was standing near him in her wetsuit, her board under her arm. She was still, as she often was, happier the longer she waited for something. He felt it was a result of her restricted teenage years, this ability to wait and wait. Her eyes were narrowed against the light. She was counting waves, he realised, waiting for the larger seventh, anticipating the right moment.

'Ready?' he asked.

She turned to him, her hair streaming backwards, and she smiled. 'I'm ready.' They walked towards the Atlantic together.

Acknowledgements

Books are never written by the author alone, and there are many people I wish to thank for their encouragement and inspiration while I worked on *The Silent Ones*. My editor, Francesca Best, and the publicity and marketing team at Hodder, have been as enthusiastic and professional as any writer could wish for. My agent, Peter Straus, has always been a trusty guiding hand. A huge thank you to my family and friends for their anecdotes and stories, which have forever improved and informed my own.

Ali Knight

UNTIL DEATH

Marriage is a prison for Kelly. Her controlling and manipulative husband Christos videos her in the house, has her followed and tracks her every move. She may be desperate to leave, but she's not stupid. If she runs, he'll make sure she never sees her children again.

Christos has a mistress, Sylvie, keen to pander to his every whim and even keener to step into Kelly's shoes, should she ever vacate them.

Kelly thinks it's stalemate for their twisted threesome, but one of Christos's container ships is about to dock in London with a secret cargo that will change all their lives forever.

If Kelly is to escape, it will be in a way she never imagined, and people *will* get hurt . . .

Out now in paperback and ebook

HODDER

Ali Knight

THE FIRST CUT

A best friend murdered.
A marriage going nowhere.
A deadly obsession.

Nicky's had more than her share of heartache.
So when she meets a hot young stranger she thinks
a little flirting can help her forget the past.
She's married, but it's innocent enough.

Except what starts as fun leads to a terrible ordeal,
and a dark secret.

Nicky's about to discover that the scars of love
can last a lifetime.

Out now in paperback and ebook

HODDER

Ali Knight

WINK MURDER

Late one night, Kate is woken by her husband Paul, drunk, covered in blood, and mumbling that he's killed something – or someone.

Afterwards, Paul denies he ever said what he did. But when an attractive young woman who works for him is found murdered, Kate's terrible suspicions about what her husband has really done send her on a desperate search for the truth.

Although as the lies multiply, and Kate's carefully constructed life comes under threat, doing the right thing is not as straightforward as it seems . . .

Out now in paperback and ebook

HODDER